TALKING ABOUT
MY BABY
Margot
Early

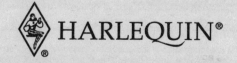

HARLEQUIN®

TORONTO • NEW YORK • LONDON
AMSTERDAM • PARIS • SYDNEY • HAMBURG
STOCKHOLM • ATHENS • TOKYO • MILAN • MADRID
PRAGUE • WARSAW • BUDAPEST • AUCKLAND

ISBN 0-373-70855-6

TALKING ABOUT MY BABY

Copyright © 1999 by Margot Early.

This edition published by arrangement with Harlequin Books S.A.

® and TM are trademarks of the publisher. Trademarks indicated with ® are registered in the United States Patent and Trademark Office, the Canadian Trade Marks Office and in other countries.

Visit us at www.romance.net

Printed in U.S.A.

PROLOGUE

I always want to control the future, but controlling the future is an illusion, and this is painful to accept. Only the present is ours and not to control but to live.

—Karen Anthony, age 35, written after Elijah's birth at Precipice Peak Hospital in Precipice, Colorado

Maternity House
Sagrado, Texas

DECEIT COULD BE BOTH survival and a way of life, and so it was for the girl who called herself Julia, who had come across the river to have her baby in the clinic, Maternity House, on the United States side of the river. Tara Marcus knew this about Julia soon after meeting her. The lies were a survival mechanism, and there was no point in arguing with survival.

"I saw the owl," Julia said. "I flew over the river as we were crossing. I am going to die. Having the baby will kill me. I know it."

Spanish had become automatic to Tara; she understood it as readily as English, and she followed the teenager's words effortlessly.

"An owl came to me the day my mother died, too," Julia continued. "But this one was for me."

The border taught respect for superstition. If Julia *had* seen an owl, Tara would have worried; owls portended death. But there was something about Julia's eyes.... Living the way Julia probably lived on the other side of the river made a person lie; it was better to invent a fiction, even a name. Truth had no purpose down there, while lies did; they increased the odds that the person who told them would live to see the next morning.

Now, even glowing in the first stage of labor, Julia's eyes were desperate, and they did not distinguish lie from truth. Every word from this woman's mouth would be a lie, perhaps even into transition, perhaps through the birth of her child.

She was not afraid, either.

Tara held her hand because it would have been natural for a girl this young, maybe sixteen, to be afraid— but where Julia had come from was so much worse.

"Promise me," said Julia. "Promise me that if I die you will take my baby and raise it. Swear on your mother's grave."

"My mother isn't dead."

"On your father's grave."

Tara grinned. "He's around, too—and so will you be." She sobered. "Julia, there are adoption services. Are you worried you won't be able to care for your baby?"

"I would never give my baby to someone else! Not unless I was dead! *I* will take care of my baby. This baby's father is a diplomat. He is descended from Pancho Villa. My mother... My mother's family was very wealthy in Mexico City."

"Relax," murmured Tara. She smoothed Julia's hair. "I'm on your side."

The touch electrified Julia. Eyes round and dark, she clutched Tara's fingers, tightly enough to make the bones crunch. "Then, promise. Swear you will keep my baby."

"I'm divorced. No man. Always broke. Midwives make no money."

"You're *rich.*"

You'll lose this argument, Tara. Where she comes from you're filthy rich, like all Americans. Just drop it. She grabbed a blood pressure cuff and fit it around the girl's arm. There had been no protein in her urine, but Tara checked for edema anyway. Julia's hair looked dry and dirty, without luster.

"Promise, please, that you will care for my baby."

I have to get away from the border. And she was going, going north to Colorado to help her mother— at least that was how Tara saw it. In any case, she was going just in time. The desensitization was happening. Another midwife at the clinic had told her, *You give and give and give, and then suddenly it's gone.* It wasn't gone yet, but...

But I look in this girl's eyes and see only deceit.

Only pointless lies instead of survival lies.

"Okay. Okay, I promise."

"Swear." She radiated strength, powerful already in labor. "Swear on the names of your mother and father."

"I swear on the name of my mother, Francesca Walcott, and my father, Charlie Marcus, that I will care for your child in the event of your death." The words sent a chill over Tara.

Especially because Julia still squinted at her with dissatisfaction.

TARA STAYED AT THE birth center for forty-eight hours, catching sleep when she could in the sleeping nook off the staff room. She attended eight births; four of the mothers had arrived with preeclampsia. These were not the uncomplicated births that her mother, Francesca, saw in her midwifery practice in Colorado. Even working in rural West Virginia, Tara's sister, Ivy, had the opportunity to give prenatal counseling.

But when women crossed the Rio Grande and arrived at the birth center to have their babies, they were often visiting the United States for the first time. They had risked their lives to cross so that their children would be born in the U.S.—and become citizens.

Like Julia.

Julia had left the clinic that evening, with her baby daughter, Laura Estrella. She had departed without telling anyone, as though afraid she'd be held to pay for the services she'd received.

You couldn't allow yourself to wonder where she'd gone or if she and her child would be safe.

The sky was starry, and as she walked to her car, a rusty dark-green Safari station wagon bought from a local rancher, Tara could make out the lights of the border patrol stations just a mile away—as well as the neon from the bars in town. In Colorado, it would be cold now. But October on the border—balmy.

Her car looked just the way she'd left it when she came out the day before to throw soiled clothes in the back seat. Bats fluttered near the parking lot's lights. One winged close to her ear as she casually checked the station wagon and got in.

Music… Rock and roll to take her home.

Jackson Browne. *I love you, Jackson.* Her fantasy man. She sang with him as she backed out of her space, ready to head home to the trailer. Her heart pounded the lonely rhythm of her nonworking hours:

I wish the best for Danny and Solange; I do not resent their love for each other, I do not resent that they have a baby. Little Kai…

It was two years since he'd told her. It didn't help that he and Solange hadn't consummated their desire for each other at the time, that they hadn't physically betrayed her. Sometimes, she wished they had. Instead, they both expected her to appreciate their self-restraint.

Now they were living in Hawaii—where Tara and Solange had practiced together, where Tara had married Danny, where Tara had been *born*—with their new baby.

The road to the trailer court was dark and poor and unpaved, and as she reached the turn, a low-rider spun out of the drive, spitting dust in the night. It backfired, and a cat meowed.

No, not a cat. Not a meow.

The short hairs under Tara's ponytail lifted.

She should pull over.

The baby cried again.

The baby was in her car.

And she didn't have to look over her shoulder at the back seat to know whose baby it was.

CHAPTER ONE

In Hawaii, I kept chickens. I had free-roaming chickens that came into the pen to roost at night or if they had problems outside. Once in a while, one of the free-range chickens—never a rooster, always a hen—would not want to roost in the pen and would find herself in a tree. If she was not lured back into the pen and retrained to come in at night, she would never return; she would go wild. She would join the group at a safe distance in the daytime, hide her nest from everyone, and climb higher and higher in her own roost so no one could get her. Somehow, in Tara, I have raised a wild hen.

—Francesca Walcott, CNM

On the road again

IT WAS PAST MIDNIGHT. Driving north, out of Texas, Tara chased off night memories and twilight ghosts, excluding everything but the road and Laura. In slumber, Laura opened and closed her soft tiny hands, holding them close against her blue sleeper.

Almost safe.

She had made it out of Sagrado. In Colorado, she would live with her mother, Francesca—and maybe make ends meet as a midwife. She wouldn't *enjoy* living with Francesca. But she had to give Laura the best life possible.

She was trying.

No one at Maternity House had questioned her buying a supplemental feeding system or taking donated breast milk from the breast bank. The birth center sometimes helped an adoptive mother get started inducing lactation. But Tara had told no one about Laura Estrella. Not then, not during the two weeks that followed. Laura would have been given to social services, and...

No way. She's mine.

Hours after finding the baby in her car, Tara had returned to Maternity House for the things she needed. Then, she'd put Laura to her breast, providing the milk through fine, flexible tubing taped to her nipple. A disposable bag hanging between her breasts, beneath her clothing, held the donor milk. She was massaging her breasts nightly and, with the help of herbs... Yes, maybe months from now, her own breasts would produce milk. But she would always need to supplement.

I'm lucky. I'm so lucky.

She had Laura. She had Laura, and she would do what she must to keep her. Anything at all.

Precipice, Colorado

THE TURNING SEASONS sprayed the mountainsides red, orange and yellow. The leaves flashed gold on red and black rocks, contrasting with the dark pitch of evergreens. Driving home at six-thirty that night, Isaac told the kids, "That whole ridge used to be green."

It was Wednesday; another babysitter was gone from his life—late getting back from a mountain bike ride. The children had been at the clinic since four-thirty. Keeping tabs on three children, ages five through thirteen, and seeing patients, and dealing with his staff… He felt the stress, readjustment to the cold and the mountains and the U.S.

Danielle cried out in Kinyarwanda, begging his help against David, who was dismembering one of her Barbie dolls.

Isaac took a breath. "English, Danielle."

She burst into tears, and both her brothers began to soothe her—in the language she'd chosen. Oliver turned around in the passenger seat to speak to her. The doll was reassembled.

"Dad," said David, behind him. "I have the coolest idea for tonight."

For D&D, Dungeons & Dragons. Isaac's brother and mother had brought the game to Rwanda years ago, along with a television and VCR that had later become bargaining chips, buying lives. In Colorado, David had discovered D&D accessories—books, boxes of dice with any number of sides—eight, ten, twelve, twenty, one hundred. David was a wizard at probability. He had written his first seventh-grade essay on chance, and his teacher had sent it to a national contest.

Isaac would have to play Dungeons & Dragons tonight. He'd enjoy it, but his life was full of have-tos, and each day he tried to unload more of them, usually at the clinic. The nurses were always dropping hints— like today. *Dr. McCrea, we're two hours behind schedule!* Then he'd heard her tell the receptionist, *Guess we're on African time again.*

He'd called an office meeting on the spot and encouraged everyone to air their feelings. They had. In a nice way.

In a nice way, he'd explained that his office wasn't an emergency room. What most of his patients needed was someone to talk to. He liked to find out what was bothering them and try to get across how they could become well.

Everyone in his office needed to relax about the clock. Precipice had one physician for every five hundred residents; Rwanda, one for every forty thousand. He worked well at great speed, but here, why race the clock?

No one had relaxed. He'd heard about the crying babies and the elderly people on oxygen, and...

There were more have-tos at the clinic. Perhaps he should record his own perceptions of time, as David had recorded his vision of chance.

Looking west at the ski lifts, hanging motionless above the rocks and grass and trees, he weighed the price of season passes against discount ski cards. Oliver and David wanted snowboards. When Isaac had left Colorado, snowboards hadn't existed. Fourteen years he'd been away.

The face of Precipice Peak bordered one side of the town. Rust-red mountains rose on the other at a gentler angle. He headed that way, east toward Tomboy, and at the top of the road, when he turned left, Danielle exclaimed, *"La sage femme! Et une dame et un bébé."*

French now.

Isaac said, "The midwife. And a lady and a baby."

"Say it, Danielle," suggested twelve-year-old David. "The midwife. And a lady and a baby."

"Yes," Oliver encouraged, *"Practice!"*

Another have-to. Isaac had to tell the midwife, Francesca Walcott, when the new owners were taking occupancy of her rented Victorian. Two years ago, when Isaac was still in Rwanda, his mother had dispersed most of her assets between him and Dan, his brother. A year later, Dan had negotiated the purchase of the Victorian and Isaac's own place—as well as empty acres and abandoned buildings sprawled over one side of Tomboy—as a package deal, acting for Isaac. Now Isaac was turning over the Victorian at a profit.

He had to.

PRECIPICE HAD ONCE been a mining town. Since then, log homes and glassy condominiums had sprung up around the turn-of-the-century painted ladies. Yet Tara still saw alpine meadows beneath the grim-faced peaks. The wildflowers were gone, the heavy snows late this year. Aspens dropped golden leaves on her mother's twenty-year-old Jeep Eagle in the gravel drive.

The sign in front of the Victorian read, *Mountain Midwifery. Francesca Walcott, CNM.* The name Ivy Walcott, CNM, had been painted over; Tara's adopted sister had moved back to West Virginia, reunited with her husband and daughter.

Tara had considered turning to Ivy rather than face their mother with Laura. Too late now.

Before she could unfasten her seat belt, Francesca stepped outside and hurried down the walk toward the Safari station wagon, picking her way on stones set in the mud and gravel between naked flower beds. Her gray-tinged auburn curls cascaded over her shoulders. To Tara, Francesca always looked like the Icenian queen Boadicea, who had avenged the rape of her two daughters by waging war against the Romans.

Francesca suited the role.

Tara cranked down her window and smelled snow, unfallen.

Her mother saw Laura.

When Tara released the buckle on the infant car seat and lifted her, Laura didn't wake, just curled her knees up to her chest. *You are so sweet. I love you. I love you.*

As Tara unfolded herself from the car with Laura, a blue Toyota Land Cruiser beat its way up the road, rocking over the bumps. The road led up to Tomboy, a ghost town recently turned real-estate speculation-ground. Though several properties were listed, her mother said only one resident had settled on the high alpine tundra, buying up half of what was there. So this must be Francesca's troublesome landlord. But first Tara saw the children, with luminous skin shades darker than the Rio Grande and wavy, shiny, black hair. A boy, a little girl, another boy.

Finally, she caught an impression of black hair, granite cheekbones and fair skin behind the steering wheel. No one had ever mentioned his looks—only that he was an obstetrician and difficult. Now, there was a real-estate sign in the yard. Was he selling the Victorian?

Where will Mom go?

Where will Laura and I go?

Evicting Francesca so that he could rent out her house to skiers. So why was there a real estate sign on the front lawn?

Francesca plastered on a grin and waved.

The driver nodded, and Tara noted the careless scrape of his eyes, eyes some murky shade of dark gray or green. The children were speaking to each other, ignoring everything else.

"Friends?"

"Shut up and smile." The hiss of a sigh escaped Francesca's lips, saying plainer than words, *What have you done now, Tara? Whose baby is that?*

The Land Cruiser halted in the rocks and mud alongside the road, beneath evergreens. As the dust settled, a car door slammed, and the driver strode toward them.

"Great," muttered Francesca.

"What?"

"Please, Tara. Let me do the talking. This is my landlord." She added, "And Dan McCrea's brother."

Dan McCrea. The *other* creep in her life who'd been christened Daniel. Why did she have so much trouble with people named Dan? There was Danny Graine, her ex-husband—

And Dan McCrea, M.D., OB/GYN.

His brother was six foot three or four. Tara rocked Laura, singing softly, *"Hush a-bye, don't you cry, Go to sleepy, little baby...."* Under the pine trees, she adjusted the receiving blanket over the tiny head in a cotton hat. She'd found the hat at Wal-Mart in El Paso, along with the infant car seat—everything but the cotton diapers she'd bought from a supplier, also in El Paso.

"Hello, Francesca."

Tara thrust out a hand. "Hi, I'm Tara. Francesca's daughter."

"Isaac McCrea." He shook her hand, then ignored her. "The buyers signed the contract today. Occupancy is set for November twenty-fourth."

His eyes were hazel, with black lashes and eyebrows. Yeah, the resemblance to Dangerous Dan was there, alongside the differences. Great chin, nice jaw, straighter hair, more interesting eyes... In Tara's arms, Laura stirred, made a soft crying sound.

She would have to get the milk and supplemental feeder from the cooler in the car. Her plan was to link up with some of Francesca's nursing moms, see if any would donate breast milk.

"Is there something I can do to change your mind, Dr. McCrea?" asked Francesca.

"No." He shook his head.

"Is it because I'm a midwife?"

Tara liked the direct question, the only relevant question. Relevant to everything when one's life was midwifery—in the United States.

"Of course not."

"Then, perhaps, when I find a new place for my home and office," Francesca suggested, "you'll be willing to serve as backup physician."

Gutsy, Mom! Incision Dan's brother serve as backup for the local midwife?

"I have no maternity insurance. I don't do births."

Didn't do births? Tara broke in. "Aren't you an obstetrician?"

"Family practice. You're thinking of my brother."

She blushed. On the phone, months and months ago, Francesca had said he was an obstetrician; but that was when he was new to town. Or maybe there was confusion with his brother, who'd lived in Precipice for years. In any case, Francesca had been getting flak from the hospital about her homebirth practice, and she always assumed the worst.

From the corner of her eye, Tara glimpsed motion. "Your car is rolling."

The Land Cruiser connected with a house-sized boulder behind it and stopped.

"Not anymore." Unconcerned about his children releasing the parking brake? Backing away, he murmured, "Enjoy your visit," and he was partway to his car before he turned and looked at Tara.

She felt to her bones what he saw.

A woman with a newborn and a slender body and flat stomach. Quelling panic, fear of discovery, she grinned. "Bye, doc."

"TARA. YOUR *ETHICS!*"

"Ethics, schmethics. This has nothing to do with being a midwife."

"You attended that child's birth! You can't just keep the baby! And you can't raise a child alone."

"What would you have done?"

Francesca thought, *We've been here a hundred times before.* Butting heads. "I would have driven straight back to Maternity House. What possessed you to do anything different?"

"I told you. I swore—"

"The mother is clearly not dead."

"Maybe, maybe not. But her wishes were obvious. She *considered* herself dead—to this child. And now, Laura can grow up knowing that her mother and I made a pact, rather than that her mother *abandoned* her, which is the story she'd hear if she was adopted by strangers."

Francesca pressed her lips together. The baby was darling, with her thatch of dark hair and huge dark eyes. *I don't dare hold her.* But Tara… Tara was nursing her with supplemental milk. Ten to twelve times a day. What was she thinking? "Tara, that baby is stolen. From the next couple in the state of Texas waiting to adopt a child."

Tara had already considered that. "I disagree. Julia fostered her out—informally—to me. People have done it forever, everywhere. Uther Pendragon handed Arthur to Merlin, who gave him to Sir Ector to raise. Dad told me about an Eskimo lady giving her second son to a woman who had none, for the strength of the community—"

Francesca rolled her eyes. She'd once heard Charlie convince a man that moose turn into caribou when they cross the Arctic Circle. "Things have changed, Tara."

"But remember how it was in Hawaii? Lots of adoption within families. Fostering and adoption are ancient traditions—"

"And this is the dawn of the third millennium."

Tara lifted the infusion of fenugreek she'd brewed. "To a bright new century. Here we are. And I can help you. I'll do the homebirths. You do the hospital births."

"I've already told my homebirth clients that I can't attend homebirths anymore. I can't risk losing hospital privileges, and there's simply too much pressure from the medical community."

"Tara to the rescue. I'll start a homebirth practice to fill in the gaps. After all, I have no hospital privileges to lose."

"*You* should not be practicing in the state of Colorado, Tara. It's not legal. In January—" Francesca began.

"Not an issue. These hands caught more than eight hundred babies just last year."

"In Texas. I know your credentials, Tara. But the answer is no."

The infant in her arms ceased sucking at Tara's nipple and the tube from the supplemental feeder. Her head dropped away in slumber, and Tara carefully turned her to burp her.

Pretending not to see the bonding between her daughter and the newborn, Francesca watered pots of cacti in the solarium. The muscles in her shoulders ached. How could Tara have done it?

Only Tara would have done it.

And Tara was fragile as a cactus. Cacti seemed hardy, but if you ignored what they were and watered them too much... Was Tara really over Danny, over his running off with her partner, *having a child* with her partner? Now ex-partner.

How can I turn her away? Wandering to the kitchen, Francesca touched the soft cheek of the sleeping newborn. Skin so fine. The smell of her so new. "Do you even have her birth certificate?"

"No." The solution—the last-gasp, avoid-losing-Laura solution—confronted Tara again. Surely it wouldn't come to that.

"How do you plan to adopt her, Tara?"

"I'm working it out. Don't worry. If I'm not worrying, why should you?"

Francesca folded her arms across her chest. Lines in her forehead deepened as she returned to the solarium. After a bit, she shook her head and muttered, "That man."

"Isaac the Greedy? His kids are cute." *Releasing the parking brake.*

"His children are in dire need of a mother."

In dire need of a mother?

Tara came alert. "Where's their mother?"

"I understand she's dead." Reluctantly, Francesca added, "In Rwanda. That's where they came from."

Rwanda?

Tara saw the terraced slopes, felt the heat and humidity, smelled the scents, the unique scents of that country, the faces of the people. She had read the newspapers and books in '94 and since, and cried for Rwanda.

She placed Laura in a sling against her chest, a style she'd learned in South America, and went to the sink. She removed the feeding system and emptied the remaining milk, then prepared for next time. Afterward, she took flour, cinnamon and nutmeg from the cupboard. "I'm going to make a couple of pies and take them up to your nemesis and his motherless children."

Francesca's eyes rounded. "You're going to do *what?*"

"It's for Laura. Here's a man who needs a wife. And I need a husband so I can get a home study and adopt Laura."

"Tara, you can't—"

Tara laughed. "Just kidding, Mom."

Francesca reminded herself to breathe. It sometimes occurred to her that Tara had been conceived in a turbulent year—oh, in how many ways—and that she'd been born on the fifth anniversary of President John F. Kennedy's assassination, and that maybe all of this was to blame for her having turned out as she had. But no. Charlie Marcus's genes—and personality, if you could call it that—were responsible.

"I'm going to try to talk him out of selling this house," Tara explained, almost as though reasoning with herself.

Francesca studied her daughter. Was Tara lying? She'd learned from the best—her father. "The house is a done deal."

"Not till closing."

"He's not going to back down, Tara. I've known him longer than you have. Not to say that I *do* know him, only that I know how he feels about selling this house. I always get the same answer."

Her daughter's smile made Francesca uneasy, as if Tara actually planned to marry Isaac McCrea. "Then maybe someone else should do the asking."

SHE DROVE SLOWLY, yet the low-slung station wagon hit rocks in the four-wheel-drive road. Her mother had offered to watch Laura, but Tara had declined. She didn't want to be apart from her. *You're so precious.* Blowing bubbles in her car seat.

Twilight bathed Tomboy. The ghostly skeleton of an uninhabited mining structure rose against the far rock walls. Closer by stood another deserted building, the Columbine, which had once been a bordello. Now the windows were boarded, like those of the houses across the road where miners had lived, but Tara drove with one elbow in order to direct an X made with her two index fingers toward the house of prostitution.

Had he bought that, too? Her mother had said "everything north of the road."

Lights shone from a house set alone at the edge of the tundra. Decades ago, the mine owner had resided there, in a two-story cabin set eight feet above the road, at winter snow level. Subsequent owners had built onto the sides and back, adding the steep rooflines of a chalet, with outdoor shutters and balconies. A snowmobile near the side porch awaited the first storms.

Isaac McCrea had chosen a high and desolate paradise for his home, and Tara envied him the alpine wildflowers that would poke through the tundra, the grasslike slivers ice formed at that altitude, the alpenglow which would turn the peaks pink each night.

He must have heard her car. A tall shadow darkened a downstairs window, then moved away.

She parked, and when the motor died, she could hear music. Drums and singing.

HIS DOORBELL RANG, and he crossed the pine floor in his wool socks, calling over his shoulder to David, "I'm going to steal the scroll."

Dice rolled on the kitchen table as he opened the door.

It was Francesca Walcott's daughter with her newborn. He remembered an observation earlier that day. She didn't look like a woman who'd recently given birth.

A black cat shot between his feet and leaped to the porch railing. Arching its back, it hissed.

"Don't take it personally. She always acts that way."

Tara heard a trace of an accent. How could she have missed it earlier? She held out a cardboard box. "I made you some pies. The bottom one might be a little crunched. I had to stack them. There's cardboard in between."

"Smells great. We're not picky." Pumpkin. Like his mom's. "Come in."

"Thanks." Her grin was raw and unbridled, radiating sexuality. When she stepped inside, he noticed she was tall, five-ten maybe. Long straight hair the shade of a walnut fell down her back, and her eyes were almost the same color. They swept the foyer, the great beams, the ancient floors, the loft. Isaac realized what she must see—the laundry heaped on a chair, the dishes in the sink, Barbie dolls and Micro Machines on the rug, a cat's kill. He grabbed a snow shovel from the porch and scooped the last outside.

The three children gathered at the table were neater than their surroundings. The little girl wore blue flannel pajamas, her long thick hair in two braids. Dirty dishes covered two counters. The music came from upstairs.

"You steal the scroll," one of the boys said to Isaac.

"Okay, I'm going to read it." Isaac remembered his manners belatedly. "Hold up, gang. We have a visitor. This is—"

"Tara." She grabbed a chair at the table and surreptitiously brushed off crumbs before sitting. In Mexico, out in the country, the women's homes had dirt floors. She'd loved visiting each home for prenatal visits and births. Years ago. "Who's who, here? And what are you playing?"

"Dungeons & Dragons," David said. As the boys dove in with answers, Isaac shut the door. Why was she here? The eviction? She couldn't possibly think this would sway his decision about the Victorian.

And that couldn't be her baby.

"Dad's a thief. We just found this scroll, and he stole it."

Isaac's thoughts drifted back to the game, and he winced. "I forgot to ask Oliver to identify it."

"That's true." David, his younger son, held their destinies in his hands. "And when you read the scroll, you begin to grow a beard. It grows at a rate of one foot per hour."

Isaac and his fellow adventurers groaned.

"It's okay, Daddy," said Danielle. "Oliver has *les ciseaux. La magique!*" Her heavily accented English turned to French, then Kinyarwanda, until she covered her mouth to keep the words inside. The gesture stabbed Isaac. He'd been too intense about her speaking English.

Daddy was easy. She'd known him as Daddy all her life. Having the children call him Dad or Daddy had been his and Heloise's main concession to the obvious fact that he was not Rwandan, not Hutu, not Tutsi, not Belgian. American.

Tara stared at Danielle with brilliant, admiring eyes. "You know more languages than me!"

"Not English." Danielle sighed.

"You shouldn't have read the scroll, Dad," said Oliver, their magician. "We'll try the magic scissors, but I think we're going to have to pay someone to remove the curse."

"Your English is very good." Tara saw something dart across the shadows in the kitchen. A mouse. Someone should let the cat back in.

You sure made yourself at home, Isaac thought. "Everyone who wants a piece of pie needs to wash a plate."

Three chairs moved in unison.

Another cat, dark gray, stalked toward the corner. *Get him. Get that mouse.* Tara glanced up at Isaac. "You have a great family."

"Thanks. Shall I wash a plate for you?"

"Oh, I can wash my own."

She began to rise, and he waved her down. "You're a guest. Dishes just aren't a high priority around here."

"They never have been with me, either." *But someone better get a handle on the crumbs.*

"And guys," he told the children, "that's a wrap for tonight. After the pie, go to bed."

None of the children chose to eat at the table, instead settling all over the rustic furniture and the tattered rug that covered the center of the distressed-wood floor. In the kitchen, the mouse had become a toy for the charcoal cat.

Isaac set a piece of pie and a fork in front of Tara. "Something to drink?"

"Water, please."

He brought it, then his own, and they were alone at the table while the kids carried on their own conversation about the game, lapsing into Kinyarwanda—then, with a glance at him, returning to English. Rules for guests.

Tara tried to kick off the conversation. "How do you like being a doctor in Precipice?" She tucked a finger into the newborn's tiny hand.

"It's nice." Calling himself to the conversation, Isaac shrugged.

Tara thought he sounded as though he was just visiting.

The baby began to wake, and she lifted the child from the sling. "Hello, Laura. Hello, hello, sweet princess."

Laura. A coincidence that this baby should share a name with one of his dead children, one of the triplets. Only Danielle had survived the birth, to become his brother's namesake three days later, when he had named her sisters, too, the sisters he'd dug up from the dirt in which they were buried. As he'd dug to find

Heloise. His hands itched to hold this Laura. Could holding her be part of healing?

He reached out.

So the doctor likes babies. Tara filed the thought away. What was his story? What had happened to the children's mother? Was she Hutu or Tutsi? One or the other, surely.

"This is Laura Estrella," she said. Her hands to his. Big, long-fingered hands, man hands, beautiful hands.

The baby was all eyes. She was also wet, Isaac observed, and Tara hadn't brought a diaper bag inside. "How many days old?"

"Two weeks." Two weeks of finishing business at Maternity House—without letting anyone know about Laura. Then, packing her birth records and midwifery texts, settling into a routine with Laura. But this man would *know,* would *know* she hadn't given birth to the child. *I'm looking after her for her mother.* Sure. Why not? Tara said the words, then followed them up. "I was working at Maternity House in Sagrado, Texas. Her mother was from Mexico and came up to have the baby. She's young and doesn't want to take care of Laura yet." A lie. It was the worst kind of lie, partly true.

Isaac's eyes belonged to Laura now—so they'd stay off Tara. A woman was a complication he didn't need, unless she liked babysitting. He'd ask her about that in a minute, seeing she'd appeared on his doorstep like Mary Poppins. "What's Maternity House?"

"A birth center. I'm a midwife, too."

"Oh."

She wanted to know what he thought. Whose side was he on? Between doctors and midwives in the

United States, there were always sides. She asked, "And do you approve?"

He glanced up. "Why should it matter?"

Only analysts should answer questions with questions; in other people, it seemed like evasion. "The medical community here. No one will provide physician backup while my mother's doing homebirths."

Not my problem, Isaac thought automatically, as automatically as he had once known no sense of "other," always seeing himself in another's eyes, always looking for the global solution. But not now and not homebirth.

With fifteen hospital beds for every ten thousand Rwandans, he and Heloise had both attended births in homes. But his boys had been born at the hospital, Danielle the only gift in a disaster at home.

When Dan visited, they'd listened to his stories of obstetrics in Precipice and sometimes of "the midwives." Dan could make you laugh.

Especially in a country with so little to laugh about.

The midwives! Isaac remembered. Dan visiting Kibuye, talking about Francesca Walcott, Ivy the Babe, Tara the... Oh, yes, he'd heard all about Tara, hadn't he?

She was the one who said "yoni" instead of "vagina," YBAC instead of VBAC... Isaac wished he could remember more. That night, Heloise had said, "Yoni. I love that word. Yes, you must call my garden my 'yoni' from now on." And he had. Except when he called it her garden.

He didn't want Tara watching his kids, after all.

Noticing that Laura had soaked the front of his shirt, Tara shoved her pie plate away from her. "Hold her, okay, while I run out to the car?"

As Tara left, Laura began to cry, and he lifted her to his shoulder and stood. *Precious baby.*

Oliver and David headed upstairs. The music went off.

Danielle came over to squint up at him and the newborn. *"La bébé est—"*

She stopped midsentence.

Crouching beside her, he smiled, teasing. *"C'est pour votre bien."*

She laughed, then tried. "You are—funny!"

"You are *smart.* My favorite girl."

Danielle touched the baby and told her, in Kinyarwanda, to stop crying, Mama would be back. Laura was momentarily silent, but by the time Tara returned, her screaming had driven even Danielle to her room.

"Sorry," Isaac apologized. "She's mad."

"There's not much you could've done. Hungry and wet." Taking the infant, Tara moved to his kitchen to warm some milk, set up the feeder. Minutes later, she sat on his couch and began to nurse, banishing any shyness about the feeder. *I'm so lucky, Laura. Lucky to have you.*

The cat dropped mouse guts at Isaac's feet. He disposed of the remains, then sat opposite Tara, on a longer, more tattered couch. "How are you doing that?"

Tara's face felt fiery for the second time that day.

He said, "Clinical interest."

She tried to forget he was Dan McCrea's brother. "Sure. It's a supplemental feeder. There's a tube. I'm not even producing milk yet."

"I've never known a woman to do that. Induce lactation." He brought Tara a fresh tumbler of water.

"Thank you." His wife must have nursed. "Actually, I'd like to see if I can get a breast-milk bank going here. And a support group for nursing mothers.''

Good ideas. None of her attitudes shocked him. Heloise's sister had nursed Danielle.

The cat rubbed his legs.

Isaac fetched their pie plates and set them on the big footstools. Between bites of apple pie, he asked, ''Will you be practicing midwifery with your mother?''

''We haven't worked that out yet.'' *Play it cool, Tara.* It was one thing to practice as an unlicensed lay midwife in Colorado; it was another thing to confess the fact to a physician. Laura watched her. ''I can't stop looking at this baby. She's irresistible.'' Time to get a hundred miles away from the topic of midwifery. ''My mom says you're absolutely set on selling that house.''

''Right.'' It wasn't her business why. Raised Quaker and practicing into adulthood—right up to Heloise's death in a country where priests had slayed or betrayed their own flocks, where anyone seemingly would kill anyone—Isaac had little trouble controlling what came out of his mouth.

''You know, my mom could probably pay a little more rent.''

''Then she shouldn't have trouble finding a new place.''

''You don't know Precipice.''

Isaac finished his piece of pie. He didn't *like* turning a woman out of her home, but he had obligations. He yawned conspicuously.

Tara seemed not to see it. She was preoccupied, her forehead creased in a frown.

Her question made him jump in his skin.

''So, you're...not married?''

CHAPTER TWO

I'm praying hard, praying I can do it.… I know I can't last much longer, that I'll end up going to the hospital, except for we have no money, no insurance. Rowdy's applied for a job at a gas station in Logan, but he doesn't think he'll get it. Gabriela talks to me, says I'm doing good. She's just a kid, younger than me, but she helps her mom with midwife stuff. She'll never do what I did, though I'll never call this precious baby a mistake. Anyhow, when Ivy checks me again the baby's coming.…

—"Alison Angelina's Birth," Devon Workman, age 16, Guyandotte, West Virginia

TARA SWITCHED BREASTS, moving the feeding tube as well. Her nipples already protruded from nursing. He noticed one of them was malformed and circled by shiny, puckered tissue. Burns?

With difficulty, he kept from staring. "Widowed."

"I'm sorry."

"It's been five years."

Silence folded in on them.

She juggled Laura and her piece of pie, trying to eat and paying more heed to the baby than to covering her breasts. If she'd been Heloise, he would have fed her bites between kisses.

As it was, he found her sexy, prodding, earthy. She'd descended on him like a forest spirit and made herself comfortable in his disordered home. Mouse-ridden—a haven for hantavirus. He shuddered slightly. Wishing her quick exit from his life, he asked, "How long will you be visiting your mother?"

"We're moving here. Need a babysitter?"

"No." He'd already decided. There was a school bus. The kids could handle it. In some ways, Oliver was older at thirteen than the adults of Precipice.

But tragedy and bloodshed didn't really mature a child.

And what to do with Danielle in the mornings?

"I have references. I went to junior high and high school here."

He pictured her employed as nanny to Sleeping Beauty and other fairy-tale children. Not his kids. *Time for this day to end.* The children would be spending the weekend with his mother in Silverton; he'd drive them over Thursday night. Friday was his extra day off before the weekend, and he'd told the schools this would be an educational absence. Only six months in the U.S.? Everything was education.

On the kitchen counter, his pager buzzed, and he found it between pie plates. "This is new for me." He eyed the device. "Can't say I love it."

Tara turned on the couch and laughed. "I love mine. A baby on the way is good news. Oh, no—I mean, I just dumped the pie on your couch."

Blood awakened his penis. Her voice? Another glimpse of her breasts? Or just having a woman in the house? "Don't worry about it. I'll clean it up." He gazed at the number. The answering service. "Excuse me."

While he was out of the room, Tara dabbed at the couch, then laid out a protective pad to change Laura. "We need to get you more clothes, kiddo." The baby watched Tara's eyes, and Tara smiled back, her mind on Isaac.

He was gone long enough to give her more chance to study the chalet. There were two primitive masks on one rough wooden wall, with a photo of a mountain gorilla between them. On the table beneath was a woven blanket.

When he returned, she asked, "What took you to Rwanda?"

"Doctors Against Violence. I was an intern and resident with them, then worked for them till last year." They'd paid his way through medical school, too, in an accelerated program starting just after high school. And they'd gotten him and his children out of Rwanda on twelve hours' notice.

Briefly, he remembered his fellow intern in Kigali fourteen years ago—twenty-four-year-old Heloise Nsanzumuhile. In three days, he'd known he was in love. With Heloise, her country and medicine.

He curtailed the conversation. "I have to go to the hospital."

Doctors Against Violence. Back in the late '80s, Tara had spent three weeks in Rwanda with her father and one of his friends, a biologist, and the mountain gorillas. On the way back to Kigali, Tara had seen the massacre of a Tutsi family. She was nineteen and had already lived in Chile for eighteen months, training in a hospital there as a *matrona*, a midwife—and reaching out, trying to create a link between the classes, between the few rich and the many poor, stirring the wrath of her friend Matilde's patrón.... That day in Rwanda, her father had clapped his hand over her mouth and wouldn't let her move. He knew her too well.

Weeks later, back in Chile, she landed in prison.

Not something she wanted to think about.

Feel the hope. Feel the possibilities. Isaac had wanted to hold Laura. *Marry a doctor, adopt Laura.* "Would you like me to stay and watch the kids?"

"We manage." There was an intense, private protectiveness in his words. Tara gathered her things hurriedly, not meeting his eyes. *Okay, he doesn't want me for a sitter.*

Which meant he wouldn't want her for a wife, either.

LAURA'S CRYING penetrated her dreams later that night. Tara's eyelids struggled open. How could any woman do this after a long labor? She'd started in great physical condition, yet she was exhausted.

She changed the infant's sodden diaper. Precious little legs. Cuddle her in a blanket. But Laura cried all the way to the kitchen. Francesca had called some other new mothers earlier that day, and the freezer and refrigerator were stocked with fresh milk. It would keep for 48 hours in the fridge, two to four weeks in the freezer.

"I'll hold her while you warm the milk and set up."

Tara hadn't even noticed her mother entering the kitchen. *I'm dead on my feet.* But it seemed important to manage alone.

As Isaac did.

"I'm fine."

Francesca was already reaching for the baby.

"Mom, you really don't have—"

"Don't be so stubborn, Tara. You don't need to prove anything to me."

Why did people always think she was trying to prove something? She'd been told the same thing before—by Danny, especially. *What are you trying to prove, Tara?*

Danny, Dan McCrea, Danielle McCrea. The little girl must be named for her uncle.

Reluctantly, Tara let her mother hold Laura while she put the kettle on for fenugreek tea. Maybe she didn't have anything to prove to Francesca, but she had much to prove to herself, especially where Laura was concerned.

Her mother turned in a slow circle, Laura against her shoulder. Gently, Francesca patted the crying newborn's back. "Tara, how *are* you going to handle her records? You can't just pretend this child dropped from space."

"I'll homeschool her." Ready to nurse, Tara took the baby from her mother and settled in a chair at the kitchen table. The immaculate house contrasted with the chaos at Isaac's.

"Eventually, someone will want to see a birth certificate." Francesca perched on the edge of another chair. Tara rarely saw her mother relax, rarely saw her sit back and just *be*. Even now, she seemed poised to spring up, to try to make Tara more comfortable.

But Francesca was right about Laura. "It'll work out," Tara promised. Laura's soft cheek was curved, her little mouth suckling hard. Long ago, Tara had adopted the philosophy that things work out. She'd been jailed in one Third World country for defending the poor and in another for—bad luck. She never spoke of those times, seldom looked back.

Look forward, Tara.

Laura's birth certificate, birth certificate... Oh, good grief! Why hadn't she thought of it sooner? "You could write a birth certificate."

"That would be fraud."

Tara heard. Francesca hadn't said, *Not on your life.* She hadn't refused.

"It's the perfect solution, Mom."

"No. I won't do it. I wouldn't even consider it, Tara."

She had considered it. Tara knew but didn't argue. Instead she began singing softly. *"Golden slumbers kiss your eyes. Smiles await you when you rise. Sleep, pretty baby, do not cry...."*

Francesca had rocked Tara to that song in Hawaii thirty years ago. Tara had been born in a homemade birthing tub beside a dolphin lagoon. She'd been born with the sac intact over her head, a symbol of good luck and strength. Francesca knew her daughter's strength—but good luck?

More than a decade ago, Tara had survived a Chilean prison. Two years later, it was Mexico. In the United States she'd been arrested for protesting a nuclear waste dump and for protecting a palm grove in Hawaii from bulldozers. Francesca could scarcely conceive of what her daughter had survived in those instances. Especially Chile. But Tara's eyes always shone, overflowing with enthusiasm, never betraying fear.

Francesca was afraid on her behalf. Always.

Tara never talked. She'd married Danny Graine, a contractor, and Danny had left her for her partner, for

a fellow midwife. Francesca knew Tara couldn't be
held wholly innocent in the desertion. But all Francesca's sympathies rested with her daughter.

Tara and Ivy. Besides midwifery, her vocation, they
were her life. With Ivy, it was a little different. Ivy
had joined their family as an adult. Brain damage, permanent amnesia, had robbed her of her past. She'd
found it now. But back when Tara had suggested
adopting Ivy, it had seemed natural. Francesca loved
Ivy as a daughter. *She is my daughter, like Tara and
unlike Tara.* Ivy's levelheadedness was a counterpoint
to Tara's Charlie Marcus ways.

Ivy lived in West Virginia now. She was reunited
with the husband and daughter she hadn't been able
to remember.

Fake a birth certificate for little Laura, precious
Laura with her mouth latched so hard to Tara's nipple?
Francesca had seen her daughter wince while nursing
Laura Estrella. *I've already helped her round up more
milk.* So many generous mothers willing to help. Was
the birth certificate so much more?

Yes.

And it was just what Charlie would have suggested.
No interest whatsoever in obeying the law. Francesca
abided by rules and regulations, had seldom found it
difficult to do otherwise.

But Tara…

Nursing a child someone had abandoned in the back
seat of her car. Holding inside the consequences of
flouting the law in other lands.

I don't want her hurt again. Not by another Danny
Graine. Not by authorities who would take little Laura
from her arms.

There must be a way to make the adoption legal.

First, a home study. But where was Tara's home? She couldn't be legally employed as a midwife in Colorado until she became licensed. Maybe it was time to convince her to take that step, if not for her own sake then for Laura's. "Tara, the law has changed. It'll come into effect next year."

"What law?" But Tara knew. Midwives would no longer be required to qualify as nurses. Instead, they'd have to verify that they'd attended a certain number of live births and take a test… "Oh, I know about it." Just as she knew there were eight or nine different titles for midwives, titles with little meaning to the consumer. Professionally, she was direct-entry, meaning she'd come into midwifery without pursuing nursing school. By choice, she held no credentials.

As far as Tara was concerned, *midwife* would do. *Matrona.*

"As of January, you can be licensed. It's just a matter of paperwork and passing the test."

"We've covered this one, Mom. No test, no certification. *Sleep, pretty baby, do not cry…*"

"*Why not?* Tara, the certification process will be *nothing* to you."

"This isn't about me. Birth is a natural process, and women should be able to have their babies however and with absolutely whomever they choose. That is a basic human right, and *that* is why I'll never certify— to uphold that right. Not my rights. The rights of mothers and fathers who want homebirths. The American College of Obstetricians and Gynecologists is out to take away *their* rights."

"Becoming licensed won't keep you from homebirths."

"You want me to go on? We could talk about how, in some states, CNMs *can't* attend homebirths and licensed midwives can, and how Colorado is becoming one of those states—"

"This isn't about me, it's about you." Francesca was a certified nurse-midwife. "And no one's asked you to become a CNM."

"Okay, me. I'm against regulating midwifery. Word of mouth is the best regulation there is. Word of mouth and *community,* something this country needs to relearn."

Francesca kept her voice even. "I can't let you do homebirths out of this house, Tara, or under my business name. It compromises my reputation, my position in this community. And I refuse to risk your going to jail when you have that child to raise."

"Ah, we're getting somewhere," Tara told Laura. "She admits you're mine."

Francesca sighed.

She might as well have said, *You're just like your father,* which Tara had always known wasn't really an insult, just something to be accepted. Like her parents' divorce, her father's desertions.

"Tara, I don't see how you can legally adopt her. You're single. You're poor. You're unemployed—"

"And I've just moved to the perfect place for finding a rich husband." She tried to banish Isaac McCrea from her mind. Isaac *and* his family, their cats and their mice.

Francesca looked thoughtful. "I suppose if you fell in love with the right man, the two of you could adopt. Not that I'd favor marrying for money—"

The phone rang.

Millie Rand was due. This must be it.

"A birth," exclaimed Tara. All thoughts of marriage and adoption fled. While Francesca answered the phone, Tara gathered up Laura and filled a new bag for the feeder. She would accompany her mother to the hospital, though she wouldn't be allowed to assist as a midwife—with or without certification. But she could help in other ways. She eavesdropped on the conversation, and when Francesca got off the phone, Tara said, "Fill me in. I'm coming along."

Her mother's lips pressed shut. Shaking her head with a rueful smile, she held Tara's head between her hands and said, "When are you going to make things easier?"

"That's why I'm here, Mom!"

Her mother's sigh could have reached the back of a stadium.

FRANCESCA'S CLIENT AND her family hadn't yet arrived when Tara and her mother reached the hospital's small labor and delivery suite. Francesca and Tara and Ivy, her sister, had provided the toys and books for the children's corner with the help of former clients whose children had outgrown the toys.

Laura was restless, so Tara walked her through the hospital. Isaac McCrea rounded a corner from the cafeteria, and they both started, between giant oil paintings of elk in the aspens.

"Hello, Tara." Uncomfortable, Isaac recalled Tara's visit to the chalet—as he had every hour since she'd left.

"I hope your emergency had a good outcome."

His emergency had been a battered wife. He and two ER nurses had talked her into going to the shelter in Montrose. It had taken four hours. Danielle, who'd begged to come to the hospital with him, was asleep on the floor of the playroom on the maternity unit; the boys were at home. He'd been about to collect his daughter, but suddenly he was in no hurry.

He nodded ambiguously as his brother, Dan, paused beside him in the hallway.

"Well, well, well. Look who's back."

Tara held Laura toward Isaac. "Help me out, doc."

A second later, he was holding the infant while Tara embraced Dan, exclaiming, "Hi, Dr. McCrea! The *other* Dr. McCrea," she added, beaming as though at a long-lost friend.

Better friends than enemies, Tara told herself. If her sister, Ivy, had been there, Ivy would have accused her of insincerity. Tara and Dan weren't friends; friendly adversaries was the best you could call it. But Tara believed you caught more flies with honey than vinegar. The midwives and Dan McCrea had often clashed over a patient's care; no doubt it would happen again tonight, at Millie Rand's birth.

Dan eyed the baby in Isaac's arms and addressed Tara. "Surely, that's not *yours?*" His gaze swept up and down her body.

Subduing an inner twinge of hurt, rising to it, Tara grinned. "Surely, *you're* not implying that it couldn't be."

"No one would imply that," Isaac cut in—and wished he hadn't.

Tara's expression was...mollified. He wanted her in a purely physical way; every man she met must want her. He couldn't forget about her nursing that child who wasn't hers. He couldn't forget *her.*

Tara saw a pregnant woman passing in the hall, her hand linked through her husband's arm. Was that

Francesca's client? Trembling, she reached for Laura, carefully taking the infant from Isaac's arms.

It felt more intimate to him than it should.

"Thanks, doc. I'd better go."

Dan's eyes had followed Tara's—then drifted to her ass. "In that case, I better go, too, to oversee this delivery."

"My mother will have this labor and delivery well under control."

"But I love to watch you in action."

Isaac's throat knotted. His brother's girlfriend of five years had moved out last winter. Still, the word "unprofessional" came to mind.

She invited it. She can deal with it.

Yet the situation violated some sanctity of mother and child—woman and child. Tara held that infant like it was her own. Checking the baby's face, tucking the blanket around her, her own eyes so involved in the child. Vulnerable.

"You know, I'm hungry," she murmured. "I think I'll get something to eat." She started in Isaac's direction, toward the cafeteria, then tossed a glance at his brother. "Join me?"

A wolf smile creased Dan's face. "I think I can spare the time."

They like each other. Fine. Isaac was glad to write her off.

Then she said, "And you?"

"Sure." *So much for writing her off, Isaac.*

Now, Dan was looking *him* up and down. "Damn, you're tall."

They loaded their trays scantily, no one genuinely hungry, and found a table at the side of the room. Realizing they'd forgotten napkins, Isaac went after them, and Dan smiled at Tara over a cup of coffee. "You know and I know that you're really trying to keep me out of the delivery room."

"The birthing suite." Tara tried some iceberg lettuce, the hospital's finest. "Whatever gave you that idea?"

"You're going to fail. You know your problem, Tara? And I mean you and—" with his fingers, he indicated quotation marks "—'midwives' like you. Everything is black and white."

As her jaw dropped, Isaac returned to the table. When he sat down, his leg touched hers, and they both scooted back their chairs.

"In your eyes," Dan continued, "all obstetricians are bad, and we all want to burn you alive. This isn't the Dark Ages. *You're* the ones who want to stay in the dark. Why won't you let us guide you instead? What gets you so riled up about technology?"

Tara felt sweat droplets gathering on her forehead. Birth was sacred. What could she say about a roomful of people staring at the Broncos instead of a woman having a baby right before their eyes? How could she make Daniel McCrea, M.D., see the difference between a vibrant, powerful woman, laboring beautifully in the peace of her own home, and a woman on an epidural, plodding indifferently through the birth of her child? These were the images she saw. And others—from her time in a Chilean hospital. In Chile, like the U.S., traditional midwifery was all but destroyed. It needed a comeback.

But all she said was, "Because technology, in my experience, leads to unnecessary cesarean sections." *Not to mention that* you *can't catch a baby without causing genital mutilation.*

Well, okay, that was putting it strongly; everyone had to do episiotomies in certain circumstances. *But every time, Dan?*

Isaac sipped his coffee, a Quaker silence keeping him out of the fray. He pictured births in Rwanda. Went far away, into himself. No, think about something else. Mice. When it turned cold, they'd flocked inside, and the local vet had given him two homeless cats. But there were too many mice for his cats to kill. He needed exterminators.

"Do you know that some women *prefer* C-sections? And some women prefer painless births."

Try vacuuming once in a while, Isaac. If the mice have nothing to eat... Right. Orkin. Pest control. That was the answer.

Tara wanted to scream. Dan was right. And probably some women had great memories of the baby arriving at halftime, and who was she to say that wasn't best? Hey, the Broncos were great. Besides, how many times had Francesca and Ivy reminded her not to judge one birth experience over another? Again and again, they'd said, *It's not your birth, Tara.*

Oh, she hated hospitals almost as much as jails—and for similar reasons. "I acknowledge the *necessity* for some cesareans, and I support the right of women who want painless births to have them, Dr. McCrea. But I also support the right of women who want homebirths to have homebirths."

"Don't get me started." With an uneasy glance at Isaac, Dan changed the subject. "Tell me about this little tyke. You seem more suited to motherhood than the role of crusader. Especially, since you're still not legal."

Dan McCrea's eyes gleamed, and Tara knew it was

all about power, about establishing power over her. Good luck. Dan McCrea wasn't scary, and she would stall him here in this cafeteria as long as she could and count on his wanting to get some sleep before office hours tomorrow.

Homebirth. Isaac had tired of the company before his coffee cooled to drinkable. He got up. "I'll see you later."

Both seemed surprised.

But he'd barely left the table before his brother said, "You know, Tara, there's such a thing as being too natural. Too earthy. Too *Eastern.* Taoist, Zen, whatever you are. Ultimately, too folksy and backward. You're all of the above."

Isaac shook his head as he left the cafeteria. Homebirth. *Have at her, Dan.*

HE LEFT! DAN MCCREA finally left.

After forty-five minutes of innuendo, a litany of the latest peaks he'd bagged, and a genuine invitation to dinner—no chance—he finally said, "Well, Tara, till next time," and departed...for the hospital doors.

Folksy and backward. She'd thought it was a compliment before he said that.

Waving at Pilar Garcia, a labor and delivery nurse, who had just filled a tray, Tara rose to speak to her old friend.

Pilar glanced at Laura, then toward the doors. "Not a new romance?"

"No. I was trying to keep Millie Rand from an unnecessary C-section. An epidural, anyway. How's she doing?"

"Just fine." Pilar's expression was mildly disapproving. Of Tara's methods? Again, her eyes drifted to the baby, almost as though she knew the state of Tara's womb.

Tara thought deliberately of other things.

There were so many Dan McCreas in the world, she was used to meeting them on their own terms, flirting right back or treating them like flies. But Ivy had told her several times that she was courting trouble.

Pilar's response made her feel worse things—that she'd teased Dan and somehow let down every woman at the hospital. She wondered how Isaac had reacted to her performance with his brother, if he saw her as Dan did—that she viewed things as "black and white." That she was a hotheaded "crusader" for a trivial cause?

Damn it, it *wasn't* a trivial cause, and she'd been trying to do the right thing.

"Okay," she told Laura as she carried the baby toward the maternity unit, "so maybe I'm a little folksy and backward. I can live with that."

DAN MCCREA HAD BEATEN her to the labor and delivery suite, and he and the anesthesiologist were busy trying to talk Millie Rand into an epidural. "You know, I just think you'll be more comfortable if you try the epidural, Millie. Maybe dilate faster."

Tara wanted to step in, to say, *This woman wants a natural childbirth. No drugs, no epidural. Too black and white for you, Dr. McCrea?*

Francesca said, for perhaps the tenth time, "My client has expressed her desire for natural childbirth."

"Francesca, what if I can't do it? I never have before."

This was Millie Rand's third child; the other two were staying with a friend. Her husband had gone to childbirth classes with her. Compared to what Tara had seen daily in Sagrado, this birth promised to be a piece of cake. If the boys would just get out of the room.

Millie's adrenaline must be pumping now. Who could have a baby with someone terrifying her? *And all this chitchat is stimulating her neocortex, just when she needs one of the older parts of her brain to take over. Time to get primal.* Why hadn't she had *this* conversation with Dan when she had the chance? As her buddy Star in Sagrado always said, *Don't fight— engage.*

Millie's husband put in, "Millie, I know what you've been talking about since you knew you were pregnant, and an epidural wasn't it."

"She's in pain," Dan exclaimed.

Tara tried to evoke some feeling of compassion for Dan McCrea. A flicker was as good as it got. The man sent her straight into radical midwife mode; Ivy called it "RMM," as in "Tara, you're in RMM." So be it. *Dan, I bet your brother was born at home and you weren't. Your mother must have been drugged, because you can't tolerate pain now.* Circumcision wouldn't have helped, either.

There. She felt better. The man suffered from hospital birth.

"You're five centimeters dilated, Millie," Francesca encouraged. "You're doing great. How about walking some?"

Millie's husband gave her an encouraging smile, and she began to climb out of bed, just as another contraction came. She moaned through it, and Francesca said, "That's right. Keep your mouth loose."

"I'm going to order a monitor, Millie. I'll feel better

about your baby if we know how it's doing all the time," said Dan.

"I can use the fetoscope, Dr. McCrea."

"We don't want a monitor." Millie's husband supported his wife's body as she labored.

Tara watched his tenderness for only a moment. It was all she could stand before unwanted emotions bubbled up. Just a man to love her like that, to want her to have his children. Down on the border, she didn't see this—just women alone, women like her.

She paused in the doorway. As the doctors in the birthing suite pressed their case, two people approached from the end of the hall.

Isaac. And Pilar, her musical laughter preceding her. Tara's heart thudded, and Laura stirred against her, then began to cry.

Isaac's gaze avoided Tara's as he peered in the door of the playroom, and the nurse continued down the hall without him.

"Back to work." Squeezing Tara's arm affectionately, Pilar sailed past, into the birthing suite.

Laura fussed, rooting for the nearest breast. There were too many people in the room, anyway, another labor-wrecker. Tara left. Noting Isaac's new coolness, she hurried by him, to sit in the waiting area and nurse. She wished she didn't care what Isaac McCrea thought of her. She *didn't* care.

Isaac checked on his daughter. Danielle was fast asleep, her braids against the green nylon of his North Face bag. He could hear a woman moaning in labor. Francesca Walcott's voice came from a room several doors down, the birthing suite. "You're doing wonderfully, Millie. You're such a good mom."

Sometime, Isaac hoped to ask Francesca how her

daughter had gotten so screwed up, but he reminded himself it was 1:00 a.m. And what had Tara really done except come on to an attractive man and talk too much about homebirth?

There were things about her he liked. Her simple clothes—corduroys, T-shirts and sweaters. Her nursing that baby. And the quality he'd once found in all beings—nobility of spirit.

Leaving Danielle, Isaac went out to the waiting room, found Tara and joined her.

He sat forward in the next seat, long forearms on long thigh bones.

Laura had not been nursing well, crying most of the time. Tara wondered if maybe the baby wasn't really hungry. Ignoring Isaac, she moved the tube away and put Laura to her nipple. As the baby latched on, she felt a strange tingling, new and unfamiliar. She was lactating! Her breasts were producing milk. Probably just drops, but... "This is incredible! I think I have milk." And much sooner than she'd ever dreamed.

Isaac felt the miracle, shared her pleasure. Inducing lactation wasn't easy. But his breath was shallow, his stomach muscles tight, as she switched the baby to the other breast, reached under her shirt and sweater, and brought out a sticky drop of milk on her finger, then licked it off. He said finally, "When is the mother going to take over?"

"What?" Tara recalled what she'd told him, that she was raising Laura for Julia. *She's not going to take over.* "I'm not sure." Why the sudden urge to level with him, to blurt the truth?

The appearance of her own mother, obviously steaming, forestalled any confession.

But Laura was still nursing, and Isaac lingered. "I

didn't mean to insult you," he said. "About babysitting. We could talk about it more."

Could we talk about marriage? *Oh, Tara, get real.* "Yes. Yes to everything."

His eyes never left her face.

Knowing Francesca wouldn't say what was on her mind in front of Isaac, Tara used her finger to break Laura's contact with her nipple. "Okay, pumpkin. Let's go see your grandma."

"Grandma?"

Tara flushed. "Sometimes I forget she's not mine." She had brought Laura's car seat inside, and she settled and strapped the newborn in it.

When she stood and lifted the car seat, he stood, too, but Tara didn't raise her eyes again until she reached her mother.

FRANCESCA SPOKE IN a low voice to Tara. "If I have to see another woman deliberately frightened by those men..." Francesca knew she was overstating the point. It was hard for physicians like Dan McCrea to see women in labor and not want to relieve their pain. Dan wasn't a drug-pusher, he was just trying to help, in the way *he* believed was best.

But it's just unnecessary interference. If Millie had *asked* for pain relief, had asked for a monitor... Francesca had seen a few women stuck at seven centimeters dilate to ten in an hour on an epidural. But most of the time she felt it slowed labor.

If only obstetricians and midwives could truly coordinate their efforts. But the American College of Obstetricians and Gynecologists said homebirth was unsafe. All over the country, midwives were attending homebirths with no physician backup—because there was none to be found. Ivy's situation in West Virginia was unusual; her backup physician, Mata Iyer, saw the need for a midwife who would visit homes in her impoverished rural area—and undoubtedly, Mata had never said the word "homebirth" to her insurance provider. Francesca's own backup physician had retired a year before, after battling endless hospital politics.

Francesca appreciated the risks. For years, she'd kept all homebirths within five minutes of the hospital, attending women at the Victorian if they lived too far from town. The more she saw, the less sorry she was to work in the hospital.

Until she actually worked in the hospital.

I am so tired of all this. Maybe it was time to quit, or take up nursing full-time.

"Did they leave?" Tara asked, knowing the answer.

"He's ordered the epidural and monitor. I'm going back to see how she's doing."

"We'll come with you." She and Laura.

"Tara, it won't help. Please go home and sleep. You need it. And *Laura* needs you."

"If Millie doesn't mind, I'd like to stay. I'll wait till the boys have done their thing and left, so we won't crowd the room."

Tara's dark eyes were eager, yet failed to hide her fatigue. Francesca knew this aspect of her daughter too well. Tara relied on births for some kind of spiritual recharge. But now she needed physical recharge.

"Tara, you're trying to produce milk, and you need rest for that."

Her mother was right. But Tara longed to see Millie's labor through to its magical conclusion. There was nothing more intense, more complete, than birth.

It fulfilled something in her that nothing else ever would. Except, perhaps, Laura.

"I'm really wide-awake, Mom."

Francesca knew that was untrue. But Tara was an adult. "Millie asked where you went." She sighed. "Let's go see how she's doing."

THE BABY'S HEAD crowned four hours later. Francesca caught the head when it emerged, and Tara guided Millie's hands toward her child. She remembered Laura's birth, Julia's apathetic eyes. But there was nothing like this joy. The experience of meeting a person never met before.

No cord. More pushing.

"Ahhh…ahhh…"

"Hey, you handsome guy." Admiring the newborn—and double-checking Francesca's quick suctioning—Dan smiled at Millie and her husband. "This one's going to play for the Broncos."

"My baby! Oh, sweet baby!"

In the bliss of seeing mother and child, Tara could even feel warmth for the obstetrician, could even appreciate that he was smiling over the newborn. She settled in a chair at the edge of the room and savored the experience of the birth.

But her eyes dropped shut.

Snow…

Walking with Isaac. He asked her why she'd become a midwife.

It's what I am. It's all I am.

There are other parts of you.

They'd stopped, and he touched her.

"Tara."

Her eyes opened. It was her mother. Laura slept in

the car seat at Tara's feet, while Millie Rand dozed on the bed, her newborn in a bassinet beside her.

No Isaac.

Just herself, aroused by a dream of him.

Francesca spoke softly. "Time to go home."

Silently, Tara gathered her things. As she lifted the car seat, Laura's eyes opened. *Don't cry.* Carrying the baby and her diaper bag, Tara slipped through the door with her mother. Outside the suite, in the bright lights of the hall, Francesca said, "I didn't want to waken you."

While Tara paused to transfer Laura to the sling, Francesca collected the car seat.

The clock at the nurses' station read five-thirty, and Pilar was talking to the nurse on the next shift. Moving on, Francesca and Tara waved, and she waved back.

"Thank you for the sleep, Mom." Tara covered her yawn with her hand.

Francesca caught her peering up and down the halls. "What are you looking for?"

Tara hid any reaction in drowsiness. "The way out."

BY THE FOLLOWING afternoon, her plan was set in stone.

She wanted to adopt Laura legally, and she knew the other midwives at the birth center in Sagrado would help her. But in her case, the authorities would insist on a prerequisite. A husband.

Tara didn't have time to "fall in love," as her mother had suggested the other night. It would take a century. But a "suitable" man to marry lived two miles away, and she had the tool to bribe him. Herself. She could care for his children, *and* she could clean that chalet. Isaac wouldn't be likely to toss his new mother-in-law out in the street, either.

Are you crazy, Tara? What made her think he'd marry her because he needed childcare—or a house-keeper? As far as she knew, he didn't even like her. His brother was a better choice.

No.

It had to be Isaac. He'd said they could talk again....

And, in some way she couldn't define, he seemed safe.

Stretching out with Laura on the downstairs couch, preparing for a half-hour nursing session, she said, "Yes, kiddo, I've got it figured out."

Francesca, who'd been working on an article for a midwifery journal at her computer, asked, "What have you figured out?"

"How to adopt Laura."

When Francesca turned her chair and waited, Tara realized her mother expected the whole story. "I'll explain after I know it's going to work."

"Why do I have a bad feeling about this?"

"Because you're a pessimist. Millie Rand's baby could have been born at home, and we both know it."

"That was a smooth change of subject, Tara. How are you planning to adopt Laura?"

"You'll feel better about it once it's accomplished. Hey, do you care if I carve those pumpkins on the counter?"

Francesca hid her alarm. "More pie?"

"Pumpkin bread."

"Not for Isaac?"

"The way to a man's heart."

Francesca was aghast. When she'd imagined Tara

finding a husband, it was something that would happen slowly. Friendship blossoming to love. But not with—

This was a disaster. She didn't know why, but it was. That reserve of Isaac's was *strong,* as strong as Tara's outgoing passion. He had lived in Rwanda, and his wife had somehow died in Rwanda—and Tara was so...*heedless.* She and Isaac McCrea were loaded freight trains that ought to pass on separate tracks. Instead, they were going to collide.

When she abruptly remembered Tara and Isaac sitting together in the waiting room at the hospital, Francesca realized something had already begun.

And there was nothing she could do to stop it.

"ISAAC, ARE YOU really all right?" Dan asked for the second time since Isaac had called, after his return from Silverton.

"Sure. Mom's giving me a breather this weekend. I'm stronger than I look."

"Yeah, right. What stunted my growth anyway?" Dan was six-one.

"I'll die sooner."

"I think Tara prefers you."

Well, he hadn't had to say her name first.

"You know, I can't stand her," Dan added. "I hate her clothes. I hate her politics. I hate the way she uses her body. She flirts with me for an *hour,* and then, I ask her out, and she says no."

"That makes my ears hurt." All of it.

"No kidding. She's a thorn in my side. I thought if we got it on, things might improve. What about you? Do you like her?"

Isaac traced the inside of his cheek with his tongue. "I don't know her."

The doorbell rang, and Isaac headed to answer it, the cordless in his hand. "Hey, Dan. I'll see you in the morning."

"I was getting around to that. I'm on call. Rich had something come up." Rich Scarborough, the Chief of Obstetrics.

They'd planned a climb, but Isaac wouldn't mind the solitude.

He opened the door, and the black cat, the one Danielle called Meow, shot in from the cold. She found the tabby kitten he'd adopted outside the market and began hissing.

Tara, with Laura in a sling against her breasts, held two foil-wrapped packages. The night had sprouted stars behind her.

Isaac spoke into the phone. "I've got to go."

The alpine cold was numbing, and he let her in. She handed him the still-warm loaves of bread and continued into the living room with its rustic furniture.

"What's the hurry?"

"I have a visitor." He shut the door behind her. The tabby had retreated to a recess beside the broom closet. Meow rubbed Isaac's legs, but he knew better than to touch her. They all did.

"You've got to be kidding." Dan found the chalet beautiful but lonely. His own place was actually farther from town, in an enclave. The locals called it "on the mountain."

"Bye." Isaac switched off the phone.

"Sorry," he apologized and sniffed the foil-wrapped loaves. Pumpkin. "What did I do to deserve this?" *My brother likes you. Even if he says he doesn't.*

"Nothing." Tara's smile was mischievous. "Yet. Where are the kids?"

"Silverton. Spending the weekend with my mother."

Tara helped herself to a seat on the ancient couch. The disarray had worsened, if anything. Lunch boxes, probably not empty, sat in various places, and the laundry mound now extended to the floor. She spotted a bread crust under the opposite couch. "He sold both houses furnished, didn't he?"

The former owner. "Yes."

Tara sensed his impatience with her visit. It gave her a bad feeling, but it was too late to stop. She *couldn't* stop—and couldn't think of a better approach. Not here, in his presence, under that gaze. "I have a proposition for you."

Isaac's eyes darkened. He pulled a footstool toward him and dropped down on it.

It would be easier to speak without that hot feeling in her chest, the feeling that wouldn't let her stop, the feeling that made her tremble. "I'd like to propose—" she waited a beat, trying to read his face "—a marriage of convenience."

CHAPTER THREE

The midwives at Maternity House treat us with respect. Tara, she holds my hand; her brow creases when I feel the pain. "Your baby will be here soon," she says, and she embraces me. She is like my oldest, Elana. I tell her she is like my daughter, and she gives more hugs.

—Inez Martinez, age 44, Maternity House, Sagrado, Texas, after the birth of Juan Diego

ISAAC HAD HEARD perfectly and didn't ask her to explain.

But she tried. "I need a husband, you need a wife. We treat it as a business decision and a business partnership—"

"Slow down. I need a wife? And that's a business decision?"

The only way to save face was by never lowering her head. Anyhow, what kind of reception had she expected? She'd known she would have to persuade him. "I'm thinking of a temporary arrangement. You can bail when you find someone you like better. You don't have a girlfriend, do you?"

He only stared.

Tara forced out the words. "I can take care of your children."

"This seems like an extreme suggestion." She knew his brother's desire for her—*and she doesn't know me at all.* He smelled sexual abuse or an absent father or both. Heloise's younger sister Dominique, the midwife, had shown similar traits. *A girl loses her father when she is ten,* Heloise had explained, *she looks for him her whole life. Maybe with her sexuality, she tries to call him, to retrieve what she lost.*

Isaac asked, "Why do you want this?"

Tara counted the chances that he would agree to her plan. Slim. In which case she shouldn't reveal the truth about Laura. "A male father figure for Laura."

"You said temporary. How will it help the *bébé?*" His control was slipping. Anger, fear, emergency. Under any of these emotions, he became *le docteur en médecine* of Kibuye, Rwanda. He was angry. "Who is her mother?"

Tara heard the change in his voice, the lapse into French followed by carefully enunciated English. She heard the anger, too, and her pulse quickened. In the past ten years, she'd learned to stand up to her fear and to anyone who frightened her. Birth had taught her that. "Calm down."

Her eyes were on his, unblinking.

Isaac returned her stare, measure for measure. "Who is the mother?"

Still angry. It was the emotion men did best, one reason she and men were a bad combination. Intimacy always led to this.

But if she wanted to adopt Laura, with Isaac McCrea, the story would have to come out. *Trust. That he won't tell his brother or the police. Trust that he's not a law-and-order kind of guy.* He couldn't be—not after the things he must have lived through.

Trembling, she began the story. She told him about the border and about Maternity House. Then, Julia. Finally, Laura.

Outside, a screech owl called. A floor lamp with holes cut in the metal shade flushed the huge room in shadowy wood tones.

When she'd finished, Isaac still waited.

"That's it." Tara eyed Laura, now asleep beside her on a plastic-sided changing blanket laid over his couch.

His head spun. She'd just…kept the baby. In other cultures, in other places, it wouldn't be an issue. For Isaac the man, it wasn't an issue. But for Isaac McCrea, M.D., it must be. He didn't even want to know about this situation.

But now he knew. "What's your plan?"

"Get married. Get a home study. Go back to Maternity House with every single thing we need in hand. I'll level with them, tell them the whole story. From that point on, I'm counting on friends, and it's a prayer, but at least I know people in the system."

"You should have talked to them before now."

"Then Laura would have gone to another home."

"That may happen anyway."

His words made her shiver. *No chance. No way.* He could help! His children needed a mother, needed her. Especially the little girl, Danielle. Kids shouldn't live…like this. She could clean up. She'd known a guy who worked for Orkin. She knew how and where to place bait and seal up a house, and she could get rid of these mice.

And she needed Isaac so she could keep Laura.

"I don't even know you, Tara."

Before he could formulate more words, she said,

"Let's have a few dates. I'll even try to find a sitter for Laura."

Her smile was full of affection, compassion for his anger. She didn't *know* his anger. Like grief, it was bigger than a man. Were all emotions the same? Isaac wondered. Could all heal with time? Lost love and rage and...

"But do I need to point out that mutual attraction isn't necessary?"

He blinked. Was she saying she wasn't attracted to him? Isaac squeezed the bridge of his nose. "This is supposed to tempt me?"

"I came prepared to offer you money."

Money? That was how much she valued herself as a potential mate? For him? "I need to think about this, Tara." And about Dan.

He was going to say yes. Tara knew it.

Isaac wished he wasn't curious. And suddenly aching for the body across from him. Just the fact that she'd chosen him, even with rodents. "What's with you and Dan?"

Regret. The cafeteria. Dan had asked her to dinner. Had he told Isaac? A lie wouldn't be smart. "We flirted. He asked me out. I didn't want to go. Look, I'm a friendly person. That was about my mother's client. And unnecessary medical intervention."

"So you flirted with the obstetrician on call?"

"He knew it. He told me so when we sat down."

It had the ring of truth; they'd gone from flirtation to argument in a heartbeat.

"I hate people interfering needlessly with women in labor. It's *oppression.*"

"I appreciate the sentiment. I don't like your tactics."

Shame overtook her. She wasn't going to stick around someone who made her feel like this. So much for Isaac McCrea. Tara moved to pick up Laura. "I'm sorry to take your time."

Everything whirled, flooding. A baby in the car. Inducing lactation. Isaac held it off. This should be the end. He didn't like her ways, didn't like women—or men—who threw their arms around people at random. But she was in a bind and so was he, handling the second-to-second immensity of caring for his children without the help of Heloise's family. And the grief and guilt. Who was he to throw stones? At anyone? "I'm sorry."

She hadn't yet lifted her child, and she faced him. "Don't be. Not everyone likes me. I can take it."

He couldn't. "Tara—" Searching for words, he covered his face with his hand. When he removed it, she was holding the child and slinging her diaper bag over her free shoulder.

He stood and took the bag from her. "I'll walk you to your car. The steps are frosty." *You might trip over a cat.*

"You're going to have six feet of snow up here before you know it."

Her voice never shook.

The alpine air was frigid. Isaac would return inside alone and try to find sanity in the company of cats and mice.

Unconsciously, he steadied Tara on the steps.

She seemed unaffected by the touch. "You ever lived in the mountains before, doc?"

"Dan and I grew up in Silverton. Our father drove the snowplow on the Million Dollar Highway."

Avalanche country. "Boy, I bet he was a local hero."

"Yes." His father had been dead three years, and his mother preferred to stay in Silverton, among her friends and neighbors.

They took his frosty path to Tara's car, and he opened the passenger door for her, so she could settle Laura in her car seat and bundle her up. Not a sound stirred the night. Tara finally backed away from the infant, and he shut the door and followed her to the driver's side.

When she was in, he crouched beside the door, close enough to feel the heat of her body. He didn't want her to leave, especially not after some of the things he'd said. Eyes on the steering wheel, he spoke from his heart, the way he'd been trained all his life. "You're too special to do what you did tonight." Any woman was.

"At the hospital—or here?"

"Both."

She laughed. "I love being alive. I love helping women have babies. I love this kiddo here, and I could love your kids, too. What can I say?"

The words sounded brittle, and he glanced at her face. She was defending who she was. He'd slandered who she was.

Standing, he tried to make his smile an apology. "I think you just said it. Good night, Tara."

BY THE TIME SHE turned the car around, to head back to the Victorian, she was crying. And it wasn't because she hadn't found a husband to help her with Laura's adoption.

It was because she'd offered herself to Isaac Mc-Crea.

And he had kept her at arm's distance and said, "No, thanks."

ISAAC COULDN'T SLEEP, and finally he rose and dressed for winter cold, and when he went outside the stars were gone. He knew the paths around the property and above the trees, the old mining trails that wouldn't disturb the fragile tundra, and he chose one of them to take him to the talus beneath the far ridge. An unnamed trail led to an unnamed peak, and he followed it, his eyes sharp for the mountain lion whose dried scat and scratch marks he'd found weeks earlier.

Cold, he zipped his parka higher. As the rocks clinked beneath his feet, the first snowflake wet his cheek. Then another.

He was thinking of her body. She was leggy and narrow-hipped, with pretty breasts— A burn on her breast? He shut his eyes, wondering.

She'd offered to marry him, offered to keep house, offered him money! How much money did she think he was worth, seeing that she was willing to buy a spouse?

Undoubtedly, she'd give her body, too, in order to adopt that child. But he wanted her to *want* him— more than desire. Much more.

He reached the peak, and a dusting of snow covered the top. Isaac tried to see the distant mountaintops and couldn't. He waited in the wind.

He'd hurt her tonight.

And she'd hurt him.

But it was less painful than hurting his own flesh and blood.

"How did Isaac like the pumpkin bread?"

Tara knew her mother didn't mean to be cruel, but she was fragile right now, still feeling the sting of rejection. "Fine. I've got to nurse Laura. Excuse me."

Francesca trailed after her to the kitchen. "You know, he might think you're throwing yourself at him, Tara."

Great. Tara didn't answer. Wordlessly, keeping her thoughts focused elsewhere—away from Isaac and her recent humiliation—Tara began the process of making fenugreek tea, getting ready to nurse. Turning suddenly, she held one hand at knee level and snapped, "You make me feel about this high, Mom."

Francesca winced. It was the last thing she'd meant to do. "Tara, I didn't mean to imply that you *were* throwing yourself at him. I'm just saying that Dr. McCrea is a little standoffish. Not everyone likes to be hugged."

"I didn't hug him."

Laura began to cry. "It's all right, sweetie," Tara murmured. "Oh, I love you."

Regarding the two of them, Francesca frowned. Had Isaac discouraged her? Was there nothing to worry about from him? "Have you looked up any of your old friends in Precipice? Tim?" Tim with his waist-length blond dreadlocks? "Scooter?" Who was thirty-two and still rode a skateboard. "Jack?" Whose claim to fame was having made the "Bartenders of Precipice" calendar.

"No, haven't had time, Mother."

But time for two rounds of baking for Isaac McCrea. Well, he was several grades above Danny Graine as husband material, several grades above anyone Tara had set her sights on before—at least, from what Fran-

cesca knew about him, which was scant. Unfortunately, Francesca couldn't see the reserved Dr. Mc-
Crea appreciating her lively, sensual daughter.

I'm imagining all this. He's not Tara's type.

The way to a man's heart?

Francesca went to the stove and hugged Tara and
kissed both her and the sweet new baby. ''I wasn't
putting you down, Tara.''

''Not intentionally, I'm sure.''

What had she said? Francesca reviewed her words
and saw what she'd implied, that Tara chased men.

''I just want to keep you from being hurt.''

Tara cast her a sharp look. ''Why don't you start
by not hurting me yourself?''

WITH LAURA AGAINST her shoulder, Tara crept out of
the house just after six the next morning. It was snowing, and she hurried to the Safari station wagon and
prayed it would start.

It took five tries and assorted prayers.

Now, to stay on the road.

She knew where to find Dan McCrea most mornings. She'd worked there more than once, steaming up
cappuccinos and lattes.

At this hour, there was still parking near the Café
International. With Laura in her car seat, Tara walked
under awnings of stone buildings, some with false
fronts, watching for ice, careful not to fall with the
baby.

She shouldered open the door, which had the name
of the café stenciled on the glass, and carried Laura
inside.

Turned out for work in oxford cloth, khaki and
Royal Robbins, Dan sipped a cappuccino and read *The*

Wall Street Journal. He saw Tara immediately, and she joined him without asking, setting Laura's car seat on the nearest table for two. She edged the table closer.

He drained his cup.

"Double, right?" she remembered. "Can I buy you something?"

His eyes shifted away and back. "You can't even buy diapers. Whose kid is that, anyway?"

"*Mine.* Good grief."

The waitress, a heavyish twenty-something blonde with homemade highlights, paused at their table. "What can I get y'all?"

"Raspberry leaf tea, please, springwater, and oatmeal. He'll have springwater, too."

"You jest. Another of these," he told the waitress, winking at her.

"You do that just like the cowboys." With a crystalline smile, the waitress wheeled away.

Tara gave no preamble. "Dan, I like your brother. He meets me in my dreams. He's my destiny, and I'm his."

Dan coughed, laughing simultaneously. "You know not of what you speak."

She examined the whites of his eyes. "More water. Eight glasses a day. Do you have a water filter? You know, with a plant diet, olive oil and lots of springwater, your energy level will increase and you'll be in better tune with everything around you."

"He doesn't like you, does he?" Dan seemed happy to twist the knife.

"I'm not sure. I think he may be under the impression that *you* like me."

"What's not to like? Your totally alien manner of communication? Your fashion sense? Your—"

"There's nothing wrong with my fashion sense!"

The waitress deposited their orders on the table.

"Is there?" Tara asked her.

"I love that sweater. Guatemalan?" She fingered it, but her eyes drifted to the baby. "What a sweetheart! Look at you! You're as pretty as your mama. Oh, God, babies, don't you love 'em?"

"Kindred spirits." Dan checked his watch. "Time to go."

Oh, no, no! "Excuse me," she said to the sweet waitress. Tara caught Dan's sleeve. "You've got to talk to Isaac. Tell him."

The waitress slipped away.

Dan waited for Tara to remove her hand, then straightened his cuff. "That you like him."

"That you don't. Like me, I mean."

Reaching out, he patted her cheek. "I have."

Oh, shit. This was a nightmare. Oh, hell, it was life, and she'd get over it. She got over everything.

Dan was on his feet. He paused beside Laura. "Who's the kid, Tara?" he asked, eyes grave.

She rose to his gaze. "My daughter."

"Say that with a little less fire, and I might buy it. Place of birth?"

"The planet Earth."

"I'm going to look into it."

Her face was going to crack from this smile. *Serenity, Tara. Be serene.* "Enjoy."

All humor had left his face. "You worked at that place down in El Paso, didn't you? The place where all the lady wetbacks have their American babies?"

A gasp. "Oh, my God! Dr. McCrea, Ah'm so

sorry!'' Cappuccino down his pants. The waitress slammed her hand to her forehead. ''Ah was just bus-sin' tables. Damn, damn, damn.'' She cast an anxious glance toward the kitchen. ''Let me get some water. Let me clean off those nice trousers.''

''I'll take care of it.'' He opened the door and left.

Tara stuck out her hand to the waitress. ''Thank you, sister of the South.''

The waitress wiped her hand and shook.

Then, spontaneous hugs.

''Hey, you risked your job,'' Tara said.

''That's all right. I got a little baby of my own, up Gunnison way. I need to get home to see her. I just came up to Precipice to find a friend, but she's moved on.''

''I'm Tara Marcus.''

''Beulah Ann Cockburn. My baby's name's Chan-tel. It means 'song.' What's yours?''

''Laura Estrella. The laurel and the star.''

''Pretty. I love Laura.''

Laura needed holding. Tara took her from the car seat to nurse. She'd have to hurry home and do it right, with the feeder.

Beulah Ann pulled up another chair. The Interna-tional was otherwise empty, except for a cook singing to Bob Marley in the kitchen. ''I nursed mine fourteen months.''

''How old is she?''

''Just two. My cousin Erin's watchin' her. Erin and Abe. He's my brother-in-law. They've got two of their own. She wants *six*.''

Tara's mouth and eyes felt watery. *Laura, Laura, baby mine.* ''Who's your friend from Precipice?''

''Ivy Walcott? The midwife?''

"That's my sister! Francesca's my mom! I'm Tara!"

"Tara! Oh, m'god. Ivy was my midwife. She came all the way to Gunnison and stayed *five days,* just waiting for my baby." Beulah Ann's eyes overflowed. "And it meant so much because, Lane, that's Chantel's— Oh, forget it, just forget it. Ivy was Erin's midwife, too, and let me tell you, did that not get a rise out of her daddy. This is a man who will not go to the hospital for a broken leg, mind you. Colorado rancher. *Real* rancher. He's my uncle Kip. Love him to death."

"Why were you looking for Ivy? Any special reason?"

Beulah Ann's eyes narrowed. "You're a midwife, too, aren't you?"

"That I am."

Beulah Ann flushed, then appealed to her with earnest eyes. "I'm lookin' for an apprenticeship. Chantel and me went to Louisiana for, oh, most of her life so far. I worked with a lady there. She knows the herbs and helps with births, and she's a Yoruba priestess? Well, I just loved her to death, but me and Louisiana have some history, so I felt it best to leave, so as not to tarnish Mam'zelle Eve. You know?"

Tara's throat was full. What was it about this woman that made her feel like crying? *Sister. I've found another sister.* She found them at midwifery conferences, at births, in coffeehouses. It was the bond of women.

And Beulah Ann wanted to apprentice with her!

This woman from the South, of ranching blood, with bleached hair, who had worked with a Yoruba priestess.

Tara said, "Why don't you give me some time, Beulah Ann? For now, we'll exchange numbers. I have to tell you right up front I'm not legal. I'm a midwife and a damned good one, but the law doesn't like me. And, neither, you might have noticed, does Dr. McCrea."

"Have you met his brother? He is *sooo* sexy, and I feel so sorry for him, losin' his wife in Rwanda."

Tara yearned to know more about Isaac, but this was gossip. Once you started saying too much about other people, that was what it became. Gossip. She wouldn't even share her opinion of Dan McCrea with anyone but Ivy and Francesca, and she couldn't sit here in public and gossip about another doctor, especially with a woman who might see her as a mentor.

An apprentice?

I need to clean up my act.

She shook her head at Beulah Ann. "I need to straighten out my own life before we could start. Let's say—can we keep in touch?"

"I talk too much, don't I?"

"Hey, you're looking at the Queen of Babble." She lifted Laura back into the car seat. "I need to get her home. Thanks again for the save, Beulah Ann. I owe you now." She grinned. "You haven't seen the last of me, sister. I live with my mom. We're in the book. Mountain Midwifery."

She was back inside seconds later. "Forgot to pay!"

AT THE CLICK OF THE latch, Francesca appeared in the foyer. The floor was littered with paper snowflakes, and she seemed as stunned to see them as Tara was. "What in the world?"

Tara shut the door as her mother stooped to pick

one up. Francesca made out some kind of printing on parts of the paper and handed it to her daughter without comment.

Drug company ads. One of those pads the pharmaceutical reps always left. The snowflakes had been cut from them. No other words.

"Tara, I want to apologize for last night. Any man should consider himself blessed to win your favor."

Tara's eyes filled, and Francesca said, "Oh, honey." As she hugged her daughter, carefully accommodating for Laura, she said, "I don't know if you'll find any messages on these, but I did see who brought them. I was getting dressed upstairs."

Oh, Tara. Your eyes are too round. Please don't care so much. Francesca immediately wished she'd left her daughter wondering.

Abruptly, she turned away, and her sigh left Tara with no doubt.

Isaac.

Isaac had brought her snowflakes.

CHAPTER FOUR

It hurt so bad inside. Not the baby pain, the heart pain. But Ivy grabbed my head on both sides and made me look at her, and she has these beautiful violet eyes and looks just like Joni Mitchell, and she said, "You're thinking about 'Someday Soon,' Beulah Ann, but this is it. This is your song, and you and your baby are going to sing it so well." And I'd already picked out the name Chantel for a girl, and I'd never told anyone but Lane.

—Beulah Ann Cockburn, age 21

I'M GOING TO LOOK into it.

Why had she ever gone to see Dan? What had possessed her?

His brother possessed her. Totally.

Isaac hadn't written a single word on those snowflakes. Who needed words?

But she'd jumped too fast, and now she was in real trouble. She needed Isaac pronto, before Dan *did* start looking into it.

Between eight and nine, she consulted with her mom on a prenatal for hospital VBAC—vaginal birth after cesarean. Tara had tried for a time to call them yoni births, but there was only so much ridicule she was willing to take from people like Dan McCrea—not to mention confusion from clients. It was only a word. A *prettier* word, one *she* preferred, but in her experience it had failed to change birth attitudes. It was simply too powerful, too ancient. Too sexy.

Tara had to drag herself from thoughts of snowflakes to focus on her mother's client. Karen Anthony had provided her medical charts. She'd had a low transverse incision after slow progression. The records indicated no emergency, but they had used pitocin to stimulate contractions—not fun for Karen. Dan McCrea had done the cesarean.

Thinking of her potential apprentice, who would be practicing in Colorado's political climate, Tara found herself saying, "The hospital's a good place for a VBAC. Docs are good to have around sometimes." VBACs *could* go well at home, but sometimes those scars didn't hold. She'd seen uterine rupture in a Mexican hospital. Awful. Awful. And she'd *prayed* for physicians then. Sometimes they'd saved babies. And sometimes they hadn't.

She gave Karen an encouraging smile. "You've had great nutrition, and you'll have your OB/GYN right on top of things." *Unfortunately, breathing down your neck and threatening another C, but…* Exhaustion swept over her.

I'm going to look into it.

She'd seen Dan's eyes. He would. Before patients. Between patients. At lunch.

No mistakes this time, Tara. This was like getting out of Chile in '88.

After the prenatal, she nursed Laura and got her down for a nap. When the baby was sleeping, Tara opened her door and crept out to retrieve the portable phone from the hall table. Returning to her room, she shut the door.

It was eleven in Colorado and would be eight in Talkeetna, Alaska. Would her father be at home or at the airport? She tried his home phone first and nearly gasped with relief when he picked up, his voice gruff and alert, keen on coffee. "Charlie here."

"Hi, Daddy. I'm glad you're there." She swallowed her guilt at what she was about to do. Her father would help her if he understood the whole story, but she wasn't up to getting it across long distance. Not now. And he would be annoyed that Isaac McCrea hadn't already accepted her proposal of marriage.

"Tara! How are you, sweetheart?"

"Pretty good, Daddy." No, don't even mention Laura. Work the problem. "Daddy, I'm really embarrassed to ask this, but the Safari Wagon's on its last legs. Or wheels."

"That car was ready to fall apart the day you bought it. If you'd held out for a decent settlement from that pond scum you—"

Danny.

Tara cut him off. "I've found something I really like, but it's pricey."

"How much?"

"Twenty."

He shouted with laughter. "I'll give you three."

Three thousand dollars? Isaac McCrea wasn't going to marry her for three thousand dollars. She swallowed. "I'd really like something reliable this time."

"All right, five."

"Dad, I'm back in Precipice, and you know how it snows here."

"You want four-wheel drive and a big engine. Is that what you're telling me?"

I want something sleek and sexy and fine. A black '65 'Vette sports car. A Porsche 928 Turbo coupe. A Jaguar XKE coupe.

When she didn't answer, he asked, "All right, what exactly is this automobile you've fallen in love with?"

She thought fast, calculating what her father would go for. "A Range Rover. Reduced."

"A Range Rover for twenty grand? How many miles are on this beast? What's the body like?"

"Pristine."

"Miles."

"Five."

"Five K?"

"Yes."

"Has a mechanic seen it?"

"Of course." *Oh, please, Daddy.*

He sighed. "Well, for this kind of extortion, I suppose I don't mind dipping into your grandfather's pockets." Grandpa Marcus.

Grandpa Marcus was dead, but the thought of him still brought a bad taste to her mouth.

There had to be a catch. Her grandfather was buying her a husband. In a sick way, it seemed appropriate. As appropriate as lying to her father, the way he'd lied to her.

"Thank you, Daddy."

"You're welcome, sweetheart. Now, what else can I do for you?"

"Nothing. You're the best."

"So are you, honey. Feel like seeing some northern lights? Got some folks coming up for a winter ascent, or I'd say let's hit the equator."

A winter ascent of Denali, and her father's Cessna would put them down on Kahiltna Glacier. "It's—not a good time. Mom needs my help, and—I'm watching a baby for someone."

"Lucky them. I can't imagine anyone being a better stand-in mom. A better mom of any kind."

His words highlighted the reason it had burned when Danny and Solange had gotten pregnant. A reason she'd never told a soul but her ex-husband—before he was ex. There was only one answer to her father's well-meant words. "Thanks, Daddy."

"I'll wire the money tomorrow. Western Union, all right?"

"Thank you. Oh, thank you."

"I always want you to have what you want, Tara. Hey, you don't need extra for tax, do you?"

"I'll make out."

"I'll throw in a little extra."

"It's really not necessary."

"Sure, it is. I know how strapped you are. Now, enjoy your new car."

"Thank you." *I will. If only he'll accept the terms.*

ISAAC WASN'T HOME. Tara thought she'd die right there. She'd found out he wasn't at the clinic on Fridays, but now here she was, cash in hand, and he wasn't home. There was just the still alpine tundra, draped in snow, and the ghostly buildings, especially the creepy Columbine, with its history of prostitution and women suffering indignities.

How was she going to stop Dan?

Carrying Laura, she wandered along the road in front of the chalet, hoping to see the Land Cruiser. But it was cold and growing dark and her Safari Wagon had barely made it up here. If Isaac refused her offer, she *would* go out and buy something with four-wheel drive. She arranged Laura in her car seat, turned the old station wagon, and backed up.

Tried to back up.

The wheels spun.

Oh, shit. She couldn't get stuck up here! He might be gone for the whole weekend.

She straightened the wheels and tried again to back out.

The engine died, and she remembered the trouble she'd had getting it started at her mother's house. The cold. It was colder up here.

She turned the key in the ignition. Nothing. Was it the battery?

She had two choices. She could bundle up Laura and walk two miles in the snow to get home, carrying twenty-three grand in her coat pockets. Or she could try Isaac's front door to see if he'd locked it before he went away.

It was dark. Where could he be? It would be the worst, the *worst* embarrassment of her life, if he came home and found her in his house. But if he wasn't home by now—good grief, he could've gone to Denver or somewhere. He could be at a medical conference. The chances of his coming home while she was here were slim, and with luck she could get her car towed, too, before he got back.

Again, she unbuckled Laura from her car seat, wrapping her warmly in case they had to walk. And *then* what if they met him on the road? This was beyond romantic pursuit.

He'd think she was stalking him.

His front stairs were snowy—it had snowed since

he'd left—and she watched her own steps as she climbed them. The bentwood furniture on the porch had collected snow, too, but the black cat slipped out from under a chair. Holding Laura close, she tried the old-fashioned door handle. It gave immediately, and she pushed the door open. She kept the cat out with her foot, wanting to leave everything as she found it.

What if he was here? What if his car was gone but he was here?

The house was cold—no fire in the woodstove, probably just a forced-air heater running barely hot enough to keep the pipes from freezing. She shut the door, remembered belatedly to stamp the snow off her boots, and searched, from where she stood, for the phone. None in sight—just the same chaos she'd seen last night. And a mouse darting for a corner. *Ugh.*

A phone had rung while she was here before, and he'd picked it up in the kitchen. All she found there now was the cradle for a cordless. When she paged the phone, it rang in a room off to the right.

She carried Laura that way, leaving wet tracks on the dirty, distressed-wood floor.

The master suite. He hadn't made his bed, but he'd sort of thrown the covers—including a hand-stitched velvet crazy quilt—over it, leaving the pillows exposed. Children's sleeping bags and pillows were heaped near a small woodstove in the corner. They seemed to emphasize that she was a trespasser. The same with the climbing guides and battered copy of René Daumal's *Mount Analogue* in the bookcase beside the bed.

The phone was on the bedside table, thankfully on top of a San Juan area phone book. She set Laura on the bed, her head and shoulders propped against the surprisingly clean pillow, and grabbed the phone and phone book. She needed a twenty-four-hour towing service. There was one in Precipice, and she dialed the number.

"High Country Towing."

"Hi. I'm up at Tomboy, and my car's stuck, blocking the road, and it won't start."

"Mm. It's going to be a while. There was an accident down on the Dallas Divide, and both our trucks are down there."

The Dallas Divide! That was forty-five minutes from Precipice, longer from Tomboy. And the trucks had to take the damaged cars wherever they were going.

Something brushed her leg, and she jumped. A tabby kitten. *Go get the mouse, kitty.*

"Can you wait where you are?"

"I...guess so." No, she'd call Francesca to get her out of here. What would her mother say when she found out where she was? Well, it was better than Isaac finding out.

The kitten wandered into the next room.

"What's the number there?"

Oh, shit, did she have to give it? Suddenly too hot, despite the lack of heat in the house, she unzipped her parka and stripped it off. What *was* Isaac's number? Checking for other animals, then leaving Laura on the bed, she hurried back to the kitchen. She slipped on the tracks she'd left. She read the number on the cradle to the towing company and hung up.

Now, take the phone and the phone book back to exactly where they'd been. She set them on Isaac's bedside table and reached down to pick up Laura.

"Oh, Laura," she moaned.

The newborn had spit up on Isaac's pillow and all over her clothes. She could have choked. Tara turned her over hastily, and the baby spit up on the velvet patchwork quilt. The rumblings from her bottom could only mean a major diaper change. *I'm going to scream.*

Get control. Get control. Think this through.

Laura's diaper bag was in the car. Tara rushed into the adjoining bathroom—she was going to be doing laundry anyway—retrieved a towel, and set it on the rug, praying for at least minimal sanitation. She placed Laura facedown on it and the baby began to scream.

"Sorry, love, I'll hurry."

Her own shirt was filthy, too. Fortunately, she kept clean clothes in her car for births. She rushed out and grabbed the diaper bag and a long-sleeved Henley T-shirt of her own, then hurried back toward the sound of the screaming baby.

Attend to Laura first. She did, on the thick black towel which then showed smears from Laura's bottom. She wished, for once, for disposables. She folded up the dirty cloth rectangle and put it on a plastic bag, but she'd forgotten to wet her washcloth to clean Laura. Leaving Laura to roll in her mess, she ran to the bathroom sink, turned on the water, and waited for it to warm.

Even diapered and dressed in a clean sleeper, Laura continued to cry, and Tara took her to the kitchen to warm milk, then sat on the edge of Isaac's bed to nurse her. *If he comes home now, there is no God.*

There was still spit-up on the pillowcase and the quilt, not to mention the poopy towel, diaper, and baby clothes on the floor.

Blessedly, after twenty minutes, Laura nursed herself to sleep. It was dark out, and Tara was thirsty. Thoroughly protecting an unsoiled area of the bed, Tara left Laura sleeping there and hurried to the kitchen to get a drink of water, then wash out Isaac's glass and take care of her feeding system.

Next—deal with the quilt. With one of his clean washcloths, she spot-cleaned the quilt, sniffed it, cleaned it some more until she was satisfied. Then she stripped the soiled pillowcase from the pillow. Rinse out the diaper and tidy it up in a plastic bag, stow it in the diaper bag. Things were coming together.

Laundry.

She gathered all the other dirty things and set about finding his laundry room. It was beside the kitchen, with a door opening onto the back porch. Detergent in sight. If she washed the white pillowcase with the black towel, the pillowcase would turn gray. Same for Laura's sleeper. Two loads? No, she'd hand wash the pillowcase, no big deal.

She dumped the towel in the washing machine, considered an overflowing basket of dirty clothes—no, she'd better not do their laundry.... She turned the setting to Small and started the washer. Oh, hell, why waste all that water? Tara stripped off her own dirty black T-shirt and her nursing bra—who cared if it turned gray—then added detergent and shut the lid.

There was no sink in the laundry room. She stooped to pick up the baby suit and pillowcase, stood, turned—and jumped, falling back against the lint-covered appliances.

Isaac lounged in the doorway in his parka, arms folded across his chest, cheeks cold-reddened and wind-tanned, eyes avoiding her naked breasts. "Tara. What a surprise."

CHAPTER FIVE

Yul and I were not having our baby in a hospital. End of story. If we had to read fifty midwifery texts and do it ourselves, we would have. See, I'm a survivor. And no one but my partner is going to touch me without my consent ever again.

—Jenny Preston, 28

TARA GRABBED HIS dirty pillowcase and drew it over her breasts, hiding. Hiding everything. "My shirt's in the other room. My car broke. I just came in to use the phone, and Laura threw up, and things became more and more chaotic. I had to put my other shirt in the wash," she added. "I mean, I didn't want to waste the water."

"Which room?"

"Which room what?"

"Your shirt. Where is it?"

The words were embarrassing. "Your bedroom."

"I'll get it for you." He left, and she covered half her face with one hand, the other half with her hair.

Then he was back, thrusting the blue Henley T-shirt toward her, his face turned away. When she took the shirt from his hand, he walked out and she dressed, abruptly remembering the twenty-three thousand dollars in her coat pocket.

And his brother. The words pounding in her head all day. *I'm going to look into it.*

She emerged from the laundry room and saw him nowhere, just a climbing pack and ice ax on the floor beside the couch. But a mountaineering boot and part of his leg showed through the bedroom doorway.

She came to the door and found him on the edge of the bed, gazing down at sleeping Laura. He hadn't removed his parka. With one hand, he reached out and touched the baby's tiny fingers.

"I'm really sorry, Isaac. I came up to—I needed to see you. Then I got stuck. I just meant to use the phone, and things got out of hand. And I had to wait for the tow truck. My car won't start."

"Do you know what's wrong?"

"The cold. Maybe a weak battery."

The mattress creaked as he rose. "Let me get the stove going, then see what I can do. Maybe you won't have to pay for a tow truck."

Boy, he really wanted to get rid of her.

"It's stuck in the ditch."

"I'll see what I can do about that, too."

"I'll...pay you." *Twenty-three thousand dollars to marry me.*

He smiled for the first time. "Save your money. It sounds like you need a new car. Not that what you drive isn't a classic." He winked and left the room.

Tara listened to the sounds of him lighting the stove, then the front door shutting behind him. Oh, hell, it wasn't too late. Tara returned to the laundry room, reset the washer, and hunted for dark clothes in his laundry basket. She put them in with the other things, then immediately regretted it. She was on his bed, her head in her hands, when he came back inside.

"Your engine is running, and your car is pointed downhill to Precipice."

If ever she'd heard a hint.

"My shirt—and, um, bra—are in your washing machine."

"You can stay until they're done. Or come and get them later."

"You don't need company now."

"I was deeply refreshed by coming home to a beautiful half-naked woman in my laundry room."

So he had a sense of humor. Okay—no better time.

"I have a dowry."

Isaac slumped against the doorjamb, then laughed. "Why are you so anxious for a husband? And why me?"

That trace of an accent again. "I told you. Because of Laura. I need to adopt her legally."

His eyes watched her, more black than hazel. She hadn't answered his other question.

Why him? *Why him?* "Well, at first, I figured that with your kids you'd have a motive for…remarrying."

"And now?"

Her emotions roiled. She wasn't going to keep this from him. "You have children of your own, and I'm infertile." She rushed on. "I've never told another soul, except my ex-husband. It's just fair to tell you."

"It will go no further."

She was glad to leave the subject. "And the last reason is, I thought you might need the money."

"How much money?"

Tara smiled. This might work. "Twenty-three thousand dollars."

His eyes widened. "Where did you get twenty-three thousand dollars?"

"From my father."

"Your father gave you twenty-three thousand dollars to buy a husband?"

She glanced at the sleeping Laura, bit her lip. "No. To buy a car. He's very wealthy—" no need to explain about her grandfather "—and I'm Daddy's girl. His only child. Sickening, I know, but there it is."

Isaac unzipped his parka and let it fall to the dusty floor. Beneath, he wore mountaineering pants, a black turtleneck and a black pile sweater. "What exactly did you tell him you were buying?"

"A Range Rover with five thousand miles on it."

His look was ironic. "Tara. I'm not a Carrera or an XKE?"

"It had to be four-wheel drive."

Isaac rubbed his hair. "Want some dinner?"

"Thank you. But is it yes or no?"

"Don't rush me." He headed for the kitchen, contemplating all he'd seen on her half-naked body. They both had stories untold.

THEY ATE IN the living room, his coffee table between them. He had made stir-fry with noodles in olive oil, and they ate it with chopsticks. While he cooked, she had called the towing company, then banished all cats outside. Carrying Laura in her sling, she'd used his six-month-old vacuum cleaner. She set out the boxes of mouse poison he'd bought but not yet used, placing them where even the kitten couldn't reach—and where the mice would. Isaac had celebrated the cleanliness by lighting an emergency candle for each end of the table.

"You're a good cook." Tara scooped up a mouthful. She glanced at his ice ax, collected with other gear in a corner. "Were you climbing?"

"Mount Wilson."

"Alone? In the snow?" He'd grown up in Silverton. Still, what he'd done was dangerous—scary.

"So." He drank some of the water he'd provided with dinner. "I saved your skin today." Isaac watched her eyes, which were intent on his.

Tara waited, motionless.

"You mean, from your brother," she finally said.

"Yes."

"Thank you."

Her simple thanks touched him more than anything else could have.

"What did he say? What did *you* say?"

"He said a lot. I said less. I said I know Laura's history and I would assess things."

"Did he talk about anything else?"

This time, when he smiled, she saw his teeth, his laugh lines. He nodded.

Her heart pounded. Her talk with Dan had worked.

"So. Your proposal."

She had trouble swallowing another bite.

"A temporary marriage would be very bad for my kids. Forget it."

She drank water. "That's fine. I mean—it can be permanent."

"Mm." He resumed eating.

She tried.

Eons seemed to pass before he spoke again, this time laying down his chopsticks. "You're attracted to me?"

Tara pretended to consider. "How do you mean?

Like—I want to be friends? Or—spiritually? Or sexually.''

Actually, he just wanted to confirm that she dreamed about him. "Oh, tell me about each. Friends.''

She was witness at her own trial. "Sure. I like you. You like babies. Even if I'm not sure you respect me.''

He sat back. "I respect you.'' *You just cleaned half my house.* But hadn't he judged her? "Spiritually.''

"I don't want to play this game.'' She picked at her food.

It occurred to him again that she believed she needed to buy a husband.

"Tara, my life's pretty full right now.''

Shit!

"But I can see that you might ease the load. If you'd like to spend some time together and see what happens—I'm agreeable.''

It was more than she'd hoped for. "Okay.''

"Tomorrow morning,'' he suggested, "let's go car shopping. We'll browse Grand Junction, Montrose, Glenwood, but we'll probably end up in Denver. We'll try to find you a car that will suit both you and your father. Let's say, I pick you up at six.''

Tara swallowed. He didn't want her money.

"Oh, Isaac, thank you!'' Abruptly, she jumped up. Over the food and the table, she threw her arms around him, feeling his muscles, his back, smelling his scent.

He caught her shoulders. "Whoa.'' Gently, he guided her warm body back to her seat. His engine was running now. "Do you hug everyone?''

"Just about.''

"Try to break that habit.'' Isaac returned to his food.

A moment of silence. "I beg your pardon?"

"*C'est pour votre bien.* For your own good. You send off pheromones the way a dandelion blows those little white tufts in the wind."

"That's me! And I *don't* like people trying to control me. That would be like me telling you not to climb fourteeners alone in the snow. Furthermore, obviously, you don't like to be hugged—"

"I don't like to mix food and sex."

She grinned, sending off a shower of those pheromones he'd mentioned. "I do."

Isaac had an erection the size of Mount Wilson. He tried to eat, then set down his chopsticks.

"You're turned on," she accused.

"*Yes.*"

"Can we start hugging and kissing? Or just kissing, since you don't like—"

"Can we finish dinner?"

But he couldn't finish his. He took it to the kitchen to put away for later. When the baby cried, he sank against the counter in relief. He heard the washing machine go off and went to throw the things in the dryer. He found his family's clothes in with a towel and a shirt and bra of hers. He switched them all over to the dryer, except the bra. Heloise had always hung hers to dry.

He thought in Kinyarwanda. *What do you think of Tara, Heloise? Will she do?*

He saw his wife give a regal nod.

It was what he wanted to see.

He'd been thinking of Tara in the wind on Mount Wilson, on the peak, on the drive home. He wanted to make love with her, wanted it as he'd wanted it with Heloise.

He wanted her entirely for himself.

HE KISSED HER IN THE open door of her car while the engine idled. It was a drawing her near by the upper arms and gently pressing his lips to hers. Everything hot washed through her as the kiss lengthened, slow and tender. He nuzzled her cheek and her hair before he released her. "Be careful driving down. We'll take your car tomorrow."

"It might not make it to Denver."

"Let me worry about that. I'll be over in the morning, and we'll have breakfast, all right?"

"All right. What time did you say?"

"Six?"

Brown eyes watched him. "Isaac. Are you telling me the truth about Dan? He's not checking up on Laura?"

"He's not."

"How do you know?"

"I know."

"In some ways," she said, "I might know him better than you do. I know him professionally in a way you don't."

"Agreed. But you don't know me at all."

"I spent three weeks with the mountain gorillas."

I spent fourteen years with my wife's family. One year was 1994. This year was worse.

He stood to shut the car door.

"On the way to the airport, I saw a family murdered," she said quietly. "They were raping the daughter."

"*Sans doute.* Your baby is cold." But he said it *"bébé est."* He was losing it, right out here in the snow, with this *girl,* this insensitive American *girl,* who would never be grown.

He shut her door, and Tara was left in another place, a bad place of bad memories. Pain. Broken bones. She touched her face.

She waited in the car as he disappeared behind the house, through the snow. She inched the wagon down the road to see him. He was splitting logs, hands bare. No coat. No hat.

He paused and pointed down the road.

She got out of the car and called, "I like you, Isaac! I'm sorry I made you angry. You better not stand me up tomorrow! You better keep your end of the bargain."

He dropped the ax and came to the car door and kissed her. Sweating.

Into her mouth, he said it. "This May, the day we left Kibuye, they killed my wife's entire family. I knew, beyond doubt, that it would happen."

"YOU'RE GOING CAR shopping in Denver with Isaac? You don't have any money," Francesca protested.

Tara had been home twenty minutes. She was faint after that talk with Isaac in the car. "Dad sent me some."

Francesca's look was pointed and more than disapproving.

"It was some of Grandpa's." No one ever called Francesca's father "Grandpa." The policy was not to mention him at all.

Her mother breathed in through her nose and released the breath hard. "Well, there's some justice in that. Though it's not enough."

Tara thought of Isaac. "It's enough."

Francesca turned.

Oh, Mom, not now.

"You don't know that man."

Silence.

"Are you taking Laura?"

"Of course."

Francesca wished she could stop her. What she said was, "I wish—just once—that you'd find a man who's good enough for you."

Tara hesitated. "Well, this one needs me, and so do his kids. And I need him." She threw up her hands. "What's good enough?"

Francesca asked, "What did he do over there?"

"For the last five years, he protected a hundred and thirty-two people. He was also a physician."

The telephone rang as Tara started for the stairs with Laura.

It was Ivy.

TEN MINUTES LATER, Tara had her sister to herself. Laura was cranky, and Tara felt a need to talk, to unburden herself—and could not. She asked about Ivy. "How's the bambino?"

"Gestating nicely."

"How is midwifery?" Francesca had said that Ivy was under too much stress from work and family. Tara wanted to know if that was true. The baby was due December first.

"Oh, beautiful. I love it here. Everything's good. I told you about Shelby's birth."

Her sister-in-law with the husband who had caused Ivy a million headaches. Tara heard the strain in her voice. Cullen's fault? Ivy and her husband had some shaky history.

But Ivy didn't elaborate on the details of her pregnancy—or her marriage. "Speaking of babies, is that Laura I hear?"

"Mom told you."

"Of course. I'm shocked. I'm amazed." The unspoken passed through the silence. *I'm concerned.*

Tara changed the subject. "Hey, you know who I met this morning? Beulah Ann Cockburn." Tara told her about Beulah Ann's looking for Ivy, wanting to apprentice. And her own response.

"I'm glad she's becoming a midwife." A pause. "Tara, what are you going to do about Laura?"

"I've got a plan, but if I tell you, then you're sworn to secrecy."

"From Mom."

"Who else?"

"All right."

"Okay, you know that the Victorian has changed ownership."

"Yes." Her voice said she suspected what was coming.

"Well, I'm planning—trying hard, that is—to marry the owner. Although he's selling the place. But he lives up in Tomboy." *You're rambling, Tara.* "Then we'll go down to Texas and make my custody of Laura legal. We'll adopt her."

"Are you kidding?"

Tara swallowed her hurt. "Did I ask if you were kidding when you announced that you were going to West Virginia to live with a man you couldn't remember marrying?"

"I'm sorry." The apology was sincere. "I'm just shocked. Isn't this guy an obstetrician?"

"Family practice. He's Dan McCrea's brother."

Ivy gasped.

"You're the one who teased me about falling in love with him!"

"You're in love with him?"

"We just met." Tara rushed on. "But he likes kids. Hey, he has kids."

"Is he apprised of your plan?"

Tara gave sound bites, never saying the word "Rwanda." She shifted Laura in her arms, trying to make the baby comfortable. "So we're going to Denver tomorrow to shop for a new car."

"Tara, do you like this guy?"

"I like this kid. I'm *nursing* her, Ivy. I'm in new-mother bliss."

"Mom told me."

More than anything that had happened in the last three days, Ivy's sober tone brought home the seriousness of Tara's situation. For a frozen instant, the threat of losing Laura, of having this baby—the only baby she might ever have—torn from her arms, loomed real and threatening. Tara blinked it away. "Look, I'd better get some sleep. Give Gabriela and Cullen hugs from me, okay?"

"Yes. Tara?"

"Mm? Shhh, Laura." Lullaby time, as soon as she hung up.

"I'm here for you. Really. If you and this guy work it out, I think it might be the best thing that could happen."

"Thanks, Ivy."

As she switched off the cordless, she glanced up to find her mother in the doorway.

Francesca said, "Honey, please don't get hurt."

How much had her mother heard? Francesca

wouldn't have deliberately eavesdropped, but if she'd come upstairs for some other reason... *And I left the door open.*

"Why do you always think *I'm* going to get hurt?"

"Are you toying with that man?"

"No."

Tara began to change Laura's diaper for the night, deliberately blocking Isaac's story from her mind.

But an hour after Laura had dropped off to sleep, Tara's eyes remained open, phrases of their talk in the idling station wagon returning to her. The story began with the genocide in '94. He had never said he'd protected anyone. He'd said that he'd told the *genocidaires* to leave. They'd left. When they came again for him and his children and for the others who'd gathered at the hospital, he had said no. Many times, from spring of '94 until last May, he'd said no.

Others were less adept with the word.

She still didn't know his wife's name.

HE WASN'T SORRY TO have involved himself.

When he showed up at seven, she opened the front door wearing jeans and a T-shirt with her Andean cardigan, and it was just the two of them, just the moment.

"I'm often late," he said. "Do you have a parka?"

"I have another sweater. I'll be fine."

Laura was bundled in her car seat, and Isaac took the seat, while Tara swung a small mountaineering pack over her shoulder. Her mother appeared in the foyer.

"Hello, Isaac."

This woman had never been late in her life.

He equaled her reserve. "Hello, Francesca."

Her voice wavered on a tense chord. "When do you expect to return?"

"Tomorrow night."

Francesca's expression remained cold, and he smiled down at Laura, then Tara. "Ready?"

She grinned, her eyes searing his.

From the shadows, Francesca watched the sparks kindle to flame and said a silent prayer that he was the right one for Tara. That he would love her as she deserved.

Yet she could not help believing this prayer would be denied. Tara always bought her blessings with time in hell.

CHAPTER SIX

One by one, they had come for all the healers, and Dominica knew they would come for her. She tried to show courage, tried not to turn from her responsibilities to the families she served, but she knew what the Inquisitors had done to her friends, to the women who had taught her what she knew. They would do the same to her. She must be brave. She must attend the birth of Carina's child without looking to the future. She must continue to care for little Angelo.

—"Burnings," Jenny Preston

BEULAH ANN BROUGHT their menus at the Café International. "Hi, Dr. McCrea. Hi, Tara. Can I get y'all somethin' to drink, to start you out?"

Coffee for Isaac, raspberry leaf tea for Tara, who was glad Beulah Ann hadn't raised an eyebrow over Tara's showing up at one brother's table the first morning and with the other brother the next. The waitress left the table without so much as a blink.

"After last night," Tara said, "I wondered something."

He held Laura, lifted her to brush his lips against her cheek.

Tara lowered her voice. "Did you finally just—give up?"

"No. We'd always had warnings. But the last were different, sent by people I believed. And I had dreams. I'd ignored them in the past and regretted it." Blood dreams. Black skin turning white in death. Waking up from his dreams and hearing Heloise tell him hers. They'd both tried to pretend the Something Terrible would not come.

"Did it occur to you to get an escort for the children and—"

"Would you have done that?"

Never. Never. They would have been murdered.

"In any case, I choose to believe that had I remained—or even taken the children to the airplane and returned to Kibuye—the outcome would have been the same."

"Except you would have died."

"No." No one had been interested in killing him. He was outside their hate. His children, by virtue of their skin color, were not.

"Did you keep the warnings?"

"To help me sleep?"

He could have meant that the contents of those letters from the *genocidaires* would give him nightmares. Or that they could never relieve his guilt.

Beulah Ann brought their drinks. They ordered.

As far as he was concerned, his guilt had been addressed. *Guilty.* If she could stomach him, he would try to get along with himself and her, which was already much harder than living just with himself and his children, who also lived with guilt, experienced it as he did. He missed his kids. "Tell me about your family, Tara."

He learned about her parents' divorce and about Ivy, the sister adopted as an adult, Ivy's amnesia and reunion with her husband and daughter.

When Beulah Ann brought breakfast, Isaac dug in hungrily. That was good, Tara observed; he needed it. "Were you sick when you came home?"

"I'm never sick. How long have you been a midwife?"

With a flash of guilt for what she wasn't prepared to say—the fact that she'd never be certified—she told him, "Well, Mom's a midwife, so I've always sort of known that was what I wanted to do. When did you know you wanted to be a doctor?"

His vocation had come to him in the silence, listening for the spirit, for "the way to open," as he'd been taught. Quaker things. Now, there was no God, or, as he'd heard an Australian doctor say, *She gave birth to the universe and died in stage three.* "I was very young."

"It must have been hard getting through school. Financially."

"DAV paid."

Doctors Against Violence. "A scholarship?"

"Yes."

"How did you get that?"

"I assisted the local physician, I raised twenty-eight thousand dollars for Nicaragua and El Salvador, and I climbed every fourteener in Colorado before I was seventeen. Set up a camera for pictures at the top to verify where I was standing."

Tara gave a little scream of delight. "That's so cool."

He shrugged, his smile part embarrassed, part

pleased. "That last bit of information was just for you."

She was touched. Again, she found her eyes on his long bones, on the slope of his nose, on his dark lashes. He was gaunt.

"How did you raise the money?"

"Dan and I hitched snowplow rides to here, Precipice, and found the rich people."

"And convinced them to part with their money?"

"That was the easy part. People like to help kids."

"How come your brother's so different from you?"

"Better upbringing. I got away with anything." Laura had dozed off, against his shoulder. "Where did you get your training, Tara?"

A chill swept over her. Still puzzling out his comparison between himself and Dan, she warned herself to speak carefully. And decided not to answer at all. "Where were you born?"

"Silverton."

"And Dan?"

"Durango."

"Hospitals."

"Ah—" He hesitated, then suddenly laughed at her. "Get lost."

Too late. She was in RMM. "You were born at home, weren't you?"

"It's too early in the morning, Tara. And I don't love your cause. Tell me where you trained."

I don't love your cause? This could turn bad. "I started with Mom, then trained in Chile, in a hospital, when I was eighteen and nineteen. Got disenchanted." That was one way to put it. "Later, I did a mix of hospital and rural stuff in Mexico, independent practice in Hawaii—" with a husband-stealing partner

"—and Maternity House. I did *tons* of births at Maternity House. The volume is incredible, and I've been there since Danny and I split, more than two years. Were you always in family practice—technically?"

"Technically. It went from obstetrics to—well, emergency medicine is all I saw for a while. Which," he admitted at last, "I like. They just lost an ER doc in Precipice, so I've offered to fill in two nights a week until they replace him." With Danielle sleeping in the maternity unit playroom—or at home with Oliver and David.

If this worked out with Tara… The thought stunned him. Her plan was nuts.

But she was flesh and blood.

And talking.

"Did you like obstetrics?"

"Not much."

"Well, I was going to look you up today, but I see you've found something better to do." Dan, set for a day's climbing.

Isaac pulled out a chair. "Where are you bound?"

"Sneffels." Sitting, he nodded at Tara, but without flirtation. Dan had ceded her to his brother.

"Dan, were you born at home?"

"Don't answer."

"Isaac was," Dan said.

"Don't ruin my breakfast, Tara." Isaac's face was wet. Sweat. Knowing the cause, loathing it, he settled Laura in her car seat and rose from the table. His pulse had doubled, making him feel like hell. "Think I'll step outside."

Tara stood, touching him. "Are you all right?"

He nodded and left her with Dan.

WHEN ISAAC'S PULSE slowed and the sweating subsided, he returned to the café to collect Tara and Laura. Dan was gone, and Isaac didn't sit down but picked up the tab, counted bills onto the table, and addressed Tara. "Ready?"

She jumped up, grabbed the car seat.

In the station wagon, she said, "So...you never get sick."

"It's a parasite. Makes cysts on my liver. If you've got a cure, I'll take it. No one else has one."

She fished a pen and day-planner from her pack. "Tell me what it's called, and describe your symptoms. Maybe there's a Nobel Prize in this."

He laughed.

"Where did you pick it up? Rwanda?"

"The Himalayas." At her look, he said, "Hey, even Doctors Against Violence get vacations."

Not in the middle of genocide, with a family to protect. "You've had it how many years?"

"Eight, nine."

"What did you climb there? K2?"

He laughed. "No."

She asked questions and wrote all the way to Placerville, but before she put away her notes, she asked, "Any other surprises? A touch of malaria now and then?"

"Right, right." A whisper of laughter came again, loosening his chest, and he saw her standing in his laundry room, falling on the dryer. His eyes were moist, things breaking up.

He realized he was afraid.

"I DON'T BELIEVE IT," Tara said.

Late that afternoon, as day turned to dusk, she and

Isaac stood in the parking lot of a Denver car dealership, ogling a two-year-old spruce-green Range Rover priced at twenty-five thousand dollars. The tag in the window didn't say how many miles were on it, and Isaac had to peer through the window to see. He whistled.

"What?"

"Fifteen. We'll have to check to make sure it's not one hundred and fifteen. Or two hundred."

A salesman was approaching through the fading afternoon light.

"Let me do the talking," said Isaac.

Tara sidled closer to him and smiled sweetly. "Maybe I should."

"Tara."

"I like to hear you say that."

FIFTEEN THOUSAND MILES. As they drove to a mechanic they'd found in the phone book, Tara said, "Isaac, I have only twenty-three thousand for taxes, everything. This deal is excellent, but I'm tight on money, and my mom and I are going to be out of the Victorian next month."

"We'll talk him down. Don't forget, you've got the station wagon to trade him."

"It's worth about five-hundred dollars."

"It's a classic. I'll convince him."

"You're not going to talk him down to twenty. In fact, I doubt you budge him a thousand dollars."

He negotiated traffic in the new vehicle. "I'll lend you the rest."

"I'd never be able to pay you back."

"You can pay me in childcare. Vacuuming."

What? He was ready to trust her with his children?

In her car seat behind them, Laura made a gurgling sound.

"You're good with her, Tara." This trip had taught him the hours and tenderness she put into nursing and caring for that baby. He'd made sure Tara slept whenever Laura slept during the drive.

Isaac's words touched her. But— "We need to look at other cars, Isaac."

"Childcare, vacuuming, extermination."

"Now, you're talking. Car or no car, I'll show you how to get rid of the mice. You're gonna need some carpentry."

"I'm not a carpenter."

"I am."

"Then you've got yourself a car."

"I don't like it, doc."

"What's not to like?"

"Borrowing money. From you."

"Tara, I'll *give* you the money."

"I like that less. Okay, it's a good car. Can we drive it home tonight?"

"Actually, I thought we'd get some dinner and stay the night at my family's cabin in the mountains. Then, drive to Silverton tomorrow to pick up the kids."

A cabin. Yes, he'd told her mother they wouldn't be home till tomorrow night.

This is what you want, isn't it, Tara?

He read her mind. "There are plenty of bunks. But if staying somewhere else would make you feel better, that's fine."

"No." She shook her head. "No."

CHAPTER SEVEN

A homebirth can bring a family together and make the father closer to his children. I saw this in the huge change in my husband, Matthew, after Jackson was born.

—Shelby Till, 35, after the birth of Jackson Renfrow Till

WHEN THE SHERIFF pulled up in front of her house that afternoon, Francesca's heart stopped. Was this about Tara? Or Laura?

Oh, please, no...

She'd been showing a client to the door, and she walked the woman to her car before joining the sheriff. "Hi, Burt. What is it?" It had to be bad news, and her head throbbed with the knowledge and the fear.

Had something happened to Tara and Isaac and Laura on the road?

The sheriff shifted his weight. "Got a call today from the Alaska state troopers, Francesca."

A line of nausea crawled from her stomach to her throat. She knew it wasn't her family, because she would have found out differently, from Charlie. But if it was Charlie—

Sweat gathered on her hairline, and she was present in the unreal. It was the summer of 1996, and she could hear the radio in her father's hangar, and Art Turner had lost contact with—

"—know a Mia Kammerlander?"

She blinked. Hugging herself, thinking, *What just happened to me?* "I know Mia." Oh, no.

Mia

Her former apprentice was a midwife in Talkeetna—

"I have some news for you."

"What?" Oh, Mia. The dogsled or the plane or... There were many things that could happen in Alaska, and why had Mia wanted to go there, why had she settled on *Talkeetna?*

"Shall we go inside?"

Mia was dead. Francesca believed it before the sheriff said she'd disappeared and the search would continue. "She asked that you be contacted in the event of an emergency."

It was ten years or more since Mia had been her apprentice. In the intervening time, they'd seen each other at midwifery conferences, worked together on a few articles and, of course, exchanged E-mails. But wasn't there someone closer? No family—Francesca knew that. Yet...

Burt went on to say that he didn't know much more, but he handed her a card on which was written a number for the Alaska state troopers.

A few numbing minutes after he left, Francesca picked up the receiver and punched the numbers, misdialing the area code, and as she disconnected, the phone rang, making her jump.

Her finger lifted, and she forgot to say "Mountain Midwifery" and only said hello.

"Francesca."

She recognized Charlie Marcus's low growl before he said another word. Pursing her mouth, Francesca sank down at the kitchen table. Her limbs tingled, and that reaction she'd had when the sheriff came didn't mean anything. But it was hard to get out a word. She shut her eyes. *Real world, Francesca.* "The sheriff was just here."

"Oh."

Mia was his neighbor up there. Indignation took hold. "Why didn't I hear this from *you,* Charlie? What's happened?"

"You were about to hear it from me. I saw no need to worry you unnecessarily. I know worry's your favorite hobby, but it's not good for you, Cesca. It'll make you old before your—"

"What happened to Mia?" She was too warm, and shaking.

"Well, it was Monday night, and she'd been to a birth— Want to know whose?"

"I want to know what happened to Mia." Charlie liked to tell stories, and he could drag this out for hours. *You might show more concern, Charlie.* She was sure he'd made a play for Mia. Mia was six feet tall and stunning, and they were both pilots, and...

"Mm. Well, Mia had a race the next day in Nome. Started loading her dogs into burlap sacks to fly them down, but stopped with two dogs in bags right by her Beechcraft. Looks like one of the other dogs got loose, and she took after it on her snowmobile. The dog's back, but Mia isn't."

Francesca's throat closed. A woman who'd been missing for five days on a snowmobile in Talkeetna was not just missing.

He said, "Sorry, Cesca."

It would not sink in. She had to call the troopers. Was there something she could do? Anxious to get rid of Charlie, she said, "I guess that's it, then. If you wanted to talk to Tara, she's not here. She's gone to Denver with a man to buy some car you gave her money for."

"Denver?"

"Yes, Denver. Did you think there's a car dealer in Precipice?"

"No. I just had the feeling she was buying locally."

Francesca grew queasy.

Charlie changed the subject. "What makes you think I called to talk to our daughter instead of the sexiest woman in the lower forty-eight?"

He wants something. Twenty years divorced was a long time to get used to having an ex-husband instead of just a runaway, alcoholic husband. "If you want something from me, the answer is no."

"Maybe I just wanted to hear the sound of your voice." A thoughtful pause. "Actually, I just wanted to tell you about Mia."

"Thank you." Five days. *Were you waiting for weekend rates, Charlie?*

"And to find out when you'll be coming up here."

"I'm not coming to Talkeetna! I wouldn't come if *you* were the one—"

"Ouch, Francesca. Go easy. Now, just put aside your animosity toward those of us up here you can't stand—and the one you can't bear the thought of seeing in a coffin. And, Cesca, I want to be cremated. A stirring memorial in the Talkeetna Cemetery does appeal to me, but it could be desecrated by your jealous relatives. Now, if you were to bring my body to Colorado where I could lie by your side—''

"We are not talking about *your* body. Do you ever think of anyone but yourself?''

"I was getting around to that theme, Francesca. Shouldn't you think of Mia? I know you're scared to see me, but—''

"Scared to see *you?*''

"Not just me. But speaking of me, think about it Cesca. I've been dry for some time, and—''

"I'm sure glad you're not landing on those glaciers drunk, Charlie. What's your point?''

"That Mia decided *you* should be the one contacted in case of emergency. Yes, Francesca, I know this because I am the font of all information in Talkeetna, Alaska. And if she cared so much about you, don't you think you should put aside your own petty grievances—''

"No grievance I have with *anyone* in Talkeetna is petty.''

He whistled. ''The apple doesn't fall far from the tree.''

"Goodbye, Charlie.''

"A moment more of your time. Just because you're frightened, Francesca, is—''

"We've covered this ground! I am *not* frightened.''

"Oh, be serious. Your fear of dogs, for instance— in particular, sled dogs—is legendary. Tara tells me you're afraid of catching babies more than a few minutes from a hospital. And for thirty years, you've been afraid of this beautiful northern rain forest you used to call home. You turned chicken when I went to Vietnam, and you've been frightened ever since. And all I want, Francesca—'' he took on the aggravating tone that was poetry and vulnerability and bush pilot's certainty all rolled into one ''—is for you to come back here and remember those long Denali summers when you were too young and in love to be afraid of me.''

Her jaw dropped.

''Now, don't deny having been young and in love. I'll lose respect for you, then, Francesca. Fear, I can understand, but not—''

''If you're about to say you can't take a lie, we can end this conversation right now! I can't believe we're *having* this conversation.''

''It's the only conversation possible when someone suggests something that scares you shitless.''

''I am *not* scared shitless!'' She was shouting. This could only get worse.

It did. It got much worse before she said, ''Goodbye, Charlie.''

''Goodbye, Goddess of Earthly Delights.''

Flushed and trembling, Francesca set down the phone. What had she done? What had she done?

THE CABIN WAS frigid. Lighting the woodstove, Isaac noticed her making up a narrow lower bunk. Tara had insisted that she and Laura would squeeze in together.

''Tara, the couch would be warmer.'' And it would be warmest if the three of them shared his parents' bed.

But it wasn't time to turn in. They huddled on oversized pillows near the stove, sipping tea he'd made, Laura snoozing in the car seat beside her. Tara shook her dark hair back from her olive skin. Her eyes darted at his and caught him staring.

''What?'' she asked.

"Tell me something. About you."

Her expression was what he'd known he'd see. She had secrets to match the scars.

"Like what?"

He tread carefully. "I just want to know you better."

"Then, you?"

"Fair."

She consulted the rafters, giving him time to admire her face, her neck, her chin...the whole shape of her stretched out on the rag rug.

"When I was thirteen—" her voice shook, and she failed to steady it "—I was supposed to go for visitation with my father. He was going to show me Alaska. But he was drinking and didn't want to do it, so he sent me to my grandfather, who was a con man. All summer, I drove around the Midwest with him, and we pulled scams. We made friends with these people in Kansas who wanted to open a restaurant, and my grandfather knew the business. He said, 'I've got to get this little girl through college.' We embezzled fifty thousand dollars from them and drove off, exchanging high-fives all the way to Seattle."

Isaac shook his head. "That's a good one." Now, his turn. He gave her something less interesting. "I haven't made love in five years."

Her eyebrows lifted. Laura had awakened, and Tara took her from the car seat. "Oh, well."

Oh, well. Too bad. He laughed. "I'm going to bring that big bed over here, closer to the stove, so you and Laura will be warmer. I'll sleep on the couch."

WHILE WIND GATHERED outside, shaking tree limbs, Tara fell asleep on his parents' bed, nursing Laura.

Isaac covered them both. Only moonlight illuminated the room. When he gently pulled Tara's T-shirt down over her breast, she rolled restlessly to her back and blinked.

"Just covering you up." He arranged the sheet and blanket over her and over part of Laura. "Good night, Tara."

Her eyes searched his face, then dropped shut. "Good night."

He watched her toss twice under the sheet and blankets, then settle down, her body outlined beneath the covers. The valley at the tops of her legs, her full breasts. She left herself open to him, and he didn't touch.

Just wondered what secrets she hadn't told.

AT NOON, SUNDAY, Francesca's phone rang. She'd been watering plants in the solarium and wondering how to break the news about Mia—and her own news—to Tara.

"Mountain Midwifery."

"This is Jenny Preston."

"Hi, Jenny." Francesca kept any wariness out of her voice. Supermodel Jenny Preston, daughter of the chief of obstetrics from his first marriage and one of Precipice's celebrity residents, was the reason the hospital had stopped tolerating Francesca's homebirth practice. Had made her choose between homebirths and hospital privileges.

Jenny, come hell or high water, wanted a homebirth.

When Francesca told Jenny she couldn't do it, Jenny had said she and her partner, Yul Vermont, would manage on their own.

No bad feelings, except Francesca's own, about her weakness.

"Francesca, I heard through the grapevine that your daughter's back. Does she do homebirths?"

The Precipice grapevine worked fast. Everything Francesca said now was spurred by yesterday's news and her own decision. "You'll have to ask her. She's not a certified nurse-midwife, and she has no plans to become licensed in Colorado. But she's attended many, many births."

"Great!"

"I can have her phone you when she gets home. It may not be today. What's the best time to reach you?"

Replacing the phone in the cradle, Francesca felt as though she'd sacrificed *her* ethics. Tara had more births behind her than Francesca did because of the sheer volume on the border at Maternity House. But she was breaking the law, and what would happen to Laura if Tara went to jail?

What would happen to that precious baby?

Her thoughts jumped from Tara and Laura to Tara and Isaac, then back to Tara and Laura. Whatever happened between her and Isaac, Tara would recover.

But she would never get over losing that baby.

"ISAAC. THERE'S NO reason for me to go to Silverton with you to pick up the kids. And meet your mother."

He watched the snow, the wiper blades. No reason? "I've got to get my kids. We're going. I'm sorry we have to take your car."

"That's not what I meant." Tara turned on the CD player, shoved in the CD he'd bought for her. *You pick,* he'd said. She'd chosen Jewel, *Pieces of You.*

Isaac switched off the music and pulled to the shoulder.

He unfastened his seat belt and hers, and they were hugging. Kissing.

She'd never known anything like it, like him. Genuine desire. *I really want this man, and he wants me.*

His eyes were on hers, his head turning to see her better. They kissed again, making love with their mouths, falling in love until she held him away.

"THIS IS TARA," he told his mother.

Tara hugged her.

Isaac embraced his own, lifting Danielle into his arms.

"*Allô, Tara.* Are you coming home with us?"

The sparkle had returned to Tara's brown eyes. "To Precipice. I'm going to my own house."

Both boys nodded with satisfaction.

Isaac's mother caught *his* eye then. Slowly, she, too, gave a nod and a smile, and she hugged him as she said, "It's so nice to meet you, Tara."

FRANCESCA HADN'T SEEN or noticed a green Range Rover when it passed her house and drove up toward Tomboy, but she saw it pull into her driveway later. *Is that the car?* She couldn't get a car like that for twenty-three thousand dollars.

When Tara came through the door carrying Laura, her eyes glowed almost feverishly. Her cheeks were pink and dusky. She wouldn't meet her mother's gaze.

"Is there anything else to carry in?" asked Francesca.

"Just her diaper bag and one other bag. I'll bring them in when I get Laura settled upstairs."

Francesca followed her. "Where did you find a car like that for twenty-three thousand dollars?"

"Um. Isaac lent me some, and I'm paying him back in childcare. And housekeeping." She shouldn't mention mice. Mom would freak about the hantavirus risk.

"Childcare?"

"Yes." She placed Laura on a baby blanket on the bed and grabbed soft cotton diapers from the pile beside her nightstand.

"Tara, be careful. How do you think a physician is going to react to your stance on never becoming licensed?"

Tara's stomach flip-flopped. The ominous loomed heavy. She was blinded with recollections. His mouth, touching his hair, him touching hers. "It…should…be okay." Okay? *She* wasn't okay. Making a stab at humor, she suggested, "Maybe you should write that birth certificate now."

"Something tells me it's too late," her mother answered wryly. "In any case, that was *never* an option." Distracted, suddenly preoccupied, Francesca sat on the edge of the bed and picked up Laura in her fresh diaper and thick flannel baby blanket. "Oh, sweetie, I missed you." She lifted her eyes. "Tara, I had some upsetting news this weekend."

Shakily, she told her about Mia.

"I'm going up to Talkeetna, Tara."

The sudden hard thump of Tara's heart responded to words more shocking than the news that Mia Kammerlander was missing, was probably— "You're going to *Talkeetna?*"

Tara's mouth was dry. Okay, Grandpa Marcus was the winner. But her *other* grandfather… Years ago, she and Ivy had gone to Alaska to visit Charlie, and Tara had been determined to meet her mother's father, Talkeetna's legendary glacier pilot Roy Walcott. She'd known she could befriend him and her uncle and—

Uhn-uhn.

She let out a long breath. "Mom."

Her mother didn't react, was staring off as though seeing a long distance—or back a long time. But all Francesca said was, "Why did she ask them to contact *me?*"

Tara kept her feelings to herself. Mia had apprenticed with Francesca while she, Tara, went to Chile. *Because I couldn't get along with my own mother.* And Mia wasn't like Beulah Ann or Ivy or a hundred other midwives Tara could name; she wasn't an instant sister. Now Mia had disappeared in the bush on a snowy Alaskan night. And Francesca was going home to Alaska.

"You'll be back soon, right? Do you need me to see your clients?"

Francesca hesitated. "Tara, I don't know...." She faltered, and she couldn't explain that it was the way Charlie had said "this northern rain forest" and she'd seen summer's lush green and autumn's reds and ambers and tasted blueberries and known such a violent longing for *place,* and her heart had changed in a minute. "This house is being sold." A small sigh. "As you know, I'm not happy with my work here."

It all dawned on Tara. Her mother was going to Alaska to stay. "But, Mom, what if they won't talk to you?"

Francesca's blue eyes hardened. "I am *not* a pariah, Tara. There are other people in Talkeetna besides—" She snorted in disgust. "It hardly matters. I'm not going back for them. I'm going in spite of them."

Tara knew the fears Francesca must be facing, the long catalogue of fears, just as she knew that her grandfather and uncle saw her own father every day of the week and never uttered a word to him, and her dad never said anything back, and that it was all based on something a long time ago, when bush pilots in Talkeetna fought over customers not just to earn the best income but to put food on the table. It was something neither of her parents liked to talk about, and whenever they did it was with hatred in their eyes. After meeting her grandfather— Whew.

All feelings mutual.

She admired her mother for doing this, but under the admiration was the knowledge that it was because of Mia Kammerlander, that Francesca was doing this for her.

Would she do that for me if I went missing somewhere?

She had gone missing.

But no one had known.

Francesca handed her a piece of paper. ''Your first client, I believe.''

''Wow! Thank you.''

''This one comes with a land mine attached.'' Francesca told her about Jenny—and about Rich Scarborough, who wanted his grandchild born in a hospital.

Tara registered the news with mixed feelings. A model, an obstetrician's daughter... *I can do it.*

Something else must be on Francesca's mind. Even holding Laura, she seemed ready to bolt. Which would be better than her bringing up physicians and midwifery licensing again.

Still, Tara was curious. "Have you talked to Dad?"
He knew Mia, too.

"Yes. He's offered to meet me at the airport and
fly me, free of charge, to Misheguk. Obviously, I can't
afford to refuse."

She sounded stiff and spinsterly and worried.

The worry was legitimate. Dad might not even show
up at the airport. Tara whispered, "I'll miss you very
much."

SHE WAS TO ARRIVE at Isaac's at seven the next morning, to pick up Danielle. She would watch Danielle all
morning, drop her at afternoon kindergarten, then pick
everyone up and take them home after school—and
begin Operation Mouse.

Tara was nervous before she got there—troubled by
the news about Mia, Francesca's departure and that
question her mother had raised. *How do you think a
physician is going to react…?* She'd spent the morning scanning want ads, looking for a room to rent, a
place that would take a woman with a baby, and praying that Isaac would make some kind of commitment
to her before she had to leave the Victorian.

When she reached the chalet, all the children were
up and dressed, and Danielle had toys and school supplies packed, ready to take down to the Victorian. She
was finishing some couscous at the kitchen table.

Dressed in a dark, olive-green sweater and black
jeans, Isaac kissed her cheek and asked, "Want to go
to the hot springs tonight? Up in Oro?"

The hot springs was known only to locals and a few
others.

The invitation jerked her from her thoughts. "Sure.
Thanks. If my mom will watch Laura."

He squinted. "Something wrong?"

She waited till the kids were out of the room before she told him about Mia—and her mother's departure. "If you'd rather not go tonight—"

"No. It'll be nice."

Isaac said, "I'll try to get out of the clinic by six, and we can go at eight. The boys will look after Danielle."

DANIELLE'S INITIAL SHYNESS as they drove to the Victorian gave way once she was inside and met Francesca. Francesca was expecting a client that morning, and Tara would need to see her, too. But in the meantime, Tara read to Danielle and colored with her and helped her with a pot holder loom. Danielle remained absorbed in her activities through the prenatal, ate every last crumb of her peanut-butter-and-jelly sandwich, and afterward prepared, with resignation, to go to school.

Tara went to the lumberyard while Danielle was at school and arrived to pick up the children at three-thirty, as planned.

The boys wanted to throw a football, even in the snow, but she lured them away with the circular saw, hammer and nails, and soon had two apprentice carpenters. They embraced the mouse cause with enthusiasm and focus, and David soon took over the task of calling the bait companies' 1-800-numbers to ask directions on the placement of bait and any other advice they would give.

Danielle sat with Tara as she nursed Laura, and Tara knew a fresh contentment—so much so that she barely noticed the clock ticking past six. When she did, she decided, *These kids are going to learn to cook.*

THE ROAD TO THE hot springs was rutted from tires that had pressed into the slick snow, now iced over in valleys and mounds. In the Range Rover, Isaac negotiated the bumps confidently, as smoothly as it could be done.

Francesca had agreed to babysit Laura. Isaac's boys were minding Danielle.

To keep her mind off Mia—and because she'd waited so long already—Tara said, "Tell me about your wife."

"Heloise?"

A name. *This is progress.*

"She was an obstetrician. I'll show you her picture when you come over again."

There were no other cars at the hot springs. Tara had worn her swimsuit under jeans and a sweater.

They grabbed their towels and got out of the truck under a rising moon. Standing by the open driver door, Isaac pulled off his sweater and long-sleeved T-shirt, and he was lean like an underfed animal, his muscles defined, the way a wolf or a lion gets from hunting its food. His skin was shadowed under his dark hair, against his hazel eyes.

She reminded herself to research that parasite. A friend in Boulder was a licensed acupuncturist and O.M.D., doctor of Oriental medicine. Maybe he could help.

Nervous, Tara peeled off first her jeans, then her own sweater. Though she'd nursed Laura before she left home, her breasts felt heavy in her black tank suit with the red trim.

Isaac peered at her over the car's roof as he removed his own sweats.

At last, they waded through the cold air and the

snow and mud around the edge of the pool, and he noticed her slim hips and long legs, her firm body that had never borne a child—and never would—yet had taken responsibility for another woman's baby.

The water was searing, wonderfully hot. Tara chose the far side of the small pool, lowering herself, concealing her breasts.

Isaac kept his eyes on her face and nowhere else.

In the sulphur fumes in the moonlight, the pool's black plastic lining beneath her, Tara drew a shallow breath. "How did Heloise die?"

"In childbirth. At home. Danielle was a triplet. Her sisters died. Heloise bled." It shouldn't be hard to explain. "In the spring of '94..."

"Yes."

"Everyone had premonitions. That something bad was coming.

"I ignored mine. I worked the day in April that President Habyarimana's plane was shot down. I stayed at the hospital with a sick boy. Meningitis. The radio was broken. People were ordered to stay in their homes. In the morning, the killing began, and people showed up to kill everyone at the hospital. I sent them away. Then people began coming in, missing arms, half-dead—

"Did I say my wife was Hutu? Her father. Her mother was Tutsi. Everyone Tutsi from my home, my wife's family, came to the hospital to hide. Including my boys. The *genocidaires* said they were the offspring of Tutsi and Belgians. I said, 'These are my sons. Go away.'

'The rest of Heloise's family begin saying they hate the cockroaches, the Tutsis—they're trying to fake it. Then, my sister-in-law, Dominique, who was a midwife and a fine human being, comes to the hospital and says my wife is dead. Three days before. She brought Danielle. She nursed Danielle.''

Tara clutched her head.

''It was five years ago,'' he repeated, as he had when he'd first revealed that his wife was dead.

His wife and two babies had died in April. A million Tutsis had been murdered by August. And five years later, this past May, his wife's family had been slaughtered.

Isaac.

She had to bare herself as he had. ''I was raped. In Chile and in Mexico. Prisons. I got a venereal disease and didn't deal with it, didn't know I had it for ages. That's why I'm infertile. Both tubes are a mess.''

Scars. His questions were an attempt to make the past go away, to pretend it wasn't real by pretending it wasn't there. ''Do you ovulate?''

''On this side.'' She pressed with her hand.

Isaac watched her, and one of her movements sent ripples across the pool to slosh gently against him. Silence of the outdoors, silence of leaves and bare branches rustling. ''Does your mother know?''

''Not that I'm infertile. Just Danny does. My ex.'' She abbreviated that story, but took her blame. ''Our sex life wasn't great. The divorce rate among midwives is high.''

Especially if they purloined each other's husbands.

The grandfather, the ex-husband, the rapists. *No one is going to hurt you again, Tara.* Except that he'd stopped believing he had the power to stop evil. ''How would you feel if I came over there?''

In the moonlight, she tried to read his eyes. ''Good.''

He came toward her through the steam, black hair falling forward over his eyes. He had a faint scar on his upper lip. She liked the hollows around his collarbone. She liked his wiry strength. He'd shaved clean for their date.

As Isaac searched her face, the steam swirled around them. He touched the smooth, lightly tanned skin of her left cheek.

His bare muscular shoulders were above her, fair and smooth.

The wet hand touched her face again, and his lips turned sideways over hers. He held each side of her head and she delved into his eyes.

Isaac's hands had disappeared into the pool and steam and settled on her waist. Their mouths opened together. His tongue slipped between her lips, and she clung harder to his back and met his erection. First time this close. "Isaac."

He kissed her again, her breasts against his chest.

"Isaac, I'm really excited." *It scares me.*

"That makes two of us. It's okay."

She rubbed against him, and his breath flattened. He lifted her, and her legs wrapped around him, and they kissed, each moment taking them further from the place where no one got hurt, toward the place where they belonged to each other.

Joy spread over him. Nectar. Touch.

He whispered to her, and Tara felt safe, safe enough to let him hear her. Though she never spoke a word. Just sounds.

Light burned through him. "Baby." God, it hurt so much to feel like this. To love. *Heloise…*

His wife nodded. And smiled.

Headlights arced through the cottonwoods and

pines, and he eased Tara away from him and got out. Snatching up their towels and shoes, he brought them to her side of the pool and shielded her from eyes in the car as she stood.

She wrapped herself in her towel.

"Hold on to me."

Tara stepped into her shoes. She carried her jeans and sweater as she held his arm on the way to the passenger door.

Another couple parked yards down the road, giving them privacy. Tara tugged on her clothes over her wet swimsuit in the front seat, her cold jeans sticking to damp skin.

He switched on the engine and the heater.

"I need to get back to Laura, to nurse her." Nervous, still feverish from their closeness, she rambled. "Now I know why you don't like homebirth."

"Yes." He reached across the front seat to hold her.

Tara's heart answered. A long kiss, because she couldn't stop now. It was too late. He was touching her face. Could he feel which bones had been broken? Why didn't he quit? Kissing her. Spreading his hands against her skin. Stroking the corners of her mouth. Their tongues gentle with each other again. Why couldn't one of them stop?

Her mother was going to Alaska. Heloise had died of third-stage hemorrhage. She, Tara, wasn't legal. Laura wasn't legally hers. Soon, they'd have nowhere to live.

And she was in love.

With a man who hated homebirth.

CHAPTER EIGHT

Ivy said to me, "You can do it, Beulah Ann. I've seen fifteen hundred women do it, and you can do it." I told her what happened in Louisiana, and she said I was very strong. When Ivy came back for a postpartum visit, I asked if she thought I was strong enough to be a midwife. She seemed to think about it, and then she said, "Yes. Yes, I do." I know she's right.

—Beulah Ann Cockburn, 21

JENNY PRESTON AND her partner, Yul, arrived at twelve-thirty on Tuesday, while Danielle was in school. Tara knew she'd have to watch the clock because she had another prenatal right afterward, another brand-new client who'd called just that morning.

Jenny was six feet tall, and even eight months pregnant, she had the look. Model. Dark blond hair and brown eyes. Mastery of her own body. Tara had never met a model before—or anyone who radiated such complete self-confidence. She controlled her space. She controlled herself.

And she was surprisingly down-to-earth in her leggings and thrift-shop sweater and down vest.

Yul was rugged and handsome—a ski patrolman.

Tara had to get some questions out of the way.

"You're aware that it is illegal for me to practice midwifery in the state of Colorado?"

Jenny looked her in the eye. "How many births have you done?"

"More than twenty-five hundred. If you like, I can give you the names of some colleagues who know me—and there are a couple of women in town whose births I've attended in the past, when I lived in Precipice before." She chose three midwives unassociated with Maternity House—because of Laura—and wrote down their names and numbers from her Rolodex. She also gave them the name of Francesca's retired backup physician, who had moved to Alta.

"Thanks." Jenny's smile dazzled. High cheekbones. Beautiful lips.

Tara tried to ease back on one of the room's impossible Victorian chairs and chose the floor instead, sitting cross-legged. "Okay, Jenny, I've looked at your records already. I want to go over some things, and then we'll see how the baby's doing. Hm. Kicking. I saw that. Come to think of it, let's do the exam now."

SHE'D ALLOWED NINETY minutes for the first visit, but Jenny was an incest survivor who had been violated by her first stepfather. Rich Scarborough, chief of obstetrics, was her biological father, and Jenny's mother had left him soon after her birth. Her second stepfather had been, she admitted, kind to her and her mother.

Jenny insisted that a homebirth was paramount. Without a midwife, Jenny said, she and Yul would handle it. He was an EMT, after all.

Tara and Jenny were still talking when she heard her next client's Humvee outside. Leila Ahmed Ibrahim had called just that morning—another brand-new client. Francesca was out right now, hunting Sorel-style boots for the Arctic, and Laura was starting to fuss at Tara's breast.

Tara thought of Beulah Ann Cockburn. She was going to *need* an assistant at this pace, and with Isaac's kids to care for.

But she and Isaac had talked last night on the way home from the hot springs. The boys could be trusted to look after Danielle; Oliver even picked her up when she cried. In a pinch, Oliver could drive. Not legal, but able. He'd learned in Rwanda, and Isaac let him practice with the Land Cruiser on the Tomboy road.

Tara said, "That's my next client. We'll have to wrap it up. Let's make an appointment for next week."

LEILA WORE A LONG gown to her ankles, a shawl covering her hair, and beautiful gold jewelry. She explained that she hadn't wanted to see a male doctor and that women in her country, Sudan, used midwives. She was young, her coffee skin like satin, and she was escorted to the Victorian by her husband.

This was her first child.

Though answering Tara's questions thoughtfully, Leila seemed uneasy. They'd already covered Tara's legal status, to which Leila had said, "Poof! Does not matter." So what was it?

Tara could only guess. "Leila, did you have an initiation ceremony as a child?"

The twenty-five-year-old's reaction was cautious. "Yes."

It took time to coax the next answer out of her. The

type of genital mutilation she'd endured was "phar-aonic circumcision"—infibulation.

Tara nodded somberly. The other woman's pain made Tara feel instantly close to her.

"It is a bad practice," Leila explained, "but I do not come from a barbaric country. If you were to come to my country, you would see the kindness of the people, the happiness of the children. My husband loves me very much. He regrets what was done to me."

Tara listened, nodding, trying to gain Leila's trust. "I believe you."

As the interview progressed, Tara finally remarked, "I have no experience with this, Leila, but I've read about it. You would be better off in the hospital."

"My mother had her children very fast. I could birth with a midwife in Sudan."

"She would cut you open with a knife." This wasn't going to be a routine episiotomy. The scar tissue would be deep. She explained the risks, from postpartum hemorrhage to fistulae causing incontinence, failure to dilate, prolonged labors, infant or maternal death.

Leila's disappointment sank her lovely features.

"I can take a look," said Tara. Leila and her husband were able to have intercourse, at least.

"Oh, thank you!"

She got the urine specimen out of the way first, then gave Leila a drape and showed her how to put it on. She and Francesca examined patients on a full-sized bed downstairs, rather than an examining table.

When she checked Leila, she knew what to expect, but the reality made her own limbs tremble. The crude scar, the hole through which Leila's husband's penis had entered, the inelasticity of tissue. Leila turned her head away and occasionally cried out during the examination and while Tara palpated her abdomen externally.

Finally, Tara peeled off her gloves. "Why don't you go ahead and get dressed? We'll talk after."

In the bathroom, she washed her hands unnecessarily and saw her own eyes. She must be strong for this woman. *I must stand beside her.*

Returning to the bedroom, she smiled warmly into Leila's eyes and drew up a chair—one more comfortable than those in the parlor—and gestured Leila to another soft chair.

The other woman sat gracefully, if gingerly.

"You said your husband regrets what you underwent?"

"Oh, he is against it. He knows it is unhealthy. My sister died during her initiation. But in Suakin, where my family lives, you are unclean if you are uncircumcised. And sometimes, it gives the man greater pleasure. My husband was educated in the United States, at Berkeley. He is an intellectual, a businessman. He says what happened to me is bad."

"So you wouldn't do this to your own daughter."

"No. Because of the pain. And it is unhealthy. That's why my husband and I married in another country and why he decided to work in the United States. In case we have daughters. My mother is very—powerful—and so is his."

And the grandmothers would demand pharaonic circumcision. Tara knew how slowly such situations changed. And now she was faced with a woman, three months pregnant, whose clitoris and labia minora had been entirely removed, probably with a dirty knife, then the excised labia majora shut with thorns or thread or a sugary egg paste, or any combination of the three, leaving a small hole through which to pee, to be opened later by her husband's or a midwife's knife. *Had* he used a knife? Someone had.

"I can't advise a homebirth, Leila. I'd like your permission to consult with a physician."

"All right."

"Leila, would you and your husband consider surgery to make intercourse less painful?"

"It has become less painful with time. But after the baby is born, he does not want me sewn up again."

The two embraced, and Tara treasured the contact, across cultures, the touch of different skin tones, the makings of friendship. "We'll talk soon," she promised and decided the first person she consulted would be Isaac. If anyone in Precipice knew anything about this kind of birth, it would be him.

THAT NIGHT, TARA read up on parasites in some of her books on nutrition and herbalism—Eastern and Western. She knew the basic approach but wanted review. Then she spent some time going through her mother's files and talking with Francesca about various clients. Finally, she took a break to phone Ivy. In just a few minutes, she'd filled her sister in on the news of Mia's disappearance and Francesca's upcoming departure for Alaska.

Ivy was shocked to silence, and Tara again faced her own emotions. About her mother's family, yes. But especially about Mia. *I never felt this ambivalence about Ivy.* But there wasn't the same history. When sane, controlled Mia came to be her mother's apprentice, Tara was the eighteen-year-old her mother *couldn't* handle—as Tara couldn't handle Francesca.

Mia was just a few months older than Tara, but it had seemed like years.

Enough of Mia. "Mom's called her clients and asked them if they'd rather have a hospital birth with a CNM—" a certified nurse-midwife "—or a home-birth with a well-qualified but uncertified DE—" direct-entry "—and they all chose homebirth. And one of them's due in two weeks, another in three weeks. Mom's leaving Thursday."

Ivy's breathing was quiet, noncommital.

Thinking of Jenny Preston and her father, the chief of obstetrics, Tara filled the silence. "You and I both know that these women have a right to have their babies any way they want."

"Tara, I'm worried about *you.* You have a child, and you're trying to marry this doctor next door. What does he think?"

That question again. "He doesn't know."

Tara couldn't talk about Isaac or how close she felt to him, how much she wanted to marry him—and not just for Laura, not just for him. In two days, she was already bonding with his kids. During a break from mouse eviction that afternoon, she'd taken the boys and Danielle to the top of a hill across from the chalet and introduced them to coasters; the coasters had come from the Precipice "free box." Danielle had sat with her brothers or Tara on the rides down the snowy slope.

When he got home, Isaac had asked her to stay for dinner, and Tara had played Dungeons & Dragons. The character she'd rolled was a girl ninja she'd named Haruko. David loved having a ninja in the game and had doled out experience points right and left, so that she'd gained almost two levels by the time they stopped. And afterward, she and Isaac had sat discussing the game. "Actually," she'd said, "the thing I like is that you have to choose an alignment, choose whether you're going to be good or evil and exactly how. It's a fun way to classify people. Take my mom. She's Lawful Good. You not only have to be on the side of right, you have to obey the law. But my dad? Maybe True Neutral. He hates an uneven fight, and he'd say who's *he* to sort out the good, the bad and the ugly?"

Isaac's mouth had been a straight line, unmoving.

"And I'm Neutral Good," she'd told him. "Forget the law, but help the good guys." Realizing where she'd headed without meaning to, she'd asked, "What about you? Isaac the Doctor, not Fitz the Thief."

"Isaac the Doctor?" He'd met her eyes, and she'd remembered his wife's family, everything he'd told her. But then he'd smiled, like he was pushing the past away. "My children will tell you I'm Lawful Good. And I wouldn't want anyone trying to convince them otherwise."

It hadn't been the answer she'd hoped for, but she'd put it from her mind.

Before she left, Isaac had showed her Heloise's picture—and kissed her beside the Range Rover. No, not just kissed. He'd teased her, saying he wanted to know her yoni—she could probably thank Dan for that.

I have a birthday coming up; how would you like to be my present? Isaac had asked.

And she'd had answers. *When's your birthday?*

November fifteenth.

She'd told him hers was the twenty-second.

Ah, you can be my present. Then, I'll be yours. How's that?

"Oh, Ivy." The anguished exclamation slipped out.

"Oh, Ivy, what?"

It was late, and the door of her room was shut, or it would have stopped there. It would never have started. "It's him."

"What about him?"

The words demanded release. "He's a doctor, and he doesn't like homebirth, but it's like if I picked out a man for myself, picked him out from the whole cosmos, it would have been Isaac." Isaac, whose wife had died in stage three. Whose daughters had died at birth.

"You did pick him out, Tara." Only a hint of a smile in Ivy's voice.

"I'm scared. It's not like with Danny. With Danny, I was safe, never afraid. Isaac's been all over Africa— even Rwanda, those places—" *his wife, his wife's family!* "—and you know the people who were there, they say when you flew in you saw the bodies floating in Lake Victoria, and the rivers are loaded with man-eating crocodiles but people jumped in rather than be slaughtered. And the genocide— Oh, shit, you're pregnant, you don't need to hear this." What'd she been thinking? Ivy should have support, beautiful thoughts, peace…

"I need to hear, Tara. I can tell you're falling in love."

Only Ivy could say it so baldly.

Tara said nothing.

"Okay, new subject. For selfish reasons, I'm sorry about your new client load. I was going to ask you to come out for this baby's birth."

"December first." She wanted to be there. But… Jenny. Leila. Beulah Ann. Was her sister really all right? Her husband's family lived in the area, and Tara had witnessed some real tension in the past. Around Ivy. "Ivy, you've got to tell us how you really are. Are things all right with Cullen's family?"

"Yes."

Tara remembered that her sister didn't tell *her* everything, either.

"Forget I mentioned it." Ivy sighed. "There's no way you can come out here; it's crazy. He has kids. You have a newborn you're nursing. This is why you're trying to marry the guy. You've got a home study to look forward to."

And Dan McCrea with his threat—waiting in the wings. If Isaac decided he didn't like her, after all.

"Tara." Here came Ivy's voice of reason again. "If you do decide to marry Dr. Isaac, you have to tell him how you feel about certification. *Before* he agrees to marry you. To do anything else would be a lie."

Tara swallowed. Ivy was right, and she could imagine how Isaac would react to that kind of lie.

But how would he react to the truth?

The moment Tara turned off the phone, it rang again. She pushed the talk button. "Hello?" The stairs creaked under her mother's tread.

"Tara?"

He still didn't know her voice from Francesca's, but she knew his. "Hi."

"I'm at the hospital. Can you meet me for lunch tomorrow? At the Riviera?"

The hotel, the finest restaurant in town.

"Will you have time?" she asked.

"I've cleared my afternoon."

No small feat for a man in family practice. It would

be the perfect time to talk to him about Leila. And to tell him the truth about her status as a midwife.

To tell Isaac the Doctor.

Lawful Good.

SHE WAS UP BEFORE SIX, to take Laura down to the Café International again. Dan McCrea would be there, but it was the only way she knew to get in touch with Beulah Ann.

The doctor's eyes were dark and disapproving when he saw her come in. She said, "Hi," but took a table as far from him as possible. Beulah Ann came right over, and Tara set a bag of midwifery texts on a chair.

With a glance at the kitchen, Beulah Ann sank down beside her. "Thanks, Tara. This is so sweet of you. When do you need 'em back?"

"Those, I don't use regularly. What we need to get you are Anne Frye's texts, but it's big money, so start with these. Hey, can you turn up the music?"

Beulah Ann eyed the kitchen again, then rose and left the table.

Dan came over and touched Laura's foot. His look for Tara left her no quarter. "Just saw Rich Scarborough's daughter. She's my next-door neighbor. Hope you're thinking things through, Tara."

One call to the Department of Health, and she was busted. Tara couldn't comment. She wouldn't discuss her clients, any more than he would discuss his patients.

"Just a friendly warning."

"Thank you." It probably was.

But good grief, Jenny and Yul were having a homebirth, with or without a midwife. It had been all Tara could do to get across that she absolutely would transport if things looked bad—and they needed to accept that. She'd given them a few stories, good outcomes and bad. Between Chile, Mexico and Maternity House, she'd seen her share of crises, most of them resulting from poor nutrition. *This part of it,* she'd concluded, *I call the shots. If that's not okay, you should find yourselves another birth attendant.*

Dan asked, "How's my brother? Every time I call, he says you're there—or he's on his way to see you."

The music went up, and Beulah Ann returned to the table.

"Happy." Tara had seen it in Isaac's eyes. If only today's lunch didn't change that.

Dan hesitated, then said, "Well, I'll leave you."

She smiled and waited till he was back at his own table before leaning toward Beulah Ann.

WHILE DANIELLE DREW in the kitchen that morning, Tara saw three of her mother's clients. Karen Anthony, due in two weeks, had planned a VBAC, but was nervous about a homebirth. Tara wasn't crazy about the idea, either. "Well, you were planning on a hospital birth. Why don't I go with you as a labor coach?"

"Oh, would you?"

"Sure. I can't assist with the birth, but I can be with you, even do some acupressure and other things to help with the pain."

"Thank you so much."

Beulah Ann showed up in time for the third prenatal. She had her own birth kit, and Tara introduced her as an assistant, let her take heart tones and maternal blood pressure, check the urine and assess the baby's lie. Mam'zelle Eve had taught her well, and Beulah Ann was a born nurturer.

She wished she had more time to talk with Beulah Ann and assess her skills after the prenatal, but Tara barely had time to dress for lunch. They made a date for Beulah Ann to return that evening at eight.

Nervous, Tara dressed as casually as seemed appropriate for the Riviera: in Precipice, that tended to be *very* casual. She wore overalls and a waffle-knit long undershirt in indigo blue.

She carried Laura in her car seat when she entered the restaurant, and arms in an olive-green cotton shirt reached out to take the baby from her.

"Oh, hi. Thank you."

At the table, facing the ski slopes, Isaac gave her a photo of him and his children. It must have been taken that summer, on the steps of the chalet. They were all smiling, with sadness in their eyes.

The waitress brought their menus, and Isaac said, "Would you like wine?"

She shook her head.

"None for me either."

When the waitress left, he said, "Can I talk you into a walk after lunch?"

"Sure. But there's something I have to tell you immediately. Something I should have told you much sooner, and I apologize for not doing so."

He waited almost with disinterest. But not quite.

Used to bad news and braced for it.

"I'm not a certified nurse-midwife. I've attended plenty of births, and if I jump through the hoops, I can be licensed to practice in Colorado when the new law goes into effect in January."

"Great."

She could see he thought it was less than great. *Homebirth.* Fighting her fear, she focused on his eyes, made sure they met hers. "The bad news is, I'm not going to do it."

His glance was impatient, as though he had other things on his mind. She knew her work irritated him. "Why not?"

"A hundred reasons. Do you want them all?"

"I'd rather you'd just get licensed." *Or find another line of work.* Isaac rubbed his eyes, fighting off irrelevant thoughts, unrelated pain. He felt the sweat starting, his heart beating faster. *Oh, come on; not now.*

"Well, that's not going to happen, so let me try to explain." She was going to have to do it well, but right now this photo was in front of her, and *he* was, and she wanted to be his birthday present and wanted him to be hers. "Okay, parents' rights," she began haphazardly. "Say the parents want Aunt Josephine to catch the baby, and Josephine's not a midwife. Then, Josephine could be busted for practicing medicine without a license. Isaac, are you all right?"

He uttered the name of the parasite.

Tara slid to his side of the booth to put her arm around him, and Laura cried in her car seat.

"Take care of her. I'm going outside. It passes."

While he was gone, she nursed Laura with the supplemental feeder, walked her about for a while, then returned her to the car seat and made notes to herself. *Call Dr. Ching, Beulah Ann at eight p.m., refresher EMT course, explore transport options.* The notes followed her everyday notes on Isaac's kids. *Danielle at two forty-five. O. and D. staying late to shoot baskets.*

Isaac slid into the booth beside her.

She pushed his glass of water at him, and he drank it. "Isaac, you need to drink a lot of water, preferably filtered or bottled. I can tell you that right off. Next, I want to try a parasite purge with you.''

He cleared his throat and refilled his water glass from the pitcher Tara had asked the waitress to leave on the table.

"And I want to take you to Boulder to Dr. Ching. He's a doctor of—''

"Let's talk about this later. We were discussing something else. Your reasons for not certifying. You said Aunt Josephine should be allowed to deliver the baby. Did I tell you that Aunt Dominique, who *was* a midwife, a good one, delivered Danielle and Laura and Judith?''

One of his daughters had been named Laura. It took her a moment to respond. "I would never assist a mother with triplets at home. I mean, I have—once— in Mexico.''

"What happened?'' No luster in his eyes.

"Grace. It went beautifully.''

She'd never seen him look so cynical. Or so bitter.

She closed her eyes. Focused. She had to make him understand. "Isaac, I consider myself part of an ancient tradition. Women helping women in childbirth. I just don't feel it needs to be regulated. Traditional midwives are trained through apprenticeship and hands-on experience. Maybe they add to their training with courses taught by health professionals. What's wrong with that? Why a license?''

"I've seen the work of some traditional midwives, Tara, and it wasn't all good and it wasn't all gentle.''

His comment made her think of Leila. The restaurant was private enough. "Isaac, that reminds me. I have a client who was infibulated in the Sudan. I wanted to consult you. To ask how the delivery should go.''

Breath moved his nostrils. His throat and jaw tensed. "She should be in the hospital. They should all be in a hospital, Tara. What is this homebirth crap, anyhow? It's not like there aren't enough beds at Precipice Peak.''

Oh, shit. He couldn't really feel that way. Even after... ''So, she needs an OB/GYN?''

''Yes. It's miserable. Send her to Dan.''

Dan. Perhaps if she approached Dan as a physician, explaining the help Leila needed, a new bond of professional respect could be established between her and Isaac's brother.

Suddenly she remembered Dan's warning about Rich Scarborough. What a headache!

''Your brother thinks I'm 'folksy and backward,''' she muttered.

''He's able to joke about it. I'm not.''

Just what she wanted to hear. ''So...you've never attended a homebirth?''

''*Hundreds.* People died. Do I need to remind you who some of them were?''

''No. But you weren't there. And in the Netherlands, for instance—''

''I'm not an idiot, Tara. I have a better picture of birth worldwide than you do. May I keep the right not to love homebirth? *Merci.* But let's assume you and your clientele are right and this is a good idea. Then why not license? You want to go to jail?''

''Been there, done that.'' Trying to ignore his anger, she rattled off the places. ''Mexico, Chile, Nevada, Utah, Texas, Hawaii.''

''*For what?* Third World countries aside.''

"Protests, environmental activism."

She had never seen such distress, or incomprehension, in his face. "What about Laura? Think of her, if you can't think of my children."

His children. *We're in deep, aren't we, Isaac?*

"Look, I'm not going to jail. If someone reported me for being unlicensed, the Department of Health would just tell me not to practice. I might have to pay a fine."

He stared. She really thought she wouldn't be arrested. No wonder she couldn't keep out of jail. Some explanation vibrated through him and flitted away, out of reach. It was replaced by thoughts of Southern midwives recently arrested in connection with a home VBAC death.

Find another line of work, Tara!

Slowing his breath, he took both her hands in his, to tell her what he'd known since the night he'd found her in his laundry room and maybe before that. Known because of that baby. Because she'd cleaned half his house and he'd cleaned the rest, and his boys were becoming carpenters. Because he believed in a core of goodness inside her. "Tara. I want to marry you." He repeated it. "I want to marry you." Slowly, he shook his head. "But I can't under these circumstances. You could become licensed—or stop being a midwife."

She drew back, and her suddenly glistening, suddenly fiery eyes reminded him of other brown eyes, and the restaurant came and went. "Never. I will never stop being a midwife."

"With four children?"

With four children... I want to marry you.

When the waitress reappeared Isaac asked her to

please come back later; they'd barely glanced at their menus.

"It's my principles," she hissed. "Women should be able to birth at home with whoever they want attending."

"Oh, come on, Tara. That's like saying anyone should be able to pass himself off as a physician." *Give it up, Tara! It's bullshit.*

"That's not what I'm saying. Look, what I saw in Mexico was that women trusted midwives and *curanderos* according to the practitioners' success levels. It's self-regulated, community-regulated." *With four children? I want to marry you. I want to marry you.* "Normal birth is *not* a medical procedure, and midwives are not physicians and have never pretended to be. My sister, Ivy, attends births in *shacks* in Appalachia. Her clients' alternative is not a doctor. It's no one. Or their own families."

Something Isaac wanted very much was going up in smoke. She was overwrought; one of them had to cool it. "Tara, let's try to work this out." Stroking the back of her neck while the world walked by outside the windows.

She escaped his touch, balling up the napkin she'd used to dab at her eyes. "Frankly, I don't see much room for compromise."

"I have compromised." Marrying a midwife was a compromise. "Come on, Tara."

"If you would excuse me from lunch, I'd appreciate it. I'm sorry, Isaac." She fished in her diaper bag and pulled out two twenties and set them on the table—with the photo of him and his children. "Your lunch is on me."

He reached across her to shove the bills back in her

diaper bag. The photo lay between them. "You owe me nothing. Except for the car. I'll see you this afternoon."

The kids! "You have the afternoon off, Isaac. Wouldn't you like to spend it with them? The boys are staying late—"

"Tara, don't do this."

"I'll resell the Range Rover as soon as possible. I don't need it anyhow; my mother's leaving her Subaru behind when she goes to Alaska. She's leaving tomorrow. And as soon as I can, I'll return your cash." A plan hatched in her mind. With the money from the Range Rover, she could hire a Texas lawyer and try to adopt Laura legally. She would come prepared with a list of her clients, a financial sheet showing what she'd be paid.

But Isaac had sold the Victorian; it would be occupied by its new owners on November twenty-fourth. Two days after the birthday she wouldn't be spending with him. She'd have to find affordable housing. What was she going to do?

I hate you. I hate you.

She finally answered him. "Tomorrow I'll pick up Danielle at the clinic when I get back from the airport, and I'll resume watching your children until I sell the Range Rover. Then I'll repay the money I owe you."

Isaac's throat was so tight he couldn't breathe. *Tara. Please.*

She replaced the two twenties beside the photo, gathered her diaper bag and Laura in the car seat, and said, "I'll see you tomorrow."

He was on his feet, trying to take the car seat.

''I don't need any help. Please sit down and enjoy your meal.''

He opened the door for her and stood watching her through the glass.

CHAPTER NINE

I knew what would happen, because I had seen
many before. But I didn't realize what it meant.
As the day approached, I was filled with terror.
I became hysterical. I was taken to the country
by my grandmothers and held down by three
women. Afterward, I was afraid to pee, because
I had heard and seen other girls scream. I did
not pee for three days.

—Leila, describing her infibulation or pharaonic
   circumcision

HER MOTHER MUST NOT get wind that anything was
wrong. If Francesca was worried about Tara, she
would postpone the trip to Talkeetna, maybe cancel it.
That mustn't happen. After a lifetime of caution, Francesca
was kicking away her safety net. *She's got to
do it.*

For whatever reason.

Tara stopped at the newspaper office on the way
home to put in an ad about the car, asking $28,000.
After placing the ad, Tara headed back to the Victorian,
deliberately focusing on her midwifery practice
and on adopting Laura. Should she call Maternity
House now and explain the situation? No, she should
do it in person, *after* hiring a lawyer. She wouldn't be

able to get anyone's advice on who to retain, but she should choose someone in El Paso.

Parking in front of the house, she braced herself.

Francesca stepped out on the porch and came down to carry in Laura. "Isaac called. He said you weren't feeling well, but he'd like you to call him at home if you feel up to it."

"I'm fine."

Francesca inspected her daughter for signs of illness. Nothing amiss. "Anything I can do?"

"No. But you must need help packing." She held her mother's arm gently on the steps.

"Believe it or not, I'm done. I hate to ask, but maybe you could hold a garage sale or take my extra things to the free box? Of course, keep anything you like. The furniture is Isaac's. It goes with the house."

Tara's heart missed a beat. *She's not coming back.* A resentment she'd been trying to suppress bubbled up again. So many times she'd begged her mother to take some risks. Now Mia Kammerlander was the instigator. *Oh, Tara, give it up.* Poor Mia was probably dead. And she'd probably been lonely as hell in Alaska, in her whole life, with zero women friends.

Except my mother.

"Sure, I'll take care of your things. And Laura and I are taking you to the airport."

"Thank you, sweetie. Oh, I'm going to miss you two."

Tara and Laura.

Tara felt tears percolating again. But she also knew hope. Had Isaac changed his mind?

Inside, she said, "Let me take Laura, and I'll go upstairs and call Isaac."

"Oh, I'll watch her, Tara." Francesca was already

lovingly removing the infant from her car seat. "Go call Isaac."

"HI." HE PAUSED. "How are you?"

Why answer that? *Because I thought we were in love.* "Well, I'm upset. You want to marry me, but not really me, or you want me to be different."

He was silent, probably thinking of his wife and daughters. She wasted one thought, that he didn't love her as he'd loved them. Perfectly natural. He barely knew her.

And what she'd said was true.

He didn't want to marry *her,* the real Tara, at all.

Useless to argue with him. Absolutely useless. "I guess I'm sorry—" *where were those tears coming from?* "—that we're so wrong for each other."

Isaac cleared his throat, away from the phone. "Look, I'll try to find a nanny for Danielle ASAP. It's unnecessary for you to sell the car—or pay me back."

"Oh, but you're so wrong. And frankly, I need the money from the car to try to adopt Laura. But I'll care for your children while you work, until you find someone you think is good enough." And whether he liked it or not, he was going to purge that parasite.

His silence was brief. "Thank you." Another pause. "Then, I'll see you."

"Fine." She hung up and burst into tears, then remembered Francesca and hurried to the bathroom to get in the shower and cry. She'd given Isaac all her secrets—and then she'd given him her heart.

And he had given it back.

As Danny had.

Isaac McCrea was the last man in her life. The last.

SHE HAD TO LEVEL with Beulah Ann about Laura.

"My gosh," said Beulah Ann. "That mother is *gone,* and she gave the baby to you. Oh, Tara, I wish there was some way I could help."

"You've already helped. Let's talk midwifery."

They did, for an hour, until Tara was satisfied that Beulah Ann was really beyond apprenticeship. She was ready to start tallying the births she needed to be licensed in Colorado. And Beulah Ann wanted to be licensed.

"You're not afraid of working with me?" asked Tara.

Beulah Ann waved away the concern.

"Would you like to bring your baby up here, Beulah Ann?" It must be hard to be so far from Chantel.

"I've got a room in a house that doesn't want kids. No one does. And I can't afford a trailer."

Tara knew the story. It was going to be her own pretty soon. Unless, after the adoption, there was money left from the Range Rover. "If you want, the two of you can stay here, with me, till November twenty-fourth. Then we'll look for a place together. You'd need to figure out your own childcare, though. Don't quit your day job, but I'm going to be sharing the money from the births with you. And, some of them, with my mom, because she's been doing prenatals." Tara gathered some client records from the table.

"There's no need for that, Tara." Francesca paused in the doorway, then stepped in.

"Hello, Ms. Walcott."

"Francesca. You must be Beulah Ann. I remember Ivy going to Gunnison for your birth."

"She's my heroine."

"Mine, too," murmured Tara. "Mom, let's talk about the money later."

"Nothing to talk about—except between you and Beulah Ann."

"That plane ticket cost you an arm and a leg."

"Enough, Tara. I have a little tucked away, and I get back a deposit from Isaac on this place. Now I'm just grateful my clients have some help." Francesca slipped out and shut the door, leaving the two young women to talk money.

And Tara to reflect again that her mother wasn't coming back.

ISAAC LAY AWAKE, wishing he hadn't called Tara after that scene at the restaurant.

What would happen to her baby? Would she be able to adopt?

Midwifery laws. Adoption laws.

As he had for the last two nights, he picked over the things she'd told him and all she hadn't. Her grandfather, raped, prison, abandoned by her husband. Chile and Mexico.

The previous night, the boys had been talking broken bones, and Tara had said, *Oh, I've had lots. This one. This one. This one....*

Mandible, maxilla, zygomatic, nasal, ribs, patella.

Remembering touching her face at the hot springs and many other times, feeling something amiss, he'd finally said, *Teeth?*

She'd grinned. *You bet.*

Isaac had left the room and stood on his own in darkness. When he'd walked her to the car, he'd said, *They beat the shit out of you.*

And made me eat shit, too. But hey—let's not talk about it. It was a long time ago.

Her voice had trembled.

This morning, he'd anticipated lunch and, face it, sex. A lifetime of sex. A half-hour's conversation had destroyed those plans.

Sleep drifted over him slowly, a black blanket.

"Daddy? Daddy?"

He saw Oliver, then made out David and Danielle. They crawled right up on the bed with him, dragging along their pillows and sleeping bags. They all curled together like wolves in a pack.

He wished for Tara.

Letting her go would be the mistake of a lifetime.

FRANCESCA KNEW WHEN her daughter withheld things, and this was one of those instances. But her plane would leave Montrose in an hour and a half, at six-thirty. They were en route to the airport before dawn. In the back, Laura slept in her car seat.

"Tara, I know something's bothering you. It would help me just to know what it is."

"It wouldn't help. You'd go to Talkeetna and worry about it, when you already have enough on your mind." She flashed a grin at her mother. "This is *minor.*"

"A broken heart?"

Tara rolled her eyes. "My heart works just fine, thank you very much. A *broken* heart is one that can't love. I *think* I've met some people like that, but you never know what they're like off duty."

Francesca wanted to scream. Broken hearts, broken bones. Tara had flown from La Paz to Quito to Miami on her father's nickel, and met Charlie in Florida for

her surgery. Surgeries. Charlie was the one she'd
called. Charlie. After Tara had engineered her own
escape by wits and will, she'd gotten from Santiago
to La Paz by various forms of ground transportation,
all notoriously uncomfortable for people *without* broken bones. And called Charlie.

Her mother had learned the truth—or the truth Tara
would tell her—only when she'd seen scar tissue on
her body. Four years after the fact. After Mexico. It
was one of the rare occasions when she'd screamed at
her daughter and one of the not-so-rare occasions
when she'd told Charlie *exactly* what she thought of
him.

I didn't want to worry you, Mom.

She said she'd walk out of the hospital if I told you.

It was all about fear. Their perception of her fear.
And she *was* afraid, damn it. What was wrong with
her family that they weren't?

"It's Isaac, isn't it?"

"Don't jump to conclusions. But I'm fine. Laura's
fine. Everything's fine."

Francesca didn't want to say how much she'd been
counting on Isaac to look after Tara. It had taken just
a few days—brief contact before he took Tara to the
hot springs, an occasional wave on the road, hearing
the praises of patients who thought he walked on water, and, most of all, contact with Danielle—but she'd
come to feel subtly different about him.

"Honey," she implored without really knowing
what she was asking. "You know I'm always here for
you. I don't want you keeping things from me."

"I know that, Mama."

But she didn't say she wouldn't keep things from
Francesca.

In the airport terminal, they waited together until boarding time, and then Francesca hugged and kissed Tara and Laura again and again, with tears in her eyes. "I'm going to make the old bugger send you a ticket to come see us between births."

"The old bugger?" Tara winked at her mother. "He says you used to call him 'Man of My Heart.'"

Francesca rolled her eyes, a parting gesture. "'Used to' ended over twenty years ago."

TARA CAUGHT DAN AT his office that afternoon, while Isaac's children were in school. Learning from his receptionist that she was waiting, he invited her in at once.

Rocking Laura, Tara told him about Leila.

He was serious and said, "Have her make an appointment."

"She was raised in an Islamic culture."

"Well, if she wants to bring her husband or you along, that's up to her." There was no real warmth from Isaac's brother, and he stood up, signaling that the visit was over. But as he showed her and Laura out, he asked, "How's Isaac?"

Another chill passed over her. Without Isaac...

Dan. Laura. Rich Scarborough.

Dan had caught her pause. "Trouble in paradise?"

Tara shrugged. "You'll have to talk to him."

His expression, rather than angry, as she'd anticipated, was disappointed. He murmured, "I will."

And waited for her to leave.

As she tucked Laura in her car seat, in the back of the Range Rover, she set aside her fears. Behind the wheel, she closed her eyes and breathed deeply, saying her mantra against fear. "Act from love. Act from love."

She headed for Precipice's natural food market.

WHEN TARA REACHED home, she phoned Leila. The woman was both excited and nervous about the doctor's visit. "Will you come with me, Tara?"

"I'm happy to."

"I want to ask you something else."

"What?"

"My husband wants to know. Can you become a legal midwife?"

"Me? Oh, sure."

Leila sounded puzzled. "Then why don't you?"

Why was her world turning upside down this way? "Let's talk about it when I see you next. In the meantime, you should make an appointment with Dr. McCrea. Here's—"

"Oh, Dr. McCrea is good! He is from Rwanda. My husband goes to him."

"This is his brother, Dr. Dan McCrea. Here's his number."

Leila took it down. "There is one more thing, Tara. I've asked my husband, and he says it is all right. I would like to learn to be a midwife. If you could help me, we would pay you."

Tara's eyes shot open. Assistants and students coming out of the woodwork. "That's something else we should discuss face-to-face. And I'd like to meet your husband," she added.

Setting down the phone, she thought how much easier her life would be if she became licensed. Why would it really hurt?

Her eyes stung. Her reasons were stronger, deeper, than she could explain.

Even to herself.

SHE KEPT A GOOD FACE as she and the boys sprayed foam insulation into cracks in the exterior of the house, places mice could get in. But her mind spun. Working in the shadow of the ramshackle Columbine, the former brothel, she wished the Range Rover was sold already, so she could give Isaac back his money. She would need the rest, every cent, to adopt Laura.

Tara had some ideas for her time with Isaac's kids over the next week; surely, he could find a nanny by then.

Finishing her section of the skirt, Tara rounded up the boys. "Let's go inside with Danielle. We've got a school project to work on."

Inside, they gathered on the couches. Before Tara could speak, David caught sight of a slow-moving mouse, probably poisoned. The charcoal cat, Batini, had seen it, too. David snatched up his father's ice ax and squished the mouse.

Tara winced, and Danielle said, with expanding English, "That's *sick,* David."

"Please clean it up." Tara unzipped her parka and held Laura on her thighs. When David returned from disposing of the mouse, she said, "Okay, friends, Halloween is only a week and a half away."

The boys nodded with interest. Danielle frowned and sighed.

"Any ideas on what you want to be? I'll help you make any costume you want, but you should know that your school—" there was only one school in

Precipice, K-12 "—has a big costume contest every year. Ideas, anyone?"

They shook their heads, shrugged.

"Okay, you can each be anything you want, but I did have an idea involving all of you, something I *think* could make you win the costume contest. And your dad will love it."

"What?" demanded Oliver.

"Dad will like it?" David exclaimed.

Their craving was bold, brazen. Isaac's love. Isaac's approval.

Danielle sat forward on her seat, eyes big.

"You could be, all three of you, fourteeners, Colorado's mountains that are fourteen thousand feet or higher."

David said, "My dad is a mountaineer."

"I know." Tara checked all three faces. "What do you think? I know how to really make you look like some of these mountains. I've got photos galore—"

"Dad has books with pictures," interjected David.

The children consulted each other and slowly smiled, even Danielle. "Okay." Oliver spoke for them all. "We'll be mountains."

ISAAC THOUGHT OF HER as he drove home, that he would see her soon, what could be said. She truly behaved as though she wanted to go to jail. Not consciously, perhaps, but— It gnawed at him. Why? After Chile?

The Range Rover was parked in its usual spot.

She met him at the door, and he dragged her outside quickly so he could hold her.

"We'll work it out," he said, kissing her forehead. "All right?"

"I made dinner. Parasite purge diet."

He smiled. Couldn't help it. "Thank you."

Tara hoped he would feel that way after facing the meal—and her instructions for breakfast.

But none of the McCreas were picky eaters. They all dished up millet and buckwheat, raw saltless sauerkraut, beets, kelp, and pumpkin seeds, and gladly dipped their sourdough rye bread into garlic olive oil. Eating with Laura at her breast, without supplemental milk, Tara explained, "We need to create an intestinal environment where the parasite can't thrive. That means, among other things, promoting healthy bacteria and creating a drier internal climate. Parasites thrive in a damp internal environment with excess mucus. And there are some herbs that may help."

He'd check them out in the new *Physician's Desk Reference for Herbal Medicines,* which he'd noticed someone had been reading while he was at work. He needed to take the book to his office. He'd give her a copy of her own for her birthday.

In lieu of better things.

"I'd like to study traditional Chinese medicine," she confessed. "It would enhance my midwifery practice. I'd go the whole nine yards. Acupuncture. Herbs."

"Great idea." That would keep her busy for three years, at least. And, hey, credentials. What did they call themselves? L. Ac., O.M.D.? At least, she wouldn't be going to jail.

Or attending homebirths.

Tara caught on—and looked down at her plate.

Thinking that someday they should have a long conversation about bacteria, healthy and otherwise, Isaac said, "So where does one get bottled water around here?"

"I circled it in the phone book."

"They'll have a mineral analysis."

"Of course."

Their eyes met over the table, and it was a long second before she realized Oliver was staring at them. But the boy quickly turned his attention to his own food.

She was wearing her mother's pager everywhere now, so she accepted Isaac's invitation to stay with them. David wanted her there for Dungeons & Dragons, anyway.

The adventurers were on a ship heading south, searching for a band of tropical islanders who held a cure that would heal the mayor of a town in the north. They encountered a sea dragon, and Isaac's character, being only a thief, stayed clear of the fray.

It gave him time to think. To watch Tara and Danielle as they announced each stroke against the dragon. Tara *was* playful. He wished he had a picture of her when she was Danielle's age. He tried to imagine her growing up.

But divorce… An alcoholic father. A con-artist grandfather.

A con.

Fifty thousand dollars.

In a flash of light, he understood.

"TARA, HAVE YOU EVER considered that your feelings about the law might come from that summer with your grandfather? That maybe you believe you *deserve* to go to jail?"

She rocked backward as though he'd hit her. Then drew herself up.

The children were in bed, Laura nursing to sleep. *I should get home.* But it was so comfortable to sit on the couch with Isaac, feet in socks rubbing each other's legs, talking about her EMT recertification, which she would be getting this weekend, primarily so she could network with locals on hospital transport. She hadn't mentioned the last, had tried not to mention midwifery at all. Just give it a rest. It had been wonderful—until now. "Well, we should have gone to jail."

"Not you."

"You weren't there."

"And you were thirteen. You weren't responsible, Tara. For anything." His green eyes looked steadily into hers.

She trembled. "Nothing happened."

Oh.

"I should get home." She swung her feet away from him, detached the sleeping infant from her breast, and stood.

Isaac walked her out. While he fastened the seat into the car and buckled Laura inside and made sure she was warm, Tara said, "Your meals for tomorrow are in the fridge. Remember to take them to work if I forget to tell you. And chew your food."

"And drink springwater." Shutting the car door, he turned to her. He held her head and kissed her, and their tongues met and their bodies pulsed as one. Embracing, they walked to the driver's side. He buckled her shoulder harness, and when she'd started the car, he kissed her again. "I love you."

The shock of the gift coursed through her. She grabbed him.

And his hand caressed her breasts and then, gently, between her legs, as they kissed again and again.

FRANCESCA CALLED THAT night.

"Mom! How are you? Where are you?"

"Anchorage."

"Didn't Dad meet you? Have you found out anything?"

"Not really." Hurriedly, Francesca asked after her in a way that Tara knew included Laura.

"We're great." Laura began fussing, and Tara could hardly focus on the conversation. "Where are you? Did Dad meet you?"

"Yes. You know what, honey, I should get off the phone. I'll call you when I know something more."

"Soon."

"Soon," Francesca promised and hung up.

Very strange. Francesca hadn't mentioned Isaac's name—or, actually, Laura's. She'd just wanted to get off the phone.

It's almost like she's *keeping secrets now.*

Incredulous, Tara wondered, *From me?*

WHEN THE CHILDREN were settled in bed, Isaac called his mother. She asked, "How are you, Isaac? Tara was nice."

"Tara is nice."

"The children mentioned her even before the two of you showed up together."

"When would you like to visit us, Mom? Tara cleaned the house, and she's almost whipped the mice."

"Remember that I said I liked her *before* she did those things. How about after Halloween? I could come the next Friday and stay through your birthday."

It wasn't what he'd had in mind. "Sure. Great. The children will love to see you."

"Will I get to spend more time with Tara?"

"I think so."

"Oh, darling, I'm so glad."

THE CHILDREN HAD named the blue room downstairs in the back the Secret Room and forbade their father to enter it. Inside, Tara had covered all the furniture with a sheet, and from Isaac's budget for the children's needs had bought chicken wire, cloth and foam to line each costume, and more cloth to be stiffened and painted to create the mountains. She might have to call a friend or two on the day of the contest, to get the costumes to school. And Danielle would want to wear hers trick-or-treating on Halloween night itself.

She met with clients while the children were in school, Beulah Ann joining her for prenatals each afternoon, as well as tutorials on nutrition. On the day of her own EMT recert, Tara let Beulah Ann borrow the Range Rover to drive to Gunnison and collect Chantel.

Tara was home for lunch when Francesca called from Talkeetna to say that Mia was dead. Her snowmobile had hit a tree.

"Mom, I'm so sorry."

Francesca took a moment answering. "Is everything all right there?"

"Actually—incredibly good." Tara filled her in on Beulah Ann, Leila—and Halloween costumes. She thought her mother sighed in relief. Almost as though

Francesca suddenly had concerns of her own, maybe as large as Tara's, and was relieved not to have to think about— "Where are you staying, Mom? Let me write down the number."

"Oh..." Her mother faltered. "I'm not sure...."

Not sure? What did that mean?

"...I'll let you know."

Tara felt helpless. She wanted to go to Alaska, to protect Francesca.

It hit her moments later, after another unsatisfactory conversation-ender, her mother suddenly saying she had to hang up.

She'd done it to her mother a thousand, a million times, herself. *And this is how it feels.*

BEULAH ANN AND Chantel moved in that night, into Francesca's old room.

Beulah hadn't brought many possessions, but one was a television. "Got to have it. Need to watch the rodeos."

Rodeos? Midwifery and rodeos weren't incompatible. Still, in Tara's experience it was a first.

Chantel was blond, wiry and rambunctious. Tara and Beulah Ann watched her together as they toddler-proofed the house, and after Beulah Ann had read to Chantel and Laura, both women got their children to sleep.

Afterward, Beulah Ann crept into Tara's room to hear what she'd arranged in the way of hospital transport.

"Okay, so we've got Perry and Carlos and Yul on the mountain—" Jenny's partner was an EMT "—and Roger and Bobby and Hillary in town. I've got some numbers for other areas as well. Here—I made a list of numbers for you for your birth kit. Depending on the situation, it may be best and fastest for you to drive and me to ride in back with the mom. But it's nice to have some of these guys in the community for extra backup.''

Beulah Ann nodded, yet seemed preoccupied. "Well, I'd best get to bed.''

"Everything go okay with your family?''

"Oh. Sure.''

Tara waited.

"Tara, I feel like there's things you should know about me.''

"Mm?'' She smiled.

"I've been to prison.''

"Me, too.''

"Not jail. Prison. In Louisiana.''

Tara reeled internally. What had this very young woman done to wind up in a Louisiana state prison? Distantly, she observed her own reaction, her own surprise, when she'd been behind bars so many times herself. *It's par for the course with me.*

She should take better care of herself.

"I'm a felon. I had to tell you that. You and my uncle Kip are the only ones who know. And Lane,'' she added glumly.

Lane. Chantel's father.

"Where is Lane?'' Absent fathers were not high on Tara's list.

"Oh, right now, he's in Gunnison.''

And?

"I wanted to get your car back. He wasn't too pleased about missing the conjugal visit, but he could come find me for once.''

Tara bit her tongue, trying to let Beulah Ann tell it—whatever it was—her own way.

But Beulah Ann sighed and prepared to stand.

"Are you married?"

"Oh, yeah. To Lane Cockburn, PRCA Rookie of the Year, et cetera. He rides bulls."

Professional Rodeo Cowboys Association.

Things were slipping into place.

"We don't see each other but a few times a year, and he's not keen on us followin' him around the country. It's expensive."

"I'd think he makes some money."

"Oh, yeah. We're savin' for a little ranch of our own."

Tara knew that closemouthed expression. This woman could tell sad stories about her husband for the next week, but she wasn't going to utter a word against the father of her child. Tara respected that.

"Well, I'll have to watch him on TV with you."

Beulah Ann smiled. "He's cute. And he's *good.*"

Good at riding bulls, Tara concluded. "Beulah Ann, you could have called me. I didn't need the car. I feel really bad that your family missed this time together."

"Oh, I offered he could follow me up here, but he declined." Beulah Ann shrugged and rose. Before she left the room, she said, "I haven't eaten red meat for three days, and Lane said maybe I'd lost a few pounds. It was hard to pass up today, but it just feels so great to have lost a little." Beulah Ann touched Laura. "She's such a sweet thing. I just love babies, don't you?"

Tara bit her lip and nodded.

She wasn't as good at confidences as Beulah Ann.

CHAPTER TEN

Dylan's birth was the only one where anyone helped me before he was born. The midwife made me quit smoking, and her husband and Chad, my boyfriend, fixed the stove and the water. Also, her husband took pictures at the birth and gave them to us, for which we gave him two bags of walnuts from the tree. They still come over a bunch. Their daughter's just in love with little Dylan.

—Rhonda Davy, 24, seven months after Dylan Jason's birth at her home up Thousandsnakes Hollow, Guyandotte, West Virginia

ON SUNDAY AFTERNOON, Dan offered to take the kids to a movie, giving Isaac and Tara some time alone, and Beulah Ann volunteered to watch Laura for a few hours.

Isaac asked Tara to bring her skis to the chalet. When she arrived, the others had already left, and he kissed her first thing, for a long time. Hands in her hair, he said, "I have a cabin farther up the road. Old miner's shack. Rustic but…warm."

"Oh."

They could talk with their eyes. They did, until he finally asked, "What do you think? Okay?"

Tara swallowed. *I'm in love with him. Surely we can work out the details.* What he was suggesting could only help.

They skied past the chalet, up beyond Tomboy. Isaac knew the cabin well. Back in May and June, he'd dealt with guilt and grief by insulating it and checking the stove. At the cabin, no one would return from the movie prematurely. No one would bother them at all.

On the way, he stopped twice to kiss her, could not keep his hands off her. Love could change hearts. Maybe it would change hers, her determination to practice midwifery, attend homebirths, no matter what.

The cold whipped Tara's face. She knew his every movement. Each touch sent blood pouring through her.

The shack. Cabin. Private. Alone on the stark white landscape, craggy peaks rising beyond.

They took off their skis.

Inside, he said, "It won't take long to warm up."

Tar paper strips on the walls and ceiling. Particle board over part of the floor. He built a fire in the oil-drum stove while she tried the edge of the iron-frame bed. Beneath the clean sheets and wool blanket was a straw mattress.

"I like this place," murmured Tara. "It's kind of…folksy and backward."

He glanced at her. *Not now, Tara. Just…not now.*

The fire was going, and he shut the door, adjusted the makeshift drafts. Joined her on the bed.

Tara knew him now. The feel of his mouth, of the limbs beneath his parka. They kissed as they shed coats and boots. Then they were entwined in each other's limbs on the bed.

Her eyes felt too warm as he kissed her, touched

her. This was lovemaking. Danny had never, never made her feel this way. No one had.

Isaac didn't make fun of her army-surplus wool pants, her best cross-country ski gear. He just got rid of them, tucking her close to him between the sheets. His eyes were close to hers, inside hers. His hand was between her legs. "So, today I kiss your yoni. Okay?"

She couldn't say a word.

Not for a while.

Each touch, and she thought, *This is intense. This is too far, too much.* She cried out, the way you could in a cabin with no neighbors but the mountains.

To him, the sound was unforgettable.

The last seduction.

Except for her shivers and crying, shuddering, waves going on and on. More when he put his body against hers to hold her. Shudders.

"I'm still coming," she whispered.

He crushed her head to his chest, kept stroking her till she was limp and flushed in his arms.

But when their eyes met again, hers were full of fear.

He didn't have to hear the truth to know it. But he said, "Nothing's changed, has it?"

Her eyes turned watery. "Nothing *will.* Not what you want me to change."

He hugged her, and it was his turn to be afraid. Nothing to be afraid of. Holding her tight, he said, "Not what *you* want to change, either, Tara."

A second later, she grabbed her clothes.

Like that.

And skied ahead of him down the mountain.

ON MONDAY MORNING, Tara took Danielle and Laura with her to the houses of two nursing mothers to collect the fresh breast milk they generously provided for Laura. Danielle loved making sure the milk made it quickly to the cooler in the car and urged Tara to hurry home so they could refrigerate or freeze it. Watching Tara nurse, and thawing milk in the way Tara had instructed her, seemed to bring her nothing but pleasure. Tara told her, "You are the *best* mother's helper I've ever met."

All afternoon, she and Beulah Ann had prenatals, and after school, Isaac's children gathered in the blue room to work on painting their costumes according to photos they'd found in Tara's and their father's mountaineering books.

Tara was no longer invited to stay for dinner—or afterward. And she knew Isaac was leaving the kids on their own when he worked the ER two nights a week. But he didn't ask her to stay.

On Thursday evening, when the costumes were complete, she rushed home to meet with a possible buyer for the Range Rover. It turned out to be a high-school classmate of hers who was now selling real estate in Precipice. He bought the car on the spot, and after the paperwork had been signed and he'd left, Tara remembered that the next day was the Halloween contest at school. Francesca's Subaru would get her up to Isaac's, but she'd need help transporting the costumes to school. The Land Cruiser wasn't big enough. Worse, it was snowing and getting heavier by the minute.

After consulting Beulah Ann, who owned no car at all and had been walking to the day-care center and to work at the International, Tara got out the phone book to hunt up some friends. She tried Jack first, at the Riviera Bar. *Bingo.* "Hey, Jack, it's Tara."

"Tara—get your butt down here and give me a proper hello. What are you doing, visiting Mom?"

"Actually, here to stay. I've got a baby and I'm watching some kids, but I'm calling because I need someone with a truck to help me transport Halloween costumes to the school."

"*Tara.* I go to sleep at two. And you want me up at, what, six?"

"You've done it before. Oh, please, Jack. I'll pay you." Or rather, Isaac would.

She was tired, so tired. Laura began to cry. "Could you hang on a minute, Jack?"

"Sure. Courvoisier?" he said to someone else. "The XO?"

She ran to the kitchen, poured milk into a sterile bag, warmed it and connected it to the supplemental feeder, then picked up Laura. Her eyes drifted half shut. *I'm going to die if I don't sleep.*

"I don't want to be paid. How about, you join me for a day of telemarking Thanksgiving weekend?"

Oh, Isaac would love that. After last Sunday? He was angry, but the relationship wasn't over. It had reached a stalemate.

In chess, that means the game's over, Tara.

"Can't do it, Jack. This baby is young. I'm trying to adopt her."

"What are you doing with a baby, Tara? Which tequila? Cuervo? You want a lime with that? No chaser, okay." He spoke into the receiver. "You got a man, Tara? If you don't, it's crazy. Kids need fathers."

"Volunteering?"

"What?"

"Forget it. I didn't mean it."

"Uh, Tara." He sighed. "All right, when do I have to be there?"

"Six. How big's your truck bed?"

"Tara!"

"I'm asking for the costumes."

"What are they, for God's sake?"

"Fourteeners. You're sworn to secrecy."

"I'll be there. But try to round up another truck so we don't have to make two trips."

"Jack, you're a prince."

WHO WERE THESE guys? The one who worried Isaac wasn't the pungent man with the dreadlocks but the young Jeremy Irons look-alike.

"These are my friends Tim and Jack. They graciously brought their trucks up to transport Halloween costumes to school." Getting them home, however...

Both men yawned.

Isaac nodded to each of them. Dreadlocks said, "Hey, man," and Jeremy Irons studied his eyes for a little longer than necessary.

Through the window, Isaac saw a battered orange mini pickup with snowchains, a gleaming silver pickup with an extended cab, and Francesca's Subaru.

Tara said, "I, um, sold the Range Rover last night." She lifted her eyebrows significantly.

He had interviewed one potential nanny that week, a mother with four children of her own who wanted to take care of Danielle, too. It might be the best thing. He had to stop comparing other women to Tara. Even if Tara had Danielle speaking English.

Tara had set Laura in her car seat on the kitchen

table and was hugging Danielle and introducing everyone to Jack and Tim.

His daughter stared in wonder at Tim's hair. "Why is your hair like that?"

"I don't comb it."

"Like some coffee, gentlemen?" Isaac moved toward the stove.

"Manna from heaven. Thank you." Jack rubbed a hand over his Jeremy Irons hair and stepped up to the table to play with one of Laura's feet in her booties.

Isaac wanted him out of his house. Now.

Tara appeared beside him to start oatmeal blueberry pancakes for everybody—except his kids, who'd placed orders for plain pancakes—and Isaac himself. Breakfast was a clove of raw garlic and one-fourth cup of raw short-grain rice, which he must chew to liquid consistency.

He didn't care. He wanted rid of the damned parasite, and he *was* feeling better.

Keeping his head lowered, he watched water stream into the coffeepot.

"Everything okay, doc?" Tara murmured.

Silence. The coffeemaker gurgled. When the coffee was brewed, he headed for his room to shower and shave for work.

HIS ABSENCE BOTHERED Tara.

He hadn't reappeared by the time she'd finished at the griddle almost forty-five minutes later. Laura needed to be nursed, and she gathered her equipment and the infant and excused herself, while the other children headed for their rooms to dress for school.

She tapped on Isaac's door, never looking back at the two men seated at the table. "It's Tara."

"Come in."

He had on jeans and a black turtleneck, his sweater and shell folded beside him.

Tara sat on the bed and prepared to nurse Laura. "I brought your money."

"Let's settle after I find a nanny." Lips tight, he moved for the door.

"Isaac, what's wrong? What did I do? Is it Tim? I know he's kind of—"

"It's not Tim."

She couldn't believe it. "Jack?"

"Yes."

She arched her eyebrows. "You're *jealous?*"

"I'm in love with you!"

She shifted away unconsciously, her heart pounding, half-oblivious to Laura's distracted fussing. "You don't want to marry me," she whispered.

"I want to marry you. I'm chewing raw rice and living on sauerkraut, taking bitter herbs, and I have an appointment to see a doctor of Oriental medicine who's booked for the next month. What other signs of my affection do you need? Since last Sunday wasn't enough."

She would not be intimidated. "How are your sweats?"

"I'm sweating right now, thank you very much."

"For the record, Jack and I are just friends, have never been anything more." She adjusted the feeding tube, tended to Laura.

"Are you going to offer *him* money to marry you?"

"No. Anyhow, he wouldn't be keen on the idea."

Isaac burned. He'd seen different. "You know, Tara, I thought you had some honor."

"Don't insult me." Laura began to wail, and Tara

let the infant cry long enough to say, "My honor is what's keeping me from certifying."

"I don't buy that. And I have a reputation and four—three—four children to support. I can't afford your ideology."

"You obviously think I come cheap."

"Nurse that baby. I'm taking the children to school, and I'll be back." He walked out and slammed the door.

The two strangers at his kitchen table stopped talking and exchanged looks.

Tara called through the bedroom door. "Tell them to dress warmly. It's snowing!"

"DADDY?" DANIELLE INTRUDED on his thoughts as he drove her back from school.

"What, sweetheart?" *Cheap.*

"Can Tara live with us? I like her, and I like Laura."

Her English had come a long way in a short time. According to Danielle, Tara was teaching her Spanish while Danielle taught Tara French. Interesting. "I'm trying to work out something like that, Danielle, but Tara has another job and…" He didn't know what else to say. "Don't get your hopes up."

Her mouth fell.

The trucks were gone when they reached the house, but the Subaru remained.

Tara was washing the breakfast dishes with Laura in a sling against her chest.

Isaac said, "Danielle, how would you like to sit on the bed with Laura while Tara and I have a talk?"

"Okay."

THEY SAT ON THE BED in the blue room, which was cold and still draped in sheets. Only the paint showed the signs of the costume making.

Isaac wasted no words. "Have I ever called you cheap?"

"More or less. When you told me you didn't like my 'tactics' with your brother. When you said you wouldn't marry me if I didn't certify. When you thought...what happened Sunday...would change my—"

"Oh, what happened. You want to talk about what happened? You want to tell me what was going through *your* mind up in that cabin?"

Tara flushed. "It was beautiful."

He was going to break something. "You know, if a judge was to hear your story and hear mine, he would agree with *me*. You aren't folksy and backward. You're on a completely different plane of reason. Not only do you want women to give birth in their homes when virtually every community in America has a hospital that can accommodate them, you want to help at births illegally."

"Midwives should not have to be licensed."

"We disagree."

"Well, this is my identity. Love it or leave it."

"Careful."

She started to cry. Everything had been much simpler before last weekend. Walking away had been easier. Saying no had been easier. "You claim I have no honor. Imagine if I go through with this. It'll be like a domino. Cave in, license, marry you, adopt Laura, no problems with Scarbor—the hospital. You will have solved all my problems, and I'll be someone I hate."

To be able to take back some words. "You have honor, Tara."

She pushed her hair off her face. She couldn't afford this, wouldn't be able to function if they kept at it. She and Danielle needed to make a breast milk run, to Samantha's house, Samantha with her three little children, and she was supposed to meet with Leila and her busy husband. *And,* because Isaac couldn't leave the clinic, she would go to the school costume contest at two.

Isaac changed the subject, blessedly. "Tara, I saw four cases of whooping cough yesterday. Has Laura received her immunizations?"

"No." Whooping cough. "Do you have the new vaccine?"

"Yes. I can start her on them now, Tara."

"Thank you. I'm not sure about the MMR, yet. I had them all when I was a baby."

Measles, mumps, rubella. Was nothing simple with this woman? "Going to jail really doesn't worry you, does it?"

"No, it doesn't!"

"But you think you should've gone there all those years ago, when your grandfather embezzled that money. You think being beaten with a phone book and gang-raped doesn't make up for it."

She gasped, more tears suddenly springing out of her. She leaned over her knees. "They used… They used…" And she stopped. Breathing too hard, high and strange, gulping sobs.

He'd seen this in Rwanda. "Stop. Don't go there, Tara. Come on. I'm here. I'm sorry." Holding her. "Just stop. You're in control. You're in control." The wails would come next.

But they didn't.

She was good, good at keeping herself together, good at slowing her breathing. He lost track of time, holding her. "That's better, Tara." She was right to never go back, never take her mind there, and he'd led her to those places because he wanted things his way—wanted her to give in and *get her damned certification.*

No. He wanted more.

Maybe more than he had a right to ask.

He barely heard her choked words and wasn't sure what she meant when she said, "I think you're right."

HE GAVE LAURA HER immunizations on the couch while Tara held the child. "You're giving her the acellular pertussis vaccine, right?"

"Absolutely. And diphtheria and tetanus." Laura wailed, and Tara and Danielle wept. "Ask Beulah Ann if Chantel has been immunized."

"I will."

Danielle demanded in Kinyarwanda, *Why are you hurting her?*

"So she won't get sick. Tara, this pertussis vaccine is much safer than the old one, but you can still expect irritability, slight fever. She may sleep a lot. Call me if you're worried about the slightest thing." He bent and kissed Laura's forehead, but she was already going for Tara's breast.

Danielle jumped up. "I'll get the milk ready."

THANKFULLY, LAURA SLEPT during the ride to Samantha's house later that morning. Tara tried to keep her thoughts off Isaac, but he was right about jail. Dead-on right. Outside Samantha's family's cedar-sided, custom-built dwelling, Danielle asked, "Can I stay in the car with Laura?"

"Oh, thank you, sweetheart. I'm going to lock you in, though, okay?" There were too many strangers, too many tourists, too many weird people in Precipice these days.

From Samantha's doorstep, Tara watched the car.

Samantha's four-year-old, Jason, answered the door, feverish, half crying, half coughing. Tara recognized the distinctive high-pitched whoop. "Mommy's busy."

Samantha appeared with her three-month-old infant in her arms. "Oh, Tara, I forgot to do it. I've been feeding echinacea and goldenseal down three throats, treating for fevers, filling the bathroom with steam every three minutes."

"Relax. Deep breath. It's okay."

Isaac—that morning—flashed in and out of her mind. He'd known what to say, what to do, to break her from the thrall of the *thing* that had overcome her. The thing people called panic or anxiety and which was neither. This morning it was a reaction *he* had caused, with his anger.

Tara eyed the infant. "How's Pamela?"

"She's got it, too, but we're going to weather the storm. Whooping cough." Samantha shook her head.

Tara had seen so many children die in places where medical care wasn't available. And she had seen *curanderos* work miracles. She was not a *curandero*.

"Samantha, Pamela looks dehydrated. You might take her to the emergency room and get some fluids in her."

"I am keeping fluids in her."

The baby coughed with a strangely deep cough, and

her mother held her belly-down, listening to the high-pitched whoop, after which Pamela vomited. "Look, I should get back to my kids." Samantha sighed.

"When was the last time she had a wet diaper?"

Samantha looked momentarily confused. "Oh, this morning."

Tara didn't want to go inside and expose herself to the bug. "Don't like hospitals, huh?"

"Hate them."

"Would you feel better if a friend went with you?" *You can't go, Tara. You can't expose Laura to this.* All Isaac's children had undoubtedly been exposed at school. Danielle was most at risk.

"Tara, this is just the way I want to raise my kids. I've made a personal vow to raise them naturally, without medical intervention."

"Rehydration isn't really unnatural, Samantha. Think about it. We're not talking drugs. If you like, I can get a needle in her, and you won't have to go to the hospital." She'd done a lot of rehydration in Mexico.

"No." Samantha shut the door.

Tara looked toward the car. It was chilly out. She needed to go warm up the car for Danielle and Laura. She had to meet with Leila and Asad, take Danielle to school, the costume contest...

She drew a breath and reminded herself not to fight. Pamela wasn't her responsibility—and maybe her strong reaction had to do with immunizing Laura that morning. Maybe she wanted to prove to herself that her views on health care weren't completely radical.

She searched for her center, her self, and for a moment couldn't find it, except in the memory of that blue room, with its Gothic windows and trim made from insets of pinecones. The room where she'd sobbed in the cold, where he'd driven her back to hell, where he'd pushed so hard.

Isaac, what are you doing to me? Why am I letting this happen?

Suddenly shivering, she hurried back to the Subaru, to his child—and to hers.

"LEILA MAY CERTAINLY study with me—and attend prenatals and births, when appropriate. But—"

"How much shall we pay you?" asked Asad, who had glanced at his watch more than once during the meeting.

Beside him, Leila asked again, "Do you need to leave, Asad?"

"Not yet. Not yet." His smile was affection for his pretty young wife.

Payment. More commitment. Tara found herself sinking in deeper, becoming more rooted in Precipice, more tied to the people here who needed her, who wanted her skills, who wanted to learn from her. Yet the medical community would fight her as they'd fought her mother. And if things didn't work out with Isaac...

Things aren't working out with Isaac.

But these people need me.

She reached into her heart, into her soul, for answers. Her mother had gone to Alaska. *Can I be that brave? Can I stay here?*

"I have to leave town—I hope briefly—in a few weeks. We can start studying before then, with no charge. If Leila finds she's still interested, we can discuss a more involved course of study—and payment—

when I return. I need to remind you again that the hospital does not support my practice.''

''But Dr. McCrea likes you!'' said Leila.

She must mean Isaac.

''Why don't you become a legal midwife?'' asked Asad. ''This puzzles me.''

''Are all midwives legal in Sudan?''

''Yes. That is—some are government-trained and some are not, but all are accepted.''

''That is the situation I want in the United States.''

''This is a different country. Even in Sudan, people avoid making trouble for themselves.''

''Always? You've chosen to do things differently.''

He considered. ''By coming here. Easier on us. But I see your point. And there are some women—'' He stopped. ''Yes. I see who you are.'' His expression mingled compassion and other things. Things she could not guess, until he said quietly, ''It is difficult to be alone.''

The words struck a gong inside her—reverberating truth.

AFTER DROPPING DANIELLE at school, Tara curled up on her bed with Laura.

When the phone rang, she reached for it, Laura crying. ''Hello?''

''How are things going? I hear her crying.''

''She's a little cranky, but she's been really good.''

''Are you all right?''

''Yes. Isaac, are the children who're coming in there with whooping cough unvaccinated?''

''About a third of them. The idea is to wipe it out. Everyone has to play.''

Right. She'd heard the song and dance. Nothing was black and white. Nothing.

A long silence between them.

He said, "Tell the kids I wish I could be there."

At the costume contest.

"I will." *Isaac, I'm so scared. I'm scared to stay here. I'm afraid of losing myself. I'm afraid of how I might change with you. Please don't ask me to change.*

But how much had he changed, easily, to fight the parasite in his body?

He said, "See you tonight. Call if you need anything."

As if she was his wife. "Thanks. I—" She breathed raggedly. "Everything's fine."

She was used to being alone.

THE GYMNASIUM WAS packed with children of all ages and their parents. Millie Rand's husband caught sight of Tara. "Hello, there. I didn't know you had children in school."

"Oh, I'm here for someone else's."

"With the baby, no less." He smiled at Laura. "Millie stayed home."

Tara had visited her at home since the birth, filling in for Francesca with postpartum visits. "Is she having a good day?"

He nodded. "I'm going to hurry home to her after this. I'd better move up there to get my photos. Nice seeing you."

Tara saw Karen Anthony next, holding her lower back in that characteristic posture of late pregnancy. Tara asked her, "How's the mom today?"

"The baby's excited by the other children. I'm glad he's kicking *now*. Maybe I can sleep later."

"Any problems?"

"Not a one. Just ready to have this baby."

Tara nodded. "Which are your children?"

Karen pointed them out—a witch and a pirate. "Hey, what are you doing here? Oh, you and Dr. McCrea have something going, don't you?"

"I look after his children."

Karen's smile was more than skeptical. "Hey, maybe you'll become a CNM and get hospital privileges."

"Mm. Hadn't thought of that."

"You should. This town needs full-service midwifery."

Full service. What did that mean? And could one woman provide it all?

The two women stood together while the children marched up on stage in groups. With Isaac's camera, Tara snapped pictures of the mountains.

"Those are some costumes," murmured Karen. "Did you do that?"

"Oh, they did a lot of it. I've got to go say hi to them. Take care, and I'll see you next week. Tuesday, right?"

"Right-o." Karen gave her that little knowing smile again. "He's a nice one, Tara."

"I've gotta see the kids. Next week, okay?"

THE MOUNTAINS WON the costume contest, followed by an ingenuous ski lift and a spectacular carrot.

"Can we go trick-or-treating to Dad's office? Please?" asked David. "We'll walk over, and you can follow us, and we'll leave our costumes there. We can pick up Danielle's on Halloween."

"I'll follow in the car," Tara agreed. "Be careful

crossing the streets—all of you. And hold Danielle's hand. You can't see that well in your costumes.''

THE WOMAN WAITING for Isaac in Room 2 had waist-length disheveled hair. Her name was Samantha, and she led two small children and carried an infant. A glance at her chart told him everything. Isaac said, ''Whooping cough?''

''Yes.''

He took a cursory glance at the children. The infant was in trouble. ''I'll be back. We're going to give this one some fluids right away. I've got a nurse who's a genius with tiny veins.''

FIFTEEN MINUTES LATER, after the children were routed to the hospital, a hand tapped on a door beside him while he was reading his next patient's chart. *Coughing, vomiting…*

''Dr. McCrea. There's a problem in the waiting room. I think you should come out.''

Jennifer, his nurse, who had come to work dressed as a clown, winked at him.

''I need to see the next patient.''

''Kelly will do it.'' The family nurse-practitioner.

Relenting, he put down the clipboard and strode out to the waiting room.

Mountains. ''Well, well, well, if it isn't some of Colorado's highest peaks.''

Mount Sneffels said, ''Hi, Dad.''

''Hello, Oliver.''

David growled at him.

''Hello, Uncompahgre.''

Avoiding the temptation to glance toward the glass, to see if Tara was outside, he moved toward Mount

Wilson and crouched beside her. He met the pair of eyes inside. ''Hello, Danielle.''

''*Allô, Daddy.*''

After he had greeted each of his children, Jennifer brought out the basket of toys the office was giving trick-or-treaters and the children who came in sick that day.

And Isaac could finally peer out the window at the Land Cruiser. Tara was nursing and didn't see him.

SHE STARTED AWAKE. The blue room was warm, and it was dark outside the pointed windows. Was it only this morning she'd fallen apart in here? She'd just planned to nap, but now Isaac was bending over her, covering her up. He must have stoked the tiny wood-stove, too.

She checked Laura first. Cheeks cool, a deep sigh in her sleep. ''I'm sorry—I slept. I left the stove on after I boiled some water, and when I saw it, I realized I had to sleep. Oliver was supposed to wake me in half an hour.''

''I called from work and said he should let you sleep.''

''Why did you call?''

He just smiled gently. ''Hungry? For a very hot Indian dish?''

She shut her eyes blissfully, then began to sit up.

''Stay where you are.''

THE PHONE RANG while he was out of the room. Ten minutes passed before he returned.

She sat up against two pillows, and he carefully set the steaming plate in her lap and two huge glasses of water beside her. "That was a nanny candidate. She'll be here in fifteen minutes for an interview."

"I should get out of here."

"No. Eat and rest. If you have everything you need, you can spend the night."

In here? Or with him?

She couldn't read his eyes.

"Otherwise," he said, "I'll drive you home."

Tara turned to her food. "Thanks."

SHE WAS SLEEPING again when he came back, and she awoke and sat up and remembered where she was. Laura had awakened, too, and Tara rolled onto her side and moved her to give her nearest breast. If it didn't satisfy the baby, she'd get the supplemental feeder. She still had enough milk frozen to get her through the weekend.

Isaac left the light off.

He crouched by the edge of the bed, checked her water glass. "Shall I bring the milk for you?"

"No. I'll do it if she needs it. She's getting something."

"Be careful with that trick, Tara. You want her well nourished."

He was right. She wasn't the baby's birth mother and couldn't provide enough milk. "I surrender."

He brought her the milk, warmed under the tap. "I hired the nanny. She's a former schoolteacher, very funny, and made Danielle laugh even when she didn't want to. Her name is Mrs. Kennedy. She's starting Monday."

"Great!" Tara wished she felt as enthusiastic as she sounded. She wanted to be part of this family, to play Dungeons & Dragons in the evenings, go skiing on

the weekends, make love with Isaac. "I owe you four, right, for the car?"

He didn't bother to argue. She'd win. "Yes."

"Bring me my coat, would you?"

"Let's settle when I drive you home in the morning, all right?"

"I should go home now."

"You seem comfortable where you are." He wanted her. But if he touched her… *Just one compromise, Tara. Just one.*

"Are you feeling better, Isaac? Any change with the parasite?"

"Some." He crouched beside her, trying to forget those few minutes in the cabin. Scent and touch and sound and taste and… Everything. *Forget it.* "I *believe* your cure's working, and that's half the battle. If your plan doesn't kill me, it's sure to kill—"

She laughed, and their eyes locked in shadows.

"For a woman willing to marry a stranger to adopt a baby, you're making some strange choices, Tara."

"I never offered to become someone else."

"Too bad. That's what marriage is."

He stood to leave, and she realized he was going.

He was right to go.

As the door shut behind him, Tara turned to the infant, checking on her again, her heart filled with love for the child. She wasn't alone at all.

And nothing would come between her and Laura.

She realized abruptly that she *would* certify in order to keep her child.

So why don't I—and marry Isaac, too?

CHAPTER ELEVEN

Sister, my womb is barren, but at your labor and birth I am fertile. Believe me when I say my presence is for you, and you are why I'm here.

—Tara Marcus, scrawled during a long labor

ISAAC STOPPED IN front of her house at six-thirty the next morning and left the engine running. He unbuckled his shoulder strap and turned to her, and Tara accepted his tight embrace. She didn't allow her mouth near his, and he did not attempt to kiss her.

Sitting back in his seat, he said, "So, it's still no." A question.

Her lips parted. How to explain? She'd be wrong to say yes. For him. Just to have him.

For many reasons.

Isaac expelled a breath. "Tara—just consider—just consider that you've carried these beliefs for so long because of what we discussed yesterday—your experience with your grandfather. Didn't you say I was right?"

"It doesn't mean you're right about my midwifery status." Tara opened the passenger door. "I'm thinking about it, Isaac. And you think about why you so badly want me to change."

"You know the answer."

"Sure. And it isn't just about my going to jail." It's about homebirth, isn't it, Isaac? "Your wife—your wife whom you loved very much—was high risk." *Triplets. Get real, Isaac.* "My clients are low risk." Except Karen Anthony, who was Dan McCrea's patient, now. And Leila. She'd sent Leila to Dan. "I'm not what you think."

Her words settled through him. High risk. Low risk.

He thought of David's essay on Chance. Odds. Probability.

As she took Laura's car seat, he was at her shoulder. "Let me carry her. The steps haven't been shoveled."

"All right."

Snow crunching under his boots, he asked, "What are you going to do in three weeks? Have you found a place to live?"

"I've hardly had a chance to think about it. But, sure, I'll find something with Beulah Ann."

"If you can't, you're welcome to the blue room. As another option, I could insulate and drywall part of the Columbine."

"A midwifery office in a former brothel? I *don't* think so. That place should be razed." She unlocked her door and took Laura's car seat from him. "Thanks for the ride. Thanks for last night, letting me rest, the meal. I'm ready to take on the world!"

Her grin was genuine, her strength terrifying.

She would never sacrifice her values for him.

He left loving her more.

HER MOTHER CALLED at noon.

"Mom!" Tara clutched the receiver. "Hi!" *Talk to me, Mom. Don't hang up.* "How are things?"

"Oh…just fine. We—I—called to see about you."

"Everything's great, Mom! Laura's gained a lot of weight." To keep Francesca's spirits up, she chatted about her client load and Beulah Ann and Leila.

"You haven't had trouble with the hospital?"

"No births yet. Of course, someone could knock on this door any day with a search warrant and that crap. I'm not worrying." *Except about you.* "Is there anything I can do for you, Mom, anything I can send you?"

"No, honey, I'm fine. Have you found a place to live?"

"I've been checking the want ads and the kiosks. I'm just not sure what to do."

"And you have no money."

"Wrong. I sold the Range Rover. I'm loaded. Don't worry about a thing." But her mother would worry. *Okay, we love each other; this is life.* "Seen anything of Dad?"

"He's right here. And wants to talk to you."

"Oh. Oh." For weeks, now, she'd dreaded this. She *had* bought a Range Rover, but if her mother had told him she'd borrowed extra money from Isaac—and about Laura—

"Hello, Tara."

Yes. He knew.

"Hi, Daddy!" she answered brightly. "Boy, you and Mom—" She was babbling. He and her mother. What *were* they doing together? *Relax, Tara. Talkeetna's a small town.*

"So, when am I going to meet Laura?" He paused. "And *Isaac?*"

Tara held her lips in an O. This could be bad. Charlie was capable of phoning Isaac and asking his intentions. She'd been five years old when she met her father. Well, her mother said they'd met earlier, when he was on leave, but Tara couldn't remember. She did remember immediately liking the man who'd crouched beside her in the crowded Honolulu airport. Just as she remembered the chaos that had always surrounded him. And their wonderful times together, sitting out on his surfboard with him, snorkling in the lagoon. Waking up one day, and he was gone, and she was sure it was because of her. Then he was back. Then...

But a few years after her parents divorced, he'd changed. He *was* there to meet *her* planes. He'd come to Florida on a moment's notice.

He'd told her not to marry Danny.

"Is the connection bad at your end, Tara? *I can't hear you.*"

Issac. "Well, you're in Alaska. And Laura and I are here." Fortunately. *Turn this around.* "How's Talkeetna? How's Mom?"

"Your mother is just fine. Tell me about *Issac.*"

"There's nothing to tell. Really. And Dad, a client just showed up. I have to go. Love you!" She hung up.

Before she could move, the phone rang again, and she let it ring and listened to the answering machine kick on and listened to her father say, "That wasn't the last word, Tara."

She snatched up the phone. "He's a physician and a widower, he has three sweet, beautiful, intelligent children, and he loves me. And, no, his first wife didn't die of neglect. All right? If there's a wedding, you'll be invited."

"Thank you." There was a gentle smile in his voice. "You've told me what I wanted to know."

A wedding. Not in this life.

When she hung up for the second time, Tara arranged Laura in a sling against her body, so that she could work, going through her mother's remaining possessions. Straightening her spine, she slowed her breathing, emptied her mind, then looked down at the precious brown eyes watching her face.

Two births to attend, after which she had a three-month respite, except for prenatals. She decided.

After those two births, she would go to Texas, keeping in touch with her clients by phone and letting Beulah Ann handle basic prenatals, which her assistant was well qualified to do.

She had to find a way to adopt Laura.

SHE WAS ASLEEP IN the dead of night Thursday when her pager went off. She had to call the answering service. Dragging herself to her feet, she dialed the number and received the message. "Karen Anthony says she's in labor, and she'll meet you at the hospital."

Happy, Tara woke Beulah Ann just to tell her what she was doing—Beulah Ann's and Chantel's presence at the hospital would not be productive—prepared Laura's things and put herself in a coaching frame of mind. She was glad Karen had decided to labor at the hospital. And at least now she and Dan McCrea were on speaking terms.

They even had something in common.

They both loved Isaac.

IT WAS SNOWING LIKE mad, almost impossible to drive, and when Tara reached the hospital, there was no obstetrician in the maternity suite and none in the hospital.

Not Dan. Not Rich Scarborough.

Karen was in labor, with no one to examine her or check her progress. "Oh oh oh."

Tara, her hands held in check by the law, coached her on keeping her mouth loose. "Would you like to walk around?"

"I can't."

"Let's help you stand up. That will bring the baby down."

"Oh oh oh!" She stood with Tara's help, and Tara focused on her eyes.

"Is there anything I can do?" Preston, Karen's husband, asked.

Tara gave some suggestions, and he was massaging his wife's body when Pilar Garcia came in. "We still haven't been able to reach Dr. McCrea, Mrs. Anthony. The phone lines are down."

Tara gritted her teeth. Where was Dan? He had another client laboring down the hall and complaining of a lot of pain, even though she was on an epidural. She kept saying she knew something was wrong.

Pilar shrugged helplessly at Tara, and Tara followed her out into the hall.

"What's going on?"

"Travel advisory. Phones down. The gondola's not running." It took people up and down the mountain. "One of the EMTs tried to go up in his car and get him and drove off the road. He skied back here."

Tara returned to the birthing suite.

"You're doing great," she told Karen. "You're a wonderful mom."

When she wasn't helping Karen try different ways

to get comfortable, Tara cared for Laura and nursed her, always with part of her attention on the mother.

Walking the baby up and down the hall, she heard the second woman in labor weeping. "I know this isn't normal pain. Why won't you listen to me? I've had a child before."

Pat, the other nurse on the unit, explained, "You're just having some discomfort, Caroline." Caroline's husband kept his eyes on a television set in the corner against the ceiling. "Shall I get the anesthesiologist and tell him the epidural isn't working?"

More aggravation. Francesca had felt that Pat should be fired. There were so many competent and dedicated nurses, *caring* nurses; why was *she* working in Precipice? *It's not like we have to beg people to come here,* Francesca had said.

Tara wanted to go into the room, to check the mother, but she had no business in the hospital except as Karen Anthony's labor coach. She felt parts of herself dying. How could any midwife work in a climate like this?

By three, the quality of screams and moans were affecting both her and Karen. Tara had seen hundreds, thousands of births, and there was something badly wrong with the birth down the hall. Where were the doctors?

She found Pilar in the hall. "Pilar, something is *really* wrong in there. You've got to get her down to ER."

Pilar eyed Tara carefully, weighing the plea and the source.

Tara nodded, carrying authority in her stance, in her eyes. *I know birth.*

"We need an order."

"Go take her vitals and palpate. Please do something." *Or I will.*

AT THREE-THIRTY, Pilar was nowhere to be found, and the woman in the room with the television saw Tara and begged weakly, "Are you a nurse?"

All bets were off. Screw the hospital. Screw Pat. Screw Rich Scarborough. Screw Dan McCrea. She walked into the room. "I'm a lay midwife, without hospital privileges."

"My baby's dying. I know it. Look at the monitor." *Oh, hell!* Tara buzzed the nurse.

"Please do something," Caroline begged.

Tara very gently felt her abdomen. No need to do more.

"What are you doing in here?" Pat's voice was hostile. Contemptuous.

"It's abruptio placentae. Get this woman to ER!"

"You have no business in this room. None."

"Help me! Please! Help my baby! Look! Look!" The woman's husband was on his feet now.

Pat left the room, heading for the nurses' station. "I'm writing this up, Miss Marcus."

AT 4:00 A.M., Karen entered transition, and after a few good contractions, Tara saw the baby's head crowning.

Tara buzzed for the nurse and stepped out in the hall. "Pilar!"

But Pat came. "What is it?"

"This baby is coming *now.*"

"Tell her *not to push until the doctor gets here!* And don't you touch her."

From the birthing suite, Karen yelled, "I have to push!"

"THERE'S NO OBSTETRICIAN in the hospital?" Isaac asked.

"Dr. McCrea, I've been trying to reach them both for five hours on another case. Dr. Dan McCrea is on call," Pilar explained. "I'm sure he can't get down in this storm."

It was one of Isaac's two nights in the emergency room, but at least the kids were at home with the new sitter, Mrs. Kennedy. In the ER, there was whooping cough everywhere. They couldn't have a birth down here. He grabbed the other doctor, Reed Wiley, as he emerged from a room where yet another child wailed and coughed. "Have you delivered babies?"

Dr. Wiley cleared his throat. "Um. Yes. Not many. Yet." He smiled. "You're the handyman."

An appellation Isaac didn't appreciate, anymore than another doctor's remark that squalor and genocide made very versatile physicians. *Right, you try fixing a ten-year-old's skewered gut when you've just learned your wife is dead.* He dumped a fresh cup of coffee in the trash can and left.

Versatile.

"I'm on my way," he told Pilar.

"DON'T PUSH!" EXCLAIMED Pat. "I've called for someone to take you to ER!"

Karen Anthony pushed, and the baby's head came out, tearing Karen's perineum slightly. "Oh, my God!"

Her husband's hands caught the baby's head.

"Check for the cord," advised Tara calmly.

"I told her not to push! What are you doing here anyway? You have no hospital privileges."

"I'm her labor coach."

Isaac stood in the doorway, saw the baby's head emerging and went to the bed. "I'm Dr. Isaac McCrea. You're doing that just right, sir." Tara watched him check for a cord. "Another gentle push—"

"Karen," supplied her husband.

The two men and Karen herself caught the baby and drew the newborn up into the mother's arms. The smells, sights and sounds of birth filled the room, and it seemed incongruous, the wonder of that small body, just come to earth—the hospital...

Isaac put a sterile, warmed receiving blanket on the baby, admired her and the parents together, and turned to Tara. "Hello."

"Isaac, there's an abruptio placentae down the hall. Her abdomen's like wood, her blood pressure's falling, fetal heart—"

Isaac held up his hand.

As moaning from the other room continued, Pat rolled in a surgical cart with sterile instruments and a pan for catching the placenta.

Isaac asked, "What's going on down the hall?"

"A woman in labor," answered Pat.

He waited.

"She feels there's something wrong. She's a multipara—"

Down the hall, the other woman screamed, "Isn't anyone going to help?"

"Pat, we need some warm blankets in here, and bring me that patient's chart."

"Her blood pressure is dropping. We called the emergency room."

"Oh, would that woman stop screaming?" asked Karen.

While Preston held the new baby boy, Elijah, Karen

pushed out the placenta, with a small rush of blood. Isaac clamped the cord and let Preston cut it, then tied it himself. He would write orders, in case of hemorrhage, before he saw the other woman, but he needed to get down there fast.

He spoke to Tara for the second time. "Let's get them warm, get the lights down, and start that baby nursing."

ABRUPTIO PLACENTAE. "This woman needs a C-section, STAT. Notify the anesthesiologist, and get me a nurse, a tech, anything you can in the way of a crew." He wasn't going to get Karen Anthony's perineal tears sutured till this was done. Ironically, Tara could do that job—but not here, not now. It was against the law.

An emergency C-section. How had he gotten into this?

Because Dan had hastily ruptured a woman's membranes to connect a fetal monitor electrode, then left the hospital? Poor nutrition?

No. Ultimately, because there was no obstetrician in the whole hospital.

Where was his brother?

"THE CASE OF the Missing OB/GYN," quipped the anesthesiologist, "goes unsolved again. Kurt Maurer—our last ER surgeon—burned out on C-sections. Went to Vail to work on skiers. You know, you don't *have* to do this. We can all wait for the obstetrician on call."

Isaac just looked at him. *And let a baby die?*

It might be too late already.

"I'm just hearing the distant thunder-roll of a judge's gavel, my friend."

Malpractice. He thought of Tara.

They scrubbed in silence until the anesthesiologist said, "You've done this, right?"

"Actually, in Africa, we just let them die. You know, maybe *that's* what I should do." Immediately, he realized what had come out of his mouth. *Heloise. Laura. Judith.*

"Isaac, it was a joke."

Right. All jokes. Quaker no more. For a moment, he sagged over the sink. God, he wished he'd never said that. What was wrong with him?

He knew.

He could do a C-section with his eyes closed. But where was Dan?

"DR. MCCREA WAS called away on an emergency," Pat told Karen Anthony. "The other doctor will suture you as soon as he can get away from the ER. They don't want you down there because of the whooping cough."

Tara needed to walk Laura. The room where the woman had been screaming was empty. Isaac's emergency.

She prayed it wasn't too late.

KAREN HAD BEEN sutured, and the other mother had just been wheeled back from surgery with her newborn; they were sleeping. Tara had already said goodbye to Karen and Preston and the baby. She slipped out of the room.

It was six o'clock, and Dan McCrea and Rich Scarborough stood at the nurse's station, getting an earful from Pat. Pilar must have joined Isaac in the OR.

Pat turned and glared at Tara, but Dan grabbed the patient's chart.

Tara waited motionless outside the birthing suite.

"You're off now?" Dan murmured to Pat.

"Yes."

A young blond nurse had come in.

"Bye." He handed the chart to Rich Scarborough and went to see his C-section patient and her child.

Tara walked carefully past them, but knew, somehow, that they weren't watching her. They were poring over the charts.

Outside the OR, she searched for Isaac. She left the hospital to check the parking lot for his Land Cruiser. It was there.

When she returned inside, Isaac, Dan and Scarborough were huddled together in the hall. Isaac looked furious.

Tara heard Scarborough utter something about "managed care." How could *that* be relevant?

"Why was there no obstetrician here last night?"

"Isaac, I tried to *ski* down, and Yul Vermont stopped me. You couldn't see four feet in front of you. This was a hundred-year snow."

"You hooked a patient to a monitor and left."

"I went to feed my dog. The nurse was supposed—"

"The nurse *did*—"

Spotting Tara, Scarborough hushed them. She expected him to turn on her, but he didn't.

And Isaac did not acknowledge her presence.

She'd known to expect that. Here, she was a nonentity.

Or worse.

If there was any way to do it, they'd blame the

midwife who didn't belong in the hospital, maybe say she dislodged the placenta with a blow to the abdomen or…

Her imagination was working overtime.

Go home and get some sleep, Tara. This one's their headache.

CHAPTER TWELVE

For when they do not kill the child, they blasphemously offer it to the devil in this manner. As soon as the child is born, the midwife, if the mother herself is not a witch, carries it out of the room on the pretext of warming it, raises it up, and offers it to the Prince of Devils.... And this is done by the kitchen fire.

—Malleus Maleficarum, handbook of the Inquisition

AT THE CHALET, Isaac lit the woodstove and phoned his mother, but she didn't answer, and he left a message. He was supposed to pick her up today, to come to Tomboy for the weekend, to celebrate his birthday, but they hadn't counted on the storm or his being in the ER all night. He'd call her again a little later. The kids were gone, anyway, Danielle on an outing to the babysitter's family ranch.

He wanted to call Tara, but she would be sleeping. Finally, he turned in himself.

He dreamed of Tara being arrested. He couldn't stop it, couldn't reach her, just learned she was in jail. He woke into the fog of the dream and grabbed the phone and called her before he was out of bed.

"Mountain Midwifery." Her voice.

"Hi."

"Hi, doc. Are they coming for me?"

"No telling." Her diagnosing abruptio placentae and telling him was fortunate. They'd had to resuscitate the baby. But she'd touched the patient.

"Apgars?"

"Don't ask." It was a nightmare. One the chief of staff had forbidden him to discuss with Tara Marcus. Someone had actually said, *We know you know her.*

"I bet you all sat down in Quasimodo's office, and Pat had convulsions from her contact with the village witch."

Isaac didn't smile.

Tara felt it through the wires. It must have been bad.

She sat downstairs in the Victorian, waiting for Leila to arrive. Leila had asked if she could pick Tara up in the Hummer truck to go to the appointment with Dan McCrea. Leila had agreed that Beulah Ann could come along, too, and Beulah Ann had arranged childcare for Chantel. Now her assistant was studying in the kitchen while Tara talked on the bedroom extension. "You could have saved some time with that C-section."

"How? I didn't know there was a problem till I reached the maternity unit."

"You could have said, 'Tara, you handle third stage here. I'm going—'"

His laugh was brutal.

"I don't even know your skill level, Tara. How could I possibly have left a patient in your care, hospital policy aside?" But in the end, he'd done basically that. He'd heard about it, too. "Wouldn't it be nice if you were a CNM? Good for both of us. Doctor. Nurse."

"Ha ha."

He began to regret the phone call. "You know, this state has given lay midwives the right to practice midwifery. Why don't you support that law instead of fighting it?" *Why don't you grow up?*

Isaac's front door opened, and a woman's voice called, "Isaac? Are you home?"

"I have to go." Tara's voice had grown neutral, impassive.

"Yeah, me, too. My mom's here." Still holding the phone, he ran a hand through his hair, pulling on sweatpants and a shirt. "She wants to see you. Will you come to dinner? I think sauerkraut, aduki bean sprouts, and quinoa are on the menu."

"Thanks, Isaac." Burn no bridges. "What time?"

"Six. See you then."

HE HUNG UP AND emerged from the bedroom. "Mom." He went to her and hugged her and received her welcoming kiss. "Did you listen to my message? How did you get here?"

"On the snowplow taxis." Hitching rides on snowplows, all the way from Silverton to Tomboy. "Wonderful, isn't it?"

"Yes. Yes. You are."

"No, I didn't get your message. Is this a bad time?"

With anger, he remembered Tara's accusation, that he could have saved time with that baby. "No, no. I'm glad you're here. The children should be home soon, and Tara's coming to dinner."

TARA'S ESTEEM FOR Dan McCrea increased with the sensitivity he showed Leila. After the examination, with apologies for the pain he must have caused, he asked her to sit up, then looked at the two other women, inviting them to leave.

Leila said, "They may stay." Earlier, she'd told Tara, *I miss my family. I wrote to them that you are my new sisters here.*

He turned his back on the midwife and her assistant. "I think you and your husband will want to discuss this together, Leila. We should make an appointment for the two of you to come in. Obviously, I can't undo what was done. But after the birth of your child, I can make some surgical corrections that will make intercourse less painful. And I don't recommend a vaginal birth."

Tara felt some regret but knew she was out of her league.

Leila surprised her. "Could we try a normal birth? And change to surgery if it is not going well? Woman do have vaginal births after this...."

Dan regarded her frankly. "Sure. We'll give it a try. But I won't take unnecessary risks." And he gave her an encouraging smile.

As the women were leaving, he asked Tara, "Would you stay a minute?"

She waited, and he shut the door when the other two were gone. "I want to thank you for last night. It was outside—" He stopped there. Tara was surprised he'd said so much.

Suddenly very grateful for what he was doing for Leila, she said, "I didn't do anything."

He studied her carefully, perhaps wondering if she feared entrapment.

She'd be crazy not to. Tara gambled. "Would you like to provide physician backup for me?"

He made a sound in his throat and showed her the door.

WHEN SHE ARRIVED at Isaac's that night with Laura, Dan was in the kitchen with his brother, inspecting canning jars of wormwood, wormseed and black walnut. It was David who let Tara in, exclaiming, "Will you play D&D tonight?"

"If that's what we're doing."

"Yes! Grand'mère and my uncle Dan wish to watch, because they gave us the game in... When they visited."

Tara hugged him spontaneously, then exchanged high-fives with Oliver, Laura in the sling against her. Danielle rushed in. "Voilà! My new Barbie doll."

"Oh, she's beautiful, Danielle. I like her brown hair. See, I have brown hair, too."

"You have pretty hair, Tara."

"Can you say that in Spanish?"

Danielle considered, then shook her head.

Isaac's mother approached for a hug. "Hello, Tara. How lovely to see you."

In the kitchen, Dan asked, "You're really taking this stuff?"

"The herbs, it's a week on, five days off, then repeat. Do it twice a year."

"But this other weird stuff. I mean, what is it?"

"Dinner."

Dan winced.

Oliver said, "*I* made apple pie."

"Thank you, Oliver. My stomach thanks you. But what is *that,* Isaac?"

"Seaweed." Isaac left the kitchen to greet Tara.

His embrace seemed lukewarm, his kiss on the

cheek cursory. In the wake of the debacle, were the boys banding together? Had Isaac already forgotten that his brother was the one who'd gone home to feed a dog?

No, Tara. You're alienating Isaac all by yourself.

Reach out. That was the answer. To both men, as doctors.

Joining them in the kitchen, where Isaac held Laura against his shoulder, Tara suggested, "I'd like you both to observe me at a birth." Her only client due soon was Jenny Preston. The celebrity with a history of sexual abuse would probably not welcome two M.D.s at her birth. But after the new year…

The brothers backed to the counter, lining up against Tara.

"Oh, come on. You don't have a clue what I do."

Dan indicated the seaweed and sauerkraut. "I'm getting a picture."

DANIELLE PULLED TARA into her room. "Guess what we're getting Daddy for his birthday. A puppy!"

Tara held her breath for a moment. Isaac's birthday. Monday. *A puppy?* Was Isaac going to like this? What about the cats? "What kind of puppy?"

"A free puppy. Oliver's friend has big fluffy dogs."

A big fluffy puppy. Should she interfere? It might be a magical thing, an occasion of joy.

"Have you told your grandmother?"

Danielle shook her head, eyes big. "It's a secret."

Tara embraced Isaac's daughter. *My daughter. She could be my daughter.* And the big fluffy puppy would be…

Why interfere? They were giving Isaac a present. Let him deal with it.

Isaac appeared in the doorway with Laura. With a warning look to Tara not to tell, Danielle darted out.

Tara tried to keep her face placid. A puppy. Birthday. Well, she could offer him one thing he'd said he wanted. "Have lunch with me Monday?"

His eyes shot to hers. Held. "Yes."

Neither of them was thinking of lunch.

She flushed, remembering the last time, in the miner's cabin.

Holding Laura, he stepped near to touch her face, kiss her mouth. It had been a very long time.

And it was a very long kiss.

Stroking her hair, he said softly, "Let's hang in there, all right?"

She nodded, trusting in the feel of his heart beneath her cheek.

LATE THAT NIGHT, in the living room, after both Tara and Dan had gone home, Isaac's mother sat with him on the couch and told him, "I brought you something. I don't know if you like it or would like to give it to a woman you love someday. But here it is. This was my mother's."

His grandmother's engagement ring, the diamond solitaire surrounded by columbines cast in white gold.

He hugged his mother and pocketed the black velvet-covered box. But he couldn't see Tara accepting the ring any time soon.

In his room, later, he stowed the ring in a drawer with his socks.

She'd been so eager to marry him because of Laura. Now they were involved and— He remembered her suggestion, that he and Dan observe her at a home-birth. And her reminder, a week ago, that triplets were high risk, her clients low risk. That emergency C-section at the hospital… Pat had been fired. The nurse had been angry, but it looked like there would be no fallout for Tara from the hospital.

Everyone at Precipice Peak wanted to forget what had happened.

Isaac wished he could forget.

Disasters could happen there, too.

Was homebirth a reasonable option for low-risk women?

You know it is, Isaac.

And, when everything went right, there *was* something special about a baby being born at home.

He'd forgotten that after what happened to Heloise, an unplanned catastrophe in the midst of genocide, mass insanity, mass terror.

Give her a chance, Isaac. Go watch her at a birth. In his mind, he could hear Heloise saying the same thing. *Give her a chance.*

Surely, if *he* could accept Tara doing homebirths, *she* would become licensed. Right?

Right.

It was fair.

SUNDAY MORNING, HIS mother said, "Isaac, it's supposed to snow tomorrow. If you don't mind, I'd rather get home today. We could have a birthday lunch before I go. You could ask Tara."

Tara was his birthday lunch tomorrow. But his mother—and the weather—had just made things easier.

IT WAS SNOWING when she arrived at the clinic Monday, without Laura. Beulah Ann was babysitting. It was twelve-thirty already, but Isaac stuck her in his office and said, "Three more patients."

Fifteen minutes later, he was back. "My kids are here. With a *dog*."

Was that a smile or a grimace? Tara wondered. "A dog?"

Isaac's glance was suspicious. "Come."

"You're getting the jargon down." She rose from his desk chair.

The children were out in front of the clinic with Mrs. Kennedy and one of the cutest, fluffiest puppies Tara had ever seen. "He's a Malamute!" she exclaimed. "I think. Hi, buddy. Look at *you!*"

The babysitter said, "I don't know anything about this."

Danielle was already petting the puppy furiously while David held the leash and told his sister to be gentle.

Danielle asked, "Do you like him, Daddy?"

Isaac missed only a beat. "I love him." He saved the evil eye for Oliver.

His eldest was charming. "He was whining at school. The principal said we must bring him over now, so we called Mrs. Kennedy."

Isaac pictured his son dickering with the principal to get them *all* out of school. He'd like to hear the principal's version.

"Alex Nolan's father chose him for you. He is the pick of the litter!" Oliver exclaimed. "We can go ski-joring with him!"

Interesting. Alex Nolan's father was the anesthesiologist who'd asked if he'd ever done a C-section. He'd give him a python for *his* birthday.

"It was a secret," said Danielle. "I only told Tara!"

"WHAT ARE YOU going to name him?"

"Is there some local indigenous word that means 'Instead of Getting Laid'?" It was almost two. Ten minutes, and he had to be back at work.

She laughed. "He's cute. Danielle said the parents were 'big fluffy dogs.'"

She had his daughter's voice down.

Isaac managed a smile for the puppy. Six months ago, his children had lost most of the people they loved and nearly everyone they knew. Five years before that, Oliver and David had learned their mother was dead.

They wanted a dog, this dog.

Tara had kept their secret, and in some way it made him love her more. But the reality of a *dog*. A big dog, who probably shed like…

He took Tara—and the puppy—back into his office and shut the door. She'd brought a picnic, and he dug in, taking a minute to leaf through his messages. He dropped one in front of her. *Dr. Nolan called. 9:15.*

"Chew slowly."

It was hard with a puppy salivating at his feet. Even rice with curry was not beneath this animal. "He'll devour the cats."

"Your cats? They'll eat him. That's why you get a puppy. Your cats will establish dominance."

"Speaking of establishing dominance." His look was weary. "My gift to *you* today was the news that my brother and I have decided to observe you at a homebirth."

What? Tara flew out of her chair to hug him. At his

expression, she dropped to her knees, embracing his.
"You alpha. Me submissive pack member."

"You? Submissive?" He drew her up, onto his lap.
"I like the pack member part. Can we work on that?"

"You want someone to walk the dog."

He fed her some of his lunch, holding her, touching
her. Relaxing.

"I don't have a present for you now," she said.

"I could suggest one."

Licensing? Changing careers? She didn't answer.
Except to say, "Look, it could be a while before you
can watch me at a birth. I'll talk to my next client
who's due, but she may say no."

"We'll preserve confidentiality. Hey, move a second. This little guy's chewing on me."

"He needs a name."

"I'm sure he needs a bowl and brush and a bunch
of other things, too." He fished for his wallet. "Here.
Go to the pet store for me, will you? I'll pay, and you
can say 'Happy Birthday.' Fair?"

"What are you going to call him?"

"Raincheck."

LEILA AND BEULAH ANN were in the kitchen the next
day, studying, when Tara approached Jenny about observers.

"*Which* two doctors?"

"Dr. McCrea and Dr. McCrea."

Yul said, "Jen, you don't have to do anything you
don't want to."

"No." Her expression grew determined. "I want to
help. Because of me, Tara's mother almost lost hospital privileges. Then I had no birth attendant. If I can
help homebirth become accepted in this community, I

want to do it. But, Tara—promise that none of them will touch me.''

"I'll ask for their word on the matter.'' She hesitated. "Jenny, how *are* things between you and your father?'' It was a stepfather who had molested her, not Rich Scarborough.

Jenny shrugged. "We talk some. My stepmother's okay, I guess. He's just never been there for me. You know?''

There were times Tara's own father hadn't been there. That made her think of Francesca in Misheguk. With Dad. She tried to put it out of her mind.

"What about your mother?''

"She lives overseas now.''

Hm. She made a note to see that Jenny had extra support after the baby's birth. It would be great if her stepmother... Well, Tara didn't know Dr. Scarborough's wife.

"Jenny, would you object to my assistant, Beulah Ann, and my student, Leila, feeling the baby's lie?''

"No. It's cool. Leila's Muslim, huh? What a trip.''

JENNY CALLED A week later, at two in the morning. She had lost her mucus plug and was having contractions. She asked if Beulah Ann and Leila could come, too, and Tara said she'd do her best. In any case, she and Beulah Ann would be there in half an hour. Beulah Ann had to drop Chantel at her sitter's.

Tara phoned Isaac; he and Dan would meet her at the client's house in an hour. Next, she called Leila, who sounded sleepy, but spoke to her husband and said she could go.

When the three women arrived, Tara let Beulah Ann check the mom and baby, then confirmed her findings.

Four centimeters dilated, baby in good shape. Jenny had decided to labor in a thigh-length T-shirt. Tara encouraged her to walk around or do whatever felt good and to drink and eat something light. Yul fixed her some tea and toast, while Leila displayed a remarkable gift for focusing with the mother, for being with her. "You are so brave, Jenny. I hope I am half so brave when my time comes."

The doorbell rang, and when Yul answered, Tara heard Isaac and Dan. The issue between her and Isaac loomed large, and she tried to forget it. She needed to focus on the birth.

When Isaac ducked his head into the master bedroom with its Craftsman-replica furniture and quilts and rocking chair and woodstove, Tara stood up. "You're just in time to hold Laura."

He took the baby. "You two haven't come over to visit my dog. Who is a *mutt,* by the way."

There was affection in his voice—for her and Laura, as well as Raincheck. Smiling, Tara said, "Didn't eat the cats, did he?"

"Not yet. Though Meow almost ate him."

Tara said, "Come meet Jenny."

Labor was progressing slowly, and Jenny moaned with her contractions. She wanted to get in and out of the bath, then stand near the blazing woodstove. She had blocked out everyone but herself and her child, and Tara did nothing to interrupt that focus.

The next time Tara checked her and the baby, she was five centimeters dilated and the baby's head had moved down.

"You're doing great, Jenny. Let's get you some more to drink."

"I'm not sure I can do this. I didn't know it would hurt so much."

Tara heard Dan's ragged breath. He left the room briefly, and Tara realized he didn't want to see a woman in pain. He'd apologized again and again to Leila at his office, for hurting her.

"Let's try some acupressure spots," Tara told Jenny. "I'm certain you can do this. You're already five centimeters dilated."

Two hours later, there had been no progress, and Tara thought she knew the problem. This stop-and-go labor felt like a cord around the neck, something that couldn't be detected even with a sonogram. She was going to let the baby take its time, move around as it needed.

"Okay, Jenny, I think I know why this labor is progressing so strangely, but it's not anything for you to worry about." She explained about the possibility of a cord around the neck. "You get cord loops about twenty percent of the time. When we let this happen naturally, it generally goes just fine. But this baby will have to come out on the baby's schedule, so I need you to just hang in there with the eating and drinking for right now."

The doctors left the room, and Tara heard Dan speaking to Isaac. "Transport," "hospital" and "C-section" all came up. Finally, she heard the raised words, "If something goes wrong here, you and I are in trouble, too, Isaac!"

Tara took a deep cleansing breath, pretending the obstetrician wasn't just outside the door.

Jenny said, "They won't touch me."

"They won't touch you." Barring a catastrophe. But she and Jenny had covered that ground. "Your baby sounds good, and I'll keep listening.'' Inventory equipment. Prepare to cut an episiotomy if necessary. And be ready to resuscitate the newborn if she had to.

In the other room, Laura cried.

Leaving Leila and a quiet Beulah Ann with Jenny, Tara took the infant from Isaac. As she prepared to nurse Laura, Yul noticed her changing milk bags. ''That's not your baby, is it?''

It hurt to have someone say that. ''Oh, yes, she is.''

He apologized. ''You're doing great, lady—with your baby and ours.''

She was starting in to sit with Jenny, when Dan appeared in her path. ''We need to transport this woman.''

''I can't stand the pain!'' Jenny yelled.

Yul stared at the obstetrician. ''Is this an emergency?''

''It's an unnecessary risk.''

''Jenny's not going anywhere,'' Yul said, ''unless she and I and the midwife make that choice. If you disturb Jenny, I'll have to ask you to leave.''

Theirs was exactly the kind of agreement that could bring the sheriff to the doorstep. With Laura at her breast, Tara squeezed around the two men and into the bedroom. Beulah Ann was coaching Jenny. ''Take a breath like this. Then let it out. Your baby's making his way out to you. You're doing so good.''

In the other room, Isaac paced with his brother. Part of him was in Rwanda, in the villages of Kibuye. He'd trusted birth the way a swimmer trusts the ocean, a climber the mountains. Incompletely. Tara must have the same level of trust; she'd seen that abruptio placentae in the works. She knew what it was.

Why do this at home when a hospital was available?

She spoke of unnecessary intervention, of stressed mothers, of bad outcomes with epidurals, of the connection between repeated use of ultrasound and low birth weight. *I love primaparas,* she'd told him once, *because we get them before the doctors wreck 'em.* With episiotomies and cesareans, she meant.

Once she'd told him, *You know the trouble with OB/GYNs? They believe the perfect body is male. Pregnancy doesn't happen to males, and therefore it is treated as a disease.*

Jenny moaned, cried out with her next contraction. "Oh, I can't stand it."

"You're doin' just fine, honey," murmured Beulah Ann. "Shall we try another position?"

Dan sank down on the couch and put his head in his hands.

Isaac joined him silently.

"You know, I'm coming to terms with something about myself," his brother admitted.

"Mm?"

"I hate to see women in pain."

"Well, there's no argument it's better this way. For the baby."

Dan stared at the fire in the hearth, spontaneously knelt to put on another log, then took his seat beside Isaac. "How does this affect you?"

Yul emerged from the bedroom and Isaac postponed answering. When the father had returned to his partner, Isaac answered, "I'm not sure. What happened two weeks ago…" The emergency C-section, Dan's absence. He shook his head. "You know, I used to do this. With Heloise."

Thoughtful, Dan slowly rose from the couch and edged toward the bedroom.

Tara set Laura in her car seat to sleep. Then she had a minute to talk to Beulah Ann and the doctors about her plans for the birth. They listened, Dan with lowered brows, as she outlined her contingencies for different situations. Beulah Ann listened carefully. In the next room, Yul and Leila soothed Jenny.

When Tara and her assistant had left to scrub, Dan said, "Isaac, this violates my principles."

"We can leave. But that wasn't the idea."

Tara could hear them from the kitchen—and tried to ignore them.

Returning to the bedroom, she apologized to the mother. "Jenny, I'm sorry. I should've known better."

"Check the baby again. Please. I feel like pushing."

Eight centimeters.

"Ahhh! Ahhh! Ohhhhhh…"

"You're doing so well. Breathe. Breathe."

Jenny cried out again.

She went to ten centimeters in four minutes. Isaac and Dan watched from the doorway. Jenny screamed with the next contraction. "I'm splitting apart!"

"Mm," Leila soothed.

Yul supported Jenny's back, kissed her hair.

Tara told him, "Is this mom terrific, or what?"

At Tara's okay, Jenny began to push, lying on her side. Tara took fetal heart tones through the push. "You're doing great. You're doing great."

The baby's heart tones dropped as the head passed through the ischial spines, but afterward came right back up. Good. "Okay, Jenny, you can go ahead and push. Take it slow."

"I want to squat."

The assistants were ready with a sheet for the floor. Isaac was behind her, but Tara focused on the mother and child, continuously taking heart tones. "Yul and Beulah Ann—that's right. Lean on them. Does that work, Jenny? Good. Push. A big one." Tara supported the perineum, then caught the baby girl as she came out, keeping the head close to the perineum and rotating the baby to loosen the cord as the body emerged. "Oh, what a pretty girl."

Three loops of cord, and Isaac, with Dan breathless beside him, watched Tara's slow dance with the infant body, untangling the cord, then suctioning the baby as Yul lowered Jenny against a bean bag cushion. She put the baby in her mother's arms.

"Is she all right?" asked Jenny. "She's so quiet."

"She's just fine." Isaac peered down to check the newborn. "Just fine."

The room had filled with the scent and feeling of birth, untouched by the sterility of the hospital. Isaac remembered from distance.

Time slowed.

Dan said softly, "She's a beautiful child."

With the delivery of the placenta, Jenny began to bleed, and Tara handled it with a cup of shepherd's purse tea prepared by Beulah Ann and uterine massage. The placenta was all there, and she dimmed the lights, asked Yul to turn on the portable heater, got the extra bodies out of the room, and encouraged the mother to nurse.

The doctors grouped at the door, where Dan zipped his coat.

Isaac waited for someone to speak.

In a low voice, Dan said, "She scared the hell out of me. I'll never be in favor of homebirth. I can't provide backup for this."

Isaac stepped out onto the porch with his brother

and shut the door. "It's what I used to do for rural midwives. They'd call me on the bad ones."

Dan's raw laugh pitied Isaac. "You've got bigger problems than me. I can just say no."

Isaac nodded without adding the rest. *And I'm in love with her.*

He was walking Dan to his car when another vehicle pulled up outside the home. Rich Scarborough's Range Rover.

Dan said, "I asked him to cover for me tonight. Told him we were doing this. See you."

Isaac went to greet the Chief of Obstetrics and was relieved to see Rich helping Mrs. Scarborough from the car. They couldn't be here to harass the midwife.

"Come to see your granddaughter?" asked Isaac. "She's a pretty one."

"Is she now?" The obstetrician smiled. "Well, I'll just have to see for myself."

TARA AND ISAAC sat by one of Yul and Jenny's hearths, Isaac holding Laura. The Scarboroughs were in with their grandchild and her parents, while Leila and Beulah Ann cleaned the house.

Tara sighed. "This didn't endear me to Dan." She lifted her gaze to Isaac's. "What about you?"

"It got my heart racing some. In Africa, it would be all in a day's work. Except, more likely, someone would have died." He put his head back. Stillbirths. Blood.

Heloise, alone in labor, while *genocidaires* ran in the streets with dripping machetes. Blood outside the hospital, outside his house, everywhere. In the hospital, you began slipping in it.

"Isaac?"

So many babies he could not save. *My babies.*

He met her eyes. "My children died this way, Tara." Later, he thought that if it hadn't been so late or so emotional, if he hadn't been thinking of genocide too, he wouldn't have said what followed. But the words came out, words from his heart. "I think you need to choose. There's this path. Or there's me."

HE DID NOT call for more than a week.

Her mother did call, and Tara told her what had happened. And for the first time, she related the deaths of Isaac's wife and children. Her mother would spread it no further.

"Oh, dear God," said Francesca. She sighed. "Tara—"

"You know, out of say three thousand births, some obviously not mine, I've seen maybe two hundred bad outcomes, Mom, and that's including Chile and Mexico—and hospital situations over which I had no control. I have—through the grace of God—never caused injury to a child in birth. With shoulder dystocia, sure, it gets dicey and the mom sometimes tears—"

"I know, Tara. I know all this." Francesca was crying.

"Is it Dad? Did he do something?"

"*No.* I'm worried about *you.* And poor Isaac. Tara, you have to allow for people to be human."

At the price of giving up midwifery? *Forget it.* She'd love him the rest of her life, comfort him any way she could, make any sacrifice—except that. And becoming licensed? She brushed the thought away. "The baby's healthy, Apgar 10; she was nursing in twenty minutes. Her name is Lorena Marie Preston."

"Honey, you're living in 1999. Get used to it. You can't fight the whole world."

What was she supposed to do with that advice? "Well, for now, I'm focusing on Laura."

"You're going to let him go?"

"Mom, he didn't say, 'Get certified, or it's over.' He said, 'There's this path. Or there's me.' He'll never feel peace with my doing homebirths."

"He's frightened, Tara. He must feel tremendous guilt over what happened to his wife and babies. I'm sure he doesn't want more blood on his hands."

Her mother didn't know half the blood Isaac saw on his hands.

"He's just not the one for me, Mom."

A pause. The backlash would come.

Francesca said, "I love you, darling."

HE FELT HER ABSENCE. He also felt the final severance.

They were too different, in a way too fundamental, a way that could not work for man and wife.

The deal on the Victorian was closing days after the birth of Lorena Preston and he wondered fleetingly where Tara would go.

She'd figure something out. She knew everyone in town.

On the twenty-second, her birthday, he took Raincheck up to the miner's shack, just to get away. He asked the puppy, "Think you could get used to being called RC?"

The puppy had grown on him, and Isaac watched him sniff around the cabin, then worry Isaac's boots.

No Tara. Get used to it.

Two days later, he took the children—and the puppy—with him to Boulder to see Dr. Ching. While the children sat in the waiting room, he sat on an examining table across from a wall covered with bottles of dried herbs.

The friendly O.M.D. felt his pulse, examined his tongue, asked interminable questions about things from sweating to stools.

Isaac described his diet, and the gentleman nodded with satisfaction.

"I'm really feeling better. I'm not sure why I'm here."

"Well, I have remedies for you. A little more thorough. But we must talk about other things, too. You are a physician, a very stressful job. How do you care for your spirit?"

Only in Boulder. "I climb mountains."

"Ah, yes. The Himalayas. You like to travel."

Isaac kept his mouth shut.

The young man sat backward on a stool and faced Isaac. "Has Tara spoken to you about emotional blockages?"

Emotional blockages?

"In healing, you must always look for the spiritual disease, too. The unhealed grief. The anger. Lack of forgiveness."

Isaac's eyes felt as though they were sinking in his head. It was a different version of what he gave his patients. *Any problems at home? How's the job?*

Anger. Lack of forgiveness. Unhealed grief.

Calmly, he told Dr. Ching of Rwanda, the genocide, of Heloise's death, the murder of her family. He concluded, "Forgiveness and healing are hard to come by. And, yes, I'm angry. You would be, too."

The doctor lifted his eyebrows thoughtfully. He was in no hurry.

Neither was Isaac. He'd come to Boulder for this.

"Do you have a relationship with a woman now?"

And Isaac told him about Tara, about homebirth, about their fundamental incompatibility.

"I see. That's difficult." Dr. Ching unstraddled the chair and begin pulling jars of herbs from the shelf. "I try to be like water. When you can be like water, you slip over and around such obstacles. And yet you reach your destination."

When Isaac left the office with the children, he found a pay phone and tried to call Tara. The line was disconnected.

TARA POINTED THE Subaru for El Paso, with Laura in her car seat in back.

She had finished postpartum visits with Jenny; Beulah Ann would see her for follow-up, and Tara would stay in touch with both assistant and client by phone. Leila was doing beautifully. Between visits with Jenny and Karen Anthony and other clients, Tara had scrubbed the Victorian from floor to ceiling and loaded the Subaru with her possessions—including a genuine Native wood carving from Alaska, the first gift she'd received in twenty years from *both* her parents. When she returned to Precipice, she would move in with Beulah Ann and Chantel, sharing the basement apartment of Leila and Asad's 6,000 square foot house, which they'd generously offered for an affordable monthly rent.

She'd shed no tears over Isaac. Impossible was impossible.

But she couldn't imagine ever risking her heart again.

Isaac had walked away when she needed him most,

just when she was ready to adopt Laura. Beulah Ann had tried to persuade her that she *should* take any help Isaac offered. *Tara, you should call Isaac. You should marry Isaac, if he wants it. For goodness' sake, become a CNM. He'll help you through school. Or at least become certified. With him on your side, your chances of keeping your baby are so much better.*

Tara had shaken her head. *He'll never support homebirth. The relationship will never work.*

And Isaac knew it, too. He hadn't called.

They were finished.

And she was back to doing things as she always had.

Not alone. But with strong women beside her and behind her.

SHE REACHED El Paso Tuesday and hunted for a hotel where she'd stayed before, cheap and fairly safe. She checked in and nursed Laura to sleep.

Tara knew she shouldn't go to Maternity House, but there was nothing wrong with *phoning* there. There was no harm in asking her friend Star if she knew a good attorney in El Paso, specializing in adoption. She wouldn't say anything about her plans or where she was calling from.

The same caution kept Tara from identifying herself when she asked for Star. Fortunately, the woman who answered didn't ask who was calling, and her friend was on the line in a minute.

"Star, it's Tara."

"Tara!" It was a whispered gasp. "Just a minute. Shutting the door."

Fear settled in Tara's womb. *Keep it short, Tara. You don't want to find out why she's acting this way.*

"I'm looking for a good adoption attorney in El Paso. Do you know one?"

"Yeah, we know the adoption guru, but his retainer is, like, insane. And, Tara—"

"How much?"

"Five thou, nonrefundable." A deep breath. "Tara, Julia is here. Now. With a Marine sergeant fiancé they say is the child's natural father. She wants her baby back."

CHAPTER THIRTEEN

I'm so excited for the baby to come—and after that for the operation Dr. McCrea will do. I don't think I will ever know genital sexual pleasure, but Asad, my beloved, has taught me love of the intellect, and we have always shared love of the spirit and soul and heart…and body.

—Leila

TARA SAT ON THE hotel bed, receiver against her ear and mouth, gazing at her sleeping daughter, her baby.

Julia's baby?

Not even sixty days had elapsed since Laura's birth. In Texas, birth mothers had sixty days to change their minds about adoption, and if she didn't go back— She dredged it up from inside her, what she knew was right and correct, though her eyes were already streaming. Isaac… But that was over.

"I'll bring her…right away." A forty-five minute drive to Sagrado.

"Oh, honey," whispered Star. "How did it happen?"

"Julia left her in my car."

"Well, she lied about that."

"It doesn't matter." Tara couldn't stop the sobs.

"She's the birth mother and she wants her child back. It hasn't been that long. I'll see you soon."

She hung up and went to warm a milk bag from her cooler and then lie down to nurse Laura one last time.

ISAAC REALIZED HIS mistake. It was the twenty-fourth. Tara had left the Victorian.

Finding her had to wait until he returned to Precipice. He drove back that night, despite complaints from Oliver, who wanted to see more of Boulder. Isaac had a sick feeling of premonition. For the past five years, he had heeded such feelings, and they'd never proven wrong.

As soon as they reached home, he snatched up the San Juan area phone book and paged through it, searching for the Café International.

Beulah Ann, he was told, no longer worked there.

"Dad?" It was David, dropping his duffel bag at his father's feet. "Are you looking for Tara?"

"Yes." Who else might know where Tara had gone?

On the couch, Danielle seemed ready to cry. She told him nearly every day that she missed Tara.

Oliver merely looked annoyed, but he was the one who said, in Kinyarwanda, that Isaac should call the lady with the baby.

"What baby?"

"You and Uncle Dan went."

Jenny Preston? No.

What about Leila? Her husband had been in his office. Isaac checked the directory.

"When can we go to Boulder again?"

"Soon."

Moments later, he was on the phone with Beulah Ann, speaking from Leila's basement apartment.

"She went to adopt Laura. She went to Texas."

Isaac's throat caught. He couldn't speak.

"Dr. McCrea?"

"Did she give you a number where she'd be staying?"

"Well, she's supposed to call with it, but she hasn't yet."

As he hung up the phone, his heart raced. He could call Maternity House, but he didn't want to risk showing Tara's hand.

"Daddy, what's wrong?"

He picked up Danielle and held her. "Nothing, honey."

"Where is Tara?"

"She went to Texas. To adopt Laura."

"Adopt?"

It was a bad time to have to explain adoption. He did it quickly.

"But Laura *is* her *bébé*."

"I know, sweetheart, but sometimes it's not as simple as that." And his gut twisted hard, as though something was being ripped from him.

TARA HAD TO PULL over three times on the way to Sagrado. Windshield wipers didn't work on tears. Laura whimpered in the car seat beside her, and Tara stopped a fourth time to nurse her again, with no supplement, to feel the tingling of the milk flow.

Julia would not nurse Laura. She would buy formula or who knew what, ignoring the advice of the midwives at Maternity House.

Well, she'll hold her and feed her. She wants her back. She's going to be married.

Tara wept, for Laura and herself. But maybe Laura would, in the long run, be happier with her birth mother. Julia was young and deceitful, but perhaps the soldier would guide her.

Maternity House loomed in sight, and she pulled into the familiar parking lot.

Lights blazed outside, giving the parking lot a surreal, science-fiction glow. A military vehicle kissed bumpers with an El Paso County sheriff's car. *Oh, God, don't let them put me in jail for this. I can't go to jail. Not now. No. No.*

I don't deserve it.

I was just thirteen.

With those kernels of truth inside her, she carried Laura, her diaper bag, and the car seat toward the door of Maternity House. Star ran out, long earrings dangling beneath her short hair. But the sheriff's deputies had already stepped from their car. One was a woman.

"Deputy Trent." The male deputy, over six feet tall and two hundred pounds, nodded to his wiry partner.

Tara tried to reach the female deputy's eyes as the woman took the car seat and baby from her. *Oh, God! Not like this! Let me kiss her! Oh, God! Oh, please…*

The officer turned away with the baby, who began to cry, and an inhuman wail cut the night. Tara's breasts produced drops of milk, and she discovered it was she who had cried out. She stitched her lips shut. She knew better than to cry, to show any weakness. Star stood feet away, tears on her cheeks, and Tara longed for her friend's arms, but her own were already behind her back. The deputies were talking to her—

about felony kidnapping. "You have the right to remain silent—"

"I know them." Her rights.

He continued.

She's gone. She's gone! The scream inside, voiceless.

Star came over with the intention of hugging her, but the deputy snapped, "Ma'am, step back! Please return inside."

Leaving, Star yelled, "I'll call you a lawyer, Tara. Anyone else?"

Isaac. He mustn't learn about Laura this way or that she, Tara, was going to jail.

But there was no Isaac. Their love was ashes in the parking lot.

"No!" she told Star. "Just the lawyer. I can pay him!" Jail. Shit. Jail. "My keys are in my car! Lock it for me!"

"Okay!"

Isaac swam in and out of her consciousness. She barely paid attention as the female officer returned and everything, even the birthing-woman pendant her mother had given her, was taken from her and put in a Ziploc bag. She breathed deeply, gathering energy she pretended was courage—for what lay ahead.

Behind the cage in the back seat, she ignored the noise of the radio, the responses of the deputy, and breathed and tried to keep her mind off Laura. Just breathe.

SHE BREATHED THROUGH the eternal waiting and the booking, and she disappeared during the strip search, splitting, floating till she was in an alpine field among wildflowers. An officer's voice brought her back, and

Tara summoned her toughness. She summoned it with the last strength in her soul and mind and body as she was marched down the hall, and she smelled the smells and heard the sounds. Moaning and yelling and women whistling, reaching out to touch her long hair.

Then she was in the holding cell, with them.

"Oh, aren't you a pretty baby?" cooed a woman twice her size, cupping Tara's cheek in her hand.

HE CALLED MATERNITY HOUSE at midnight. "Hello, I'm trying to find Tara Marcus."

"Oh, God, who is this?"

"Isaac McCrea, M.D. And who is this?"

"Star Kelly. I'm her friend. Why do you need her?"

Isaac didn't want to play games. He wanted to know where Tara was. "Because I'm her friend, too. Her good friend."

"Oh, God." Star breathed audibly into the receiver. "Swear you're telling the truth."

What was going on? "Where is she?"

Star told him. She started to tell him more, and he said, "I'll find out when I get there." But he knew. He already knew—that Laura was no longer theirs.

THE FIRST FLIGHT HE could get was Friday evening, out of Durango—a city three, almost four hours' drive away. Thanksgiving weekend. There was nothing else from Precipice, nothing from Montrose, nothing from Grand Junction. He'd get there faster driving. He'd have to rent a car, but so what? Mrs. Kennedy had agreed to stay overnight with the children—and Raincheck—as long as she was needed, and he phoned his answering service and canceled all appointments at the clinic, citing a family emergency. Which it was. Tara was part of his family, and he was bringing her home.

He barely slept, and in the morning, Danielle cried to learn he was going. Even the dog looked worried— but maybe that was just at the sight of Meow, appearing around a corner and arching her back. Raincheck scurried to a corner of the kitchen and began licking the orange tabby.

Another time, Isaac would have laughed.

Oliver said, ''You'll find her, Dad.''

Isaac wished he could bring them all but knew he shouldn't. Tara might be in bad shape. He'd loaded his backpack with emergency medical supplies and with what remained in his cabinets of her favorite herbal teas. Nettles, fenugreek— No, not that one. *Oh, Tara.*

Laura.

In the solitude of his room, he held back emotion, preparing. She might not want to see him.

Precipice's one rental car company picked him up at 6:00 a.m., after he'd hugged the children and kissed them again and again and seen more tears, even from David.

But once he was headed for the rental car agency, his thoughts returned to Tara. He remembered that morning in the blue room, her meltdown. *What was she going through now? What had she been through last night?*

Oh, Tara, baby, hold on.

IN THE NIGHT, the big woman approached her cot. ''Here, pretty baby.''

Tara sat straight up, putting her feet on the floor. ''Hey, sister, I'm not interested.''

"Everyone likes Devora, honey."

"She's a stuck-up bitch, Devora!"

"Shut up, Elaine."

Tara left her cot, went to the cell bars to call for a guard when arms grabbed her from behind, a hand covering her mouth. She stepped back into them and tripped one of them. As they all fell in a heap to the floor, she screamed, "*Help!* I'm being attacked!"

"She won't listen. They never do, little sister."

I'll survive. I'll fight, and I'll survive, no matter what.

PARKING WAS A problem outside the county building, and once Isaac grabbed a spot, he locked the doors and ran. He'd long since shed his parka and winter sweater, stripped down to a T-shirt and jeans.

He found the jail in seconds. "I'm Isaac McCrea. I'm here to see a prisoner. Tara Marcus."

The deputy behind the desk said, "You just missed her. She's out of here. Charges dropped."

"Do you know where she went?"

"She called a cab."

"The Sajuarro Motel," called another officer.

He nodded, unable to utter even a thank-you, and was gone.

SHE WAS RUBBING her wet hair when a fist pounded on the door. "Tara, it's Isaac!"

The phone. The phone she'd ignored. Maybe he'd knocked and she hadn't heard. Isaac.

Trancelike, tall, she walked to the door and opened it.

Isaac saw her uncombed, damp hair, the eerie peacefulness of her face, her hollowed eyes. He came in with his backpack and shut the door, then dropped the pack against it. She'd chosen to stay in this place alone?

He approached her carefully, and Tara backed away.

"Don't touch me." Isaac. Isaac. "What are you doing here?"

He rubbed his lips together. Silence. "Too little, too late."

Tara sank down on the edge of the bed, numb. Those were his hiking boots. It was Isaac. She saw him with Laura against his shoulder.

Nightmare, nightmare.

The mattress beside her moved. His warmth, his arms, broke through her strange state. She knew his smell, the feel of him, and trembling began. Hard. *Not this!* Tara tried to move back to the trance, the other realm, but he was here, real and warm. Her breath went out of her control, coming hard and fast through her mouth.

Isaac saw, heard. *Here we go.* "Tara, come back. Come on."

She jumped up and began to pace.

"I brought meds. You want them?"

"No." She'd retreated to the far side of the room. "She's Julia's baby. Julia wants her."

"Did anyone hurt you, Tara?"

"No." A guard had come. Finally.

"Did anyone assault you?"

"Do you think I care? I just lost my baby!" She sank to the floor, and the violent breathing resumed. Her tears rose, her voice climbing to a wail for the child she'd lost.

He crossed the room in a second. "Tara." Holding her. "Tara."

"I have a right to cry!" It was a scream.

"Yes." He could only embrace her through her anguish until her sobs broke him, and he cried, too. Not just for the baby he'd held, the baby he'd loved, who'd touched the unspeakable in his life and begun to heal it. Tara's baby. But for his own and Heloise and her family. Her family, his family.

A knock sounded at the door, breaking into his thoughts, into the intimacy of pain, and Isaac released her to answer. It was the Hispanic gentleman who'd dialed her room but refused to tell him her room number. Isaac had peered into rooms with curtains open, working by process of elimination until he found her.

"Miss Marcus. Miss Marcus, you okay? This man bothering you?"

Isaac stepped out of the way, so the hotel owner could see her.

"No." Tara shook her head, still weeping, her head over her knees. "I just…had to g-g-give up my baby. This is Isaac. He's my friend."

The hotel owner seemed to see his face for the first time, to see that they were together in their distress.

"Okay, you call you need anything, Miss Marcus."

"Thank you, Mr. Alvarez."

When Isaac shut the door, she was calmer. So was he. He found a dry towel in the bathroom, then came to sit beside her on the carpet. He draped the towel over her hair.

Tara had spent four hours in the shower. She shut her eyes. Everything hurt so much, and his presence made it hurt more. Made it more real. More true.

Here was Isaac. No Laura.

She couldn't bear sympathy. In Miami, her dad had understood that. She saw him standing over her hospital bed, sober. Casually eyeing her IV line. He'd put up his feet on the steel bed frame and read her the news, interjecting, *What a crock of shit,* or whatever he happened to feel about particular statements. Many times, she'd had to beg him not to make her laugh.

"Isaac, I've got clients. I need to get home." To Leila and Asad's house.

"Anybody due?" If so, someone else would have to handle it.

"No, but…" *I need you to leave.*

She would die if he went. He was… Francesca and her dad were so far away. Ivy in West Virginia. Beulah Ann and Leila—not close enough. At the moment, it seemed that he was all she had.

All she had in the world.

"When was the last time you slept, Tara?"

She answered slowly. "I need to go to the health-food store."

He began drying her hair with the towel. "Hungry?"

Crying. Crying against his shoulder.

Isaac said, "I'll drive you home."

"I brought the Subaru. It's at Maternity House."

"I'll drive it. I'm in a rental."

"You'll pay through the nose to get it back to Precipice."

"Tara?" He held her head.

"What?"

"Are you trying to get rid of me? Are you angry with me?"

She shook her head.

"Then we'll go to the health-food store. You can buy whatever you want. And after that, we'll curl up

on this bed for a few hours. Then we'll take off.
Fair?''

Curl up on the bed with Isaac? Her limbs felt loose
and tense, her mind raw. She didn't want him to touch
her. Because human contact was healing. And healing
would hurt.

HE CARRIED THE basket through the store, helping her
fill it. A natural-bristle vegetable brush, olive oil,
honey, clay, apple cider vinegar. She chose a valerian
root tincture, spirulina, arnica massage oil, springwater, springwater.... The clerk was giving away dried
sage, to burn.

On the way back to the hotel, she said, ''I don't
want to lean on you. I hate sympathy. I want to take
care of myself. It's what I've always done.''

Isaac held his tongue and tried not to imagine her
having one of those episodes of rapid breathing, sob-
bing and trembling—alone.

SIXTY DROPS OF tincture in springwater in a motel
glass. Drink. Cry. Too tired.

''Okay. Okay. I love you,'' she said.

His hands lifting her shirt.

''They j-just took her.''

Her corduroys, ancient Salvation Army Levi's jeans
that his brother had made fun of. Her underwear. No
bra.

Under the heat lamp in the bathroom. Burning sage
in the air.

The dry brush on her skin, all over. She shivered.
Would that her skin be peeled away. Oh, he was see-
ing. Scars and... ''Okay, okay,'' she said again.
''These women...''

Brush her body, getting the old skin off. Crying. Breasts leaking.

A tablespoon of honey in the bath. Sleepy. Clay and apple cider vinegar on her face. Getting a new face. Tears. His hands soothing her.

"Isaac." Like the cry of a woman pushing the baby's head out. *"Isaac!"*

Washing her face.

Towels and olive oil.

On the bed, arnica massaged into her sore limbs, her bruises.

Wrapped in his T-shirt and sweatpants.

Cuddled close.

"It hurts."

Breath and heartbeat and kisses.

Sleep.

SHE WHIMPERED IN her sleep, then cried out. He'd heard a louder version of that sound in the scream of a mountain lion. He woke her. "Tara."

She blinked. The drapes. The hotel smell. Not just a dream. Real. *They took Laura.*

His arms, gathering her close.

"Isaac."

She tugged at his sweatpants, those he wore, and he let her, let her touch him, gave all control to her, even though he felt her anger.

She was infertile.

Not the time to suggest that things might be done. Time to kiss. She led, her tongue meeting his. *I should have married her. I should have been here.*

"Help me," she whispered.

Slide off her clothes and his.

This wasn't how he'd imagined it. Not in this nightmare, another nightmare. Raw. The world of numb unreality.

Life was the heat of her skin.

Tara eased on top of him and worked to join him, sinking over him, the soft cries of love rising from within her. "Isaac. Isaac. It feels so good." It made her cry. To have his baby. To have Laura, hers.

She came on him. Hard. Powerful woman.

Isaac let go, taking the release, the endorphins. His mind hung in limbo between a time when they'd been happy—and this. She'd made him happy from the first...and he hadn't realized it.

He heard her crying. Her tears wet his skin. "It was the right thing," she said. "You don't take a baby from the birth mother who wants her."

Isaac would have tried to intervene, would have insisted on meeting the parents, would have set some facts straight. He'd thought of nothing else on the long road to Texas. But they would have lost.

She'd taken Laura back just because she was brave and good.

And gone to jail.

They'd put her in jail.

His muscles were tight wire.

Hold her, Isaac. Just hold her.

"Why did they drop the charges?"

Tara recognized that tone, the accent coming stronger. Angry. *Don't be angry now.* She would fall apart again. She could hardly breathe. "Because she'd abandoned the baby in my car. I called Star, and she told me."

"You called Star." Had she hoped, somehow, that she could have Laura back? She ought to have Laura back. "But Julia has Laura."

"Julia and her fiancé."

Isaac left the bed, went to the bathroom. Nearly smashed the mirror.

Cool it, Isaac.

It took some time. Time to think. Time for resolve to harden.

After several minutes, he brought a warm cloth to wash her face. He felt for lumps in her breasts. Soft. Her milk had dried up, that fast.

That flimsy thread to the world of fertility and child-bearing.

He rethought what he'd planned to say.

No. He was right.

"Tara. Sit up, babe."

She did, slowly.

"Listen. We need to talk. About midwifery."

Her face lifted, and a spark of fire lit in her eyes.

Well, that got her attention, Isaac.

Kali the destroyer was back, ready to hammer him.

His Quaker upbringing pressed for caution. He picked his words. Uttered them slowly. "Tara, I just can't get worked up about the supposed injustice of you having to get licensed. But I'm really—really—" He was shaking suddenly. "I'm very angry about the night you spent in jail."

She opened her mouth, and he said, "Don't. I don't care. Whatever it is, I don't care. Your ideological gripe with a very generous state law *does not matter to me.* You matter. I don't want to see you in jail again. No. Don't say anything. Let me finish.

"You know how I feel about homebirth. But I want you for my wife. So I can compromise. And I want you to certify. I want you to establish conservative protocols for hospital transport. When you do that much, you might find you have physician backup. Maybe. If not, at least you'll have a husband in the ER once in a while. That's where I'm going full-time, as soon as I can.'' He'd already been accepted. It was just a matter of getting out of family practice. ''That's it, Tara. Solution. Like it?''

Her breath was gone. Compromise. Compromise. He still didn't like homebirth, but... *Laura. Laura!* How could he give her an ultimatum now? ''This isn't fair.''

''Fair is just what it is. You want to fight the world, you fight alone. There's still enough Quaker left in me that I prefer peace.''

That's the last word, Tara. He left the bed. His breath was rough as he opened his pack. For a moment, he held his head. She had to stop fighting. She had to stop.

He returned to the bed and knelt beside it to offer her the box containing his grandmother's engagement ring.

She didn't take it. ''I never knew you were Quaker.''

''I grew up that way. In Rwanda, I changed.'' *Take the ring. Take the ring, Tara.*

But she didn't, just whispered, ''I can't.''

They heard cars on the road and someone sigh in the next room.

Isaac yanked on his clothes, jammed the box in his pack and went out into the night.

CHAPTER FOURTEEN

The egg came first!

—Tara Marcus

WHILE HE WAS GONE, Tara tried to sleep. No way. She got up and dressed and packed. She'd have to get a ride to Maternity House to pick up the Subaru. She'd find out what she could about Laura, then head home.

Brushing her hair, she found it smooth and remembered Isaac had combed through it. *He loves me.* Where had he gone?

I hurt him.

She couldn't remember ever in her life having hurt someone that way.

He's never going to forgive this, Tara. He'll never forgive you.

Her instinct was to call a cab, leave a note.

But if she did, it would be burning another bridge.

She waited, wishing for someone to talk to. But Ivy was pregnant and would be sleeping. Her mother would be sleeping in Alaska, and she couldn't talk to Francesca about this. Beulah Ann needed her sleep in Colorado to deal with Chantel, and, anyway…

It was hard to open up.

There was really just one person left.

She wished he'd come back.

ISAAC HADN'T TAKEN her key, and he felt more like breaking down the hotel room door than knocking. But the door opened before he'd even turned off the lights in the rental car.

She stepped back as he came inside, then shut the door behind him.

She was packed.

He showered, changed and threw together his own belongings.

Neither of them spoke, and they each carried their own luggage to the car.

When he'd started the ignition, Tara said, "I'm going to drive myself home."

"Fine."

Blackness circled her stomach. *What have I done?* "Isaac, it would be wrong for me to change my values for you."

"I understand." Under his breath, he added, "Better than you."

"What's that supposed to mean?"

"Tara, I have *this much* patience left."

"I just want to know what you meant. What do you understand better than me?"

"Love."

"Did Heloise ever ask you to change who you are?"

At a stoplight, he stared at her. "Tara, I *did* change. Rwanda changed me. My children changed me. My in-laws changed me. So what? 'I am that I am; for this I came.' Change doesn't destroy the self."

The light turned green.

Silence.

"Well, this change would destroy me."

"How?"

"Do you really need me to spell it out? You know where I've been. People take pieces. People have taken pieces of me since I was a little girl. Now Laura's gone. I've got one piece left, and you want it. And not to cherish. You want to chew it up and spit it out, just like everyone else."

AT MATERNITY HOUSE, Star gave Tara the keys to the Subaru and hugged her again.

Tara held off the hug and grinned. "Hey, I'm fine."

But when she saw the nursing system, left in its bag on the front seat, her knees turned to jelly and her mouth loosed, a precursor to a voiceless cry.

Beside her, Isaac said, "Let me take care of everything. Go back to the Jeep, and I'll be there soon."

"No. I'll take care of it. I'm going inside to talk to Star and the others. I want to know just what's become of Laura."

Isaac leaned against the Subaru. "I'd like to know that myself."

"OKAY," Star said, pouring coffee for Isaac and tea for Tara. "So I told them the baby had been abandoned in your car, and you could see Julia's fiancé was pissed, though he didn't show it. Frankly, I think he's a guy who's going to take responsibility for his child even if things with Julia *don't* work out. He's Hispanic himself and has a big and apparently loving family. But he wanted the charges dropped after he heard the whole story."

Tara's heart fell. She knew she should be happy that Laura would be with her natural family. She tried to imagine the baby on a grandmother's lap and to feel joy for Laura.

Yes, it was there. The love.

"If you want, you two could go through a home study," Star suggested.

Neither Isaac nor Tara bothered to correct her, to say that there was no "you two."

"But I don't think this baby's coming back. I'm telling you, the sergeant has a whole bunch of relatives up in Farmington, New Mexico. I talked to him for quite a while, and he's a good guy, even if Julia is a piece of work."

"She's the birth mother. Star, if you can find out anything, anything about that baby, I'll always want to know."

Star hugged her. "I'll do the best I can, and I'll spread the word here. Does this mean you're in the market for *other* babies?"

Tara shook her head.

On the way out of Maternity House, Star motioned to Tara that she wanted a word alone with her.

Tara told Isaac, "You may as well hit the road. Get back to your kids."

"Thanks for your help, Star. Tara." He nodded goodbye. The birth center door opened, then shut behind him.

"What's the story, Tara?"

A mother cried out in labor, in the birthing area. Familiar sound, oh, so beautiful and familiar.

"What story?"

"Him."

Tara shrugged. "We don't mesh that well." Oh, hell, this was Star. "He wants me to become an LM. I don't want to."

Star laughed, then embraced her friend. "You've

always got people who love you, Tara. Just the way you are.''

IT WAS LATE WHEN she reached Precipice. Beulah Ann welcomed her at the apartment door of Leila and Asad's house. ''Where's Laura?''

Tara told the story as quickly as she could, stumbling over the hard parts, leaving out a great deal.

Beulah Ann asked, ''What about Dr. McCrea? He was looking for you.''

''He found me.''

''Seems he likes you a lot.''

Tara shrugged, wishing she could level with Beulah Ann. They'd suffered some of the same things. But not the same.

Beulah Ann had dragged her inside the spacious basement apartment, where Chantel was sleeping on a futon on the floor. ''I want to do something, Tara. You must feel awful.''

''I've just got to look forward, you know?''

She was cold. Grief and trauma. She started unpacking and made herself a strong infusion of warming herbs. She wrapped herself in sweaters and wool socks and slippers and sat close to the pellet stove, but it was very difficult to warm up. ''How is Leila?''

''Oh, she's just sweet as they come, and Asad's so crazy about her. Leila's told me all these amazing stories about Sudan. Like, a woman is never *forward* with her man, but if she's in the mood for love, she does a smoke ceremony with sandalwood and myrrh and other spices, and he smells it and *knows*. Oh, Tara, I'm just running on, because I don't know what to say. I know how you loved that baby, like she was yours.''

Tara did cry then.

Beulah Ann brought her the infusion. "Drink this, and you'll warm up. Can I draw you a hot bath?"

Isaac scrubbing away at her skin. Bathing her.

Tara felt dizzy. She wanted to call him. But there was nothing left to say.

Was there?

In the kitchen of the apartment, Beulah Ann worked at the stove, filling the place with smells. She brought her food. Placed something around Tara's neck.

"What's this?"

"A charm." Beulah Ann smiled. "Don't ask what for."

Tara reached up and hugged her friend.

THE NEXT MORNING, she and Beulah Ann had a post-partum visit scheduled with Jenny. This, Tara knew, would be a test. Seeing a newborn and mother.

Before the visit, Tara called Ivy and told her almost everything that had happened in Texas, making light of the time in jail and saying as little of Laura as she could and nothing at all of Isaac.

Ivy noticed the omission. "What happened with Dr. Dan's brother?"

"It's over."

Ivy was quiet.

Tara wanted to cheer her sister, help her look forward to the birth. "How's the baby doing? Has Mata checked you? Head's engaged? All systems go?"

"You know, Tara, I wish you'd talk about how *you're* feeling. You just lost *your* baby, and you were in love with this guy. What happened?"

Nothing more to say about Laura. Briefly, Tara repeated what Isaac had said about becoming licensed. "You know I can't do that."

Again her sister was silent.

"This is why I didn't tell you." At least, Ivy wouldn't tell Mom.

"Tara, I believe in direct-entry midwifery—as you do. Good grief, I learned from my grandmother, and Gabby's learning from me. But there are lawsuits igniting all over the country—over *nothing*—nothing even went wrong. We need to build a force of positive service. We need to assist at births."

"I *am* assisting at births."

"But they won't *let* you, Tara. Not in Precipice. I know those people. They'll string you up."

"A good reason not to get married." She bit her tongue, too late.

"He asked you to marry him?"

She couldn't answer that.

"Do you love him?"

"Yes! But no more than my values." She found herself echoing Isaac's words. "'I am that I am—for this I came.'"

Ivy said suddenly, "All right. New subject. I was going to ask a favor. I want to come to Colorado—we'll rent a condo for a month or something—and I'm hoping you'll attend my birth. We were going to do it here at the cabin, ourselves, but I'm not twenty years old anymore. And Mata Iyer only does hospital births."

Tara understood. Though Ivy's thirteen-year-old daughter was studying midwifery and wanted to assist at her mother's birth, she needed an experienced midwife in charge. But— "You're pretty ripe to travel across the country."

Ivy didn't answer.

This must be important to her.

Finally, she said, "I want Gabriela to help. I want some privacy with Cullen. Everything has to be *right*."

Oh, we're getting somewhere. "Why does everything have to be right?"

No comment.

Tara retraced Ivy and Cullen's history and thought she'd hit on the answer. "Are you trying to make something up to him with this baby?"

"You don't need to know."

Tara sat back a bit. Rearranged the phone. She had her answer. "Of course, I'll attend your birth." If they made it as far as Colorado. "And I'll try to round up more affordable accommodations. And Ivy—everything's going to be okay. Cullen *loves* you."

Ivy was slow to answer. "We love each other. Thanks for helping, Tara. I'll call you to say when we're coming. It'll be soon."

"And I'll find you a place to stay."

JUST A FEW MORE phone calls. Twenty-five minutes till they'd leave for Jenny's. She realized abruptly that she'd never gotten her mother's number, never learned where Francesca was staying. *I'll call Dad.*

She tried his home phone, and a woman answered. Her mother.

"Tara? Oh, God, is that you? Your telephone was disconnected, and I called Isaac, and he told me what happened. Dad and I have been haunting this phone, scared to death you'd run off to Mexico again or something. But Isaac said you were on your way home."

Dad and I. This was going to take some getting

used to. "Well, I'm here. Let me give you the number."

"Tara, I'm just aching for you, sweetheart. I wish I could take the pain on myself."

Tara's eyes shifted to Beulah Ann's television, where Chantel was watching *Sesame Street*. Her mother was going to make her cry. *Please stop.* "Dad's there?" She fingered the charm around her neck.

In a moment, her father was on the phone. "You need to learn to stay out of jail."

"Yeah, yeah. Look, I sold the Range Rover, and I want to send you back your money."

"Keep it. You can start your midwifery practice with it. I sure don't need it." A pause. "I'm real sorry about the baby, honey. If you say the word, I'll get her back for you."

The dreamer, the schemer, ready to do anything for his daughter, anything at all. He was the father she'd loved in childhood—when he wasn't drunk or missing, or the kind of drunk that meant missing, which was every kind.

Francesca took the phone back before Tara could answer. "I wish I was there to hold you, Tara. Will you be all right handling Ivy's birth?"

"Oh, sure." She just hoped Ivy would.

AFTER SPEAKING WITH her parents, Tara phoned all the mothers who had donated milk and told them the milk would no longer be needed. By the end of those calls, her thoughts were locked on Laura. She was numb, without energy.

The grief had truly begun.

IT WASN'T HARD. It wasn't hard at all to see this beautiful, happy couple and their little daughter. Mother and baby were nursing fine. Nursing...Tara excused herself from the room. Allergies.

"SO, I CAUGHT everything on the phone about the baby. And picked up some more from Tara. I ran into her yesterday."

Isaac lifted his eyebrows. It was Sunday morning, and he'd agreed to join his brother for a cup of coffee. Precipice was into ski season. The Café International was bustling, the other patrons making their own clatter and din.

His brother asked, "Want me to watch the kids while you get away together for a while?"

"That's a very nice offer. No."

Dan studied his face. "How's that parasite?"

"History." Like Tara. As long as he lived, he would never forget the night she'd sat on the hotel bed and looked at the box containing his grandmother's engagement ring and said, *I can't.*

Dan said, "Well, her sister's coming here to have a baby. Tara's looking for a place for her to spend the month."

"And have the birth?" Isaac tossed back his coffee.

Dan turned up his hands.

Isaac said, "I've gotta go. My dog's outside. Learning 'Stay.'"

He went out in the bracing wind. Raincheck wagged his tail and strained at his leash. Crouching, Isaac stroked the puppy's thick fur and was slobbered with kisses. He wondered how long he'd be haunted by his own dog's name.

TARA WALKED ALONE in the snow that afternoon. When she returned home, Isaac's voice was on the machine. "Dan said you're looking for a condo for your sister to stay in for a month. The new owners of the Victorian want to lease it. They said a thousand dollars. Get back to me."

When Tara called, Oliver answered the phone. Hearing who it was, he said, "You don't like us anymore, do you?"

"I like you!" Good grief. "Your dad and I don't agree about something. That's all. I'm crazy about you. All of you."

"But not him."

"Him, too."

"I am the leader of the Conflict Resolution Team at school. Perhaps I can help resolve your conflict."

Tara laughed. "I wish you could."

"You tell me your side. Dad will tell me his. I will resolve your conflict. *Voilà!*"

"Do you specialize in mediation or arbitration?"

"Both. But with you and Dad, arbitration. Much better."

"Oliver, I think your dad and I—just need to have our differences."

"He wants the phone, anyhow. Here."

"Tara?"

His voice. His voice. Maybe it was Oliver's words that had swayed her. Maybe seeing Jenny and Yul and their baby. Maybe Beulah Ann's charm. So she had one piece left. She'd give it to Isaac and maybe get something new in return. She wanted something new. Something besides pain.

The words expelled from her mouth like afterbirth. "I'll get licensed." *There. There. I've agreed.* Tears broke through as she spoke. At least he couldn't see her face.

A part of herself, maybe all of her, was gone.

He said, "I want to see you."

SHE TOOK HER pager, and by starlight they skied the Tomboy road up to the miner's cabin, Raincheck running in the snow beside them.

Tara felt flimsy. *At least, I should be able to stay out of jail now.*

His skis beside hers.

Poles in the icy snow.

Hooves clattered on the snow ahead of them, deer dispersing into the forest, and the dog panted and strained at his leash.

In his first glimpse of Tara tonight, Isaac had seen the difference. It was what they said happened to a child who underwent pharaonic circumcision. One day joyful, strong, secure. Then solemn. Changed.

For as long as he could, he'd pretended it was his imagination.

But you couldn't pretend forever.

He stopped skiing to hug her. "You okay?"

She nodded, eyes shimmering.

Shit.

"Laura?"

"Can we just ski?" And she did. "Raincheck. Come here, silly. You're tangled in your leash."

He wasn't supposed to see her wipe her eyes, so he acted as though he hadn't.

They reached the shack.

Isaac gave her herbal tea in a thermos. His hands to steady hers. His hands making sure her headband covered her ears.

He gently grasped the leather thong hanging around her neck, with the small bundle dangling from it. His head was light. He tried to kiss her, and she let him, her response weak. *That's two of us.*

How was he ever going to say the word "marry" to her again?

He released their bindings, stuck their skis in the snow.

They went into the dark cabin. While the puppy shook out his fur, Isaac threw logs in the stove and started a fire.

Leaving Raincheck busy with a bone, they snuggled between the sheets on the lumpy old mattress. No light but the stars in the single window.

Being close to him hurt. Tara thought she understood the expression "coming unglued." *My body feels like one big ache.* And the tears came again, hard, as they had in El Paso. With no one else could she really grieve. Not this whole-body, whole-being insanity of longing.

She trembled in his arms, and Isaac heard and felt the sobs become hysterical, blending with rhythmic, gasping breaths. He spoke the litany. Even. Firm. Caring. "Tara. Don't do it. Stop. Stop now." Several rounds, the same words and others. "Hey, look who's worried."

He lifted the puppy onto the bed, and the wagging tail and the dog's attempts to get closer drew Tara's attention. She petted him. Took a deep breath. "Hi, cutie."

When Raincheck began exploring the rest of the bed and settled in to chew on the pillow, Isaac put him back on the floor. "Those meltdowns can be habit-forming, Tara. Don't get the habit."

"Right." She nodded. "Thanks."

His shoulder felt good under her cheek.

I've got to be strong. He's in love with a strong woman. She started an inner pep talk. *You've agreed to be a licensed midwife, Tara. No big deal. You're going to go on and attend births.*

She clung to him.

There was his mouth.

Isaac.

"I'm sorry," she said. "For that night. It was awful."

"I was…upset." The bed was warming up, and he opened her parka. Found her waist.

One of her legs worked between his. She said, "I think it's time for that rain check."

The puppy on the floor lifted his head, looked at them and resumed licking his bone.

CHAPTER FIFTEEN

When Tara was born, the midwife caught her in
the water, yet she seemed to swim to the surface
on her own power. She's done the same thing
ever since.

—Francesca Walcott

HER SKIN AGAINST HIS, heat around him. "Tara."

She held him harder, felt his muscles and her own
scars, warrior marks she'd learned to live with. She
didn't want to remember coming by them and for survival had learned to forget.

But someone had stolen her armor.

He had.

"No." She broke away.

Isaac sat up partway. Her mouth was open, her anguish spilling out. She started talking, almost lucidly.

"Always a matter of eyes... Be no one. Hide your
eyes. Look dead. You needed to be no one, hold your
spirit where no one could get it. They would break
it...." She squeezed her eyes shut, her face closing
things out. "No one I loved...has ever tried so hard
to break me...as you." Her eyes sprang open. She sat
up and was suddenly spitting fury and profanity.
"Thanks so much! Thank you so very much for trying
to make me into someone else, Isaac!"

She was a grenade, pulling her own pin, and he grabbed her. "Cool it."

She hit him once, hard, on the neck. "Let me go! I will *not* cool it! I will not! You're the lover from hell! And heaven." She was climbing over him, away from him, on the bed. She swore at him viciously. "License. Play the game. Okay. For you. I love you that much. Happy?"

He shook his head. "Tara."

The same voice that could reach into her when the meltdowns came.

Her breath shook. A gasp.

Then she was back under the covers with him, grabbing him. "Once in a lifetime. Most people don't ever get it. Maybe it's not that way with you."

"You need to speak more clearly."

Her eyes beseeched him. "I'll do *anything* for you. Don't you see?"

He saw.

His gaze dropped from hers.

"The feeling really isn't mutual, is it?"

He released a long-held breath. How did a person talk about this? "We've had…a battle of wills. I see there was a price. Let's not be making wrong assumptions."

Raincheck whined at the door.

Isaac got up, threw on some clothes and his boots. He snapped on the dog's leash. "Don't go anywhere. Don't do anything."

"You mean, like get dressed?"

It was a hit, and he wanted to double over. *"The feeling is mutual. I love you!"*

He went out and slammed the door.

When he returned, she was dressed.

He said, "You're not going *anywhere*."

A LONG WHILE LATER, he was deep inside her, and she cried out as she had on an afternoon weeks ago, verbalizing every emotion she felt for him in sounds that weren't words.

He shook, shattering against her, banging the bed into the wall while the ancient mattress seemed to disintegrate beneath them.

After she saw his tears, she could talk.

She couldn't not talk.

She vomited up the past.

TARA WENT HOME to her own bed, in Leila's basement apartment, and woke in a sweat, her stomach roiling, knowing she'd screamed. She'd been in Chile, and so had Isaac and Laura. Miserable place of the unconscious. All kinds of doors in her mind were flying open, releasing predators.

Beulah Ann crawled onto the bed to hold her. "It's all over now, Tara. I'm going to bring you Mam'zelle Eve's Stop Shaking Tea."

"I talked to Isaac. I told him everything." *Her stomach.*

"Well, you don't need to tell another soul unless you want to."

Tara ran for the bathroom, and when she returned she told things to Beulah Ann, and Beulah Ann's eyes said the secrets would stay with her.

Hot tea and clutching her charm and concluded her story, saying, "So, I'm infertile."

"What about in vitro fertilization?"

"No, thanks."

"Well, I know someone with at least three children who're missing their mother."

Stop Shaking Tea. Was it helping her stomach? It didn't feel like anything would. "Is there more of this?"

"You bet."

Bang, bang, bang. A fist on the outside door. "Beulah Ann!"

At the sound of the male voice, Tara instinctively grabbed some corduroys and a sweater to wear over her long T-shirt.

Beulah Ann didn't bother to tie on a bathrobe. Her face was hard to read as she left Tara's side and marched to the door. The apartment was one big room with a bath and kitchen, two futon beds, some free-box chairs and Beulah Ann's TV. Cold wafted from the door.

"Hey, wife, have you missed me?"

"I miss you more often than you're here. You can't come in, Lane."

Tara glimpsed the cowboy hat and a boyish face, fair with a scattering of freckles.

"Ah, Beulah Ann. Me and Steamboat just wanted a place to crash for the night. And I wanted to see you and my baby girl. We're headed down Cortez way. You look so good, Beulah Ann."

"I don't need you to tell me that, Lane Cockburn."

"Beulah Ann?" Tara's interjection was tentative.

"I'll be back." Beulah Ann shut and latched the door, bolting her husband out.

"I can go somewhere," Tara volunteered. "I can go up to Isaac's."

"You're in no shape to drive."

"You're not afraid to be alone with him, are you?"

"With Lane?" Beulah Ann rolled her eyes. "He wouldn't hurt a fly."

"Is he drunk?"

"No. He acts it though, don't he?"

"What about Steamboat?"

"Steamboat's a horse. But this is your home."

"I wouldn't let that interfere with a conjugal visit. Let me grab some stuff and I'm out of here."

ISAAC WAS AWAKE when she tapped on his bedroom window. He let her in the back door, through the laundry room, and stole her back to his room, where he locked the door. "Raincheck, enough." He had to restrain the puppy from jumping, licking her to death.

"Beulah Ann's husband showed up, and there's not much privacy."

"Well, there's plenty here."

His bed. His sheets.

His arms.

She had to get up to use the bathroom. Body fluids pouring from every orifice, to the strobe of a private slide show. Images flashing. A flood, all through a strange, manageable haze. The Stop Shaking Tea.

Isaac sat on the edge of the bed, petting Raincheck and listening. *Talk about a purge.*

When she came out, he said, "I guess you don't need any garlic and raw rice to chew on."

"Ha ha." She clutched her stomach and sank down beside him.

"Let's get you something to drink. Anything sound good?"

She wished she knew Mam'zelle Eve's recipe.

LANE WAS GONE when Tara returned home in the morning after little sleep. Though weak, she brought

Danielle with her. Danielle had asked to come, and no one had objected, nor had the children seemed surprised by Tara's presence. Isaac asked her to bring his lunch to the clinic. *Just need to see your face,* he said. It had been a very long night.

At the apartment, Beulah Ann was washing dishes and singing "Someday Soon," and Danielle sat down on the floor and began to play with Chantel.

Beulah Ann said, "Leila wants to talk to you when you get a minute. Nothing urgent."

"Thanks." Tara needed to call the state registry, make some contacts, figure out what hoops she'd have to jump through come January. An internal voice spoke over the numb of survival, calling her spineless.

Ghost pains, her former self, followed her everywhere, calling her whore. For Isaac, for Isaac she had done this.

The feeling's mutual.

But he had won, her tender, strong-willed lover. The healer ministering to her all night while her body released rapes she couldn't count, while her mind saw forgotten faces. Impossible to hold anything against Isaac. It was enough to hold the shell of her former self in one piece and know she still had a body and heart and mind and soul and that he loved them without reserve.

Just certify, Tara. She must do it and get over it.

But she had no peace, even reading to Danielle and Chantel, even when Beulah Ann exclaimed, "I had the best idea last night, Tara!"

"Hm?"

"A way to link with the hospital!"

Tara's laugh was mirthless. Eye-stinging.

"We need to make a women's center. We need to—"

Feet on the stairs. Leila's soft knock. Tara let her in.

"Hi, Leila," called Beulah Ann. "Tara, we need to give birth classes and breast-feeding support. We'll inform people about hospital birth and homebirth."

"That is a good idea," said Leila. "Tara, I saw your car, and I wanted to hug you. Beulah Ann told me about little Laura."

Tara accepted her embrace. "She's with her mother, now."

Leila shook her head sadly. "You and Dr. Isaac will have a baby now?"

Not this again. "No. I can't have children."

"You have me, Tara."

Tara picked up Danielle and chased away the ghosts. She held the little girl tight and tugged one of her braids.

She'd never seen the glass as half-empty before. And now Isaac's daughter was in her arms. Where was her own heart?

"What do you think of my idea? I thought also, we could have women write about their birth experiences…"

Beulah Ann stopped at a harsh look from Leila.

Tara smiled at Beulah Ann. "It's a cool idea."

SHE BROUGHT ISAAC'S lunch—and Raincheck—to the clinic.

He had flowers for her, and he said, "I'll make dinner tonight, okay?"

She nodded, knowing she would spend the night again.

Every night, forever.

THE NEXT DAY, Ivy's family was due in Precipice. Isaac had made arrangements with Tara to help ready the Victorian for them. An excuse to see her.

When he picked her up at Leila's house, she climbed into the Land Cruiser with her birth bag and said, "I'm not going to do it."

Isaac took a breath. "What? What aren't you going to do?" Six hours ago, they'd awoken together in his bed.

But, all right, in the past twenty-four hours he'd sensed her backbone rising. Was glad to see it.

"I'm not going to become a whore to you and your brethren in Precipice. I'm not participating." She swallowed. "Sorry. Sorry I said it like that. Sorry."

"It's fine. It's okay."

She met his eyes. He nodded and held her, kissing her hair.

There would be a price for this, too, he knew.

But it was his turn to pay.

Again.

They'd both been paying all along.

WHEN IVY SAW HER sister and Isaac McCrea outside the Victorian, it was with waves of relief. *I'm here. Tara's here. Tara, I need you now.*

Gabriela had left the car first, was the first into Tara's arms. Cullen opened the passenger door for his wife, reached over to unfasten her seat belt. "Doing okay?" Kissing her, eyes in hers. "I love you."

A cramp started low in Ivy's back, inching up her spine. The pulse. The pulse of birth.

Feeling otherworldly, haunted by a telephone ques-

tion she'd never answered, Ivy embraced her husband.
"This baby matters so much," she whispered.

He drew back. *"Ivy."*

The hurt on his face both eased her mind and
stabbed her with guilt. Tara had known. Tara had
known and tried to talk her out of what she was feeling.

As he helped her from the car, Ivy felt his distress.

"I love you," he repeated.

There was guilt in his eyes, too.

Ivy went to her sister and embraced her. Tara
looked so thin. But she had someone beside her, someone who looked strong enough, strong enough for her.
Tara was saying, "This is Ivy."

A contraction. Not prelabor or false-labor or...

Her water broke, splattering over Isaac McCrea's
canvas pants and hiking boots.

The tingling started through him, the awareness of
things happening, of knowing exactly what to do. He
felt Heloise caressing his head, loving him forever,
somewhere else and inside him. *Be with Tara. Work
together on this, like you used to work with me.*

She's a midwife. Uncertified.

A pregnant stranger was vomiting on his shoes.

He was wholly present.

"Ivy," he said, "do you have babies fast or slow?"

Her husband said, "Fast."

"Let's go inside."

IVY'S CRIES BECAME intense. Panting wails as she
pushed the baby's head toward her daughter's waiting
hands.

Isaac stood by, ready to deal with what might come.
That wail of birth.

"Here's her head, Mama. There's a cord. It's one loop. I can get it."

Isaac McCrea's gloved hands closed over Gabriela's as she moved the cord, loosening it.

"Push?" Gabriela asked him.

"Gently."

Ivy grimaced, groaning, crying, as the baby slid through her birth canal, slid out. In her hands now. "Oh, baby. Oh, my baby! Oh, my baby!"

"He's a boy, Dad."

Tara made a sudden movement beside him. As a current of knowing passed between them, she grabbed him, whispered, "She's going to bleed."

The placenta came in a rush of blood. It was incomplete.

Tara was on her sister's uterus, then, massaging the sides. "Turn off the lights, Isaac. Just leave the lamp."

He watched the blood gather in Tara's stainless steel placenta bowl. Still coming.

Isaac caught the mother's gaze. "Ivy, the placenta is incomplete. I'm going in for the rest. Just hang in there. I've done this before."

Cullen took his wife's hand.

Keeping light tension on the cord with one gloved hand, Isaac worked the other up inside the vaginal canal, constantly aware of her pain level. He found her cervix, found the remaining piece of placenta, searched for a loose edge. He lifted the remainder of the placenta away from the uterus, balling it into a mass. Membranes trailed out after his hand. "Ivy, cough for me. There you go."

She expelled the membranes.

"Tara, get an IV going, and Cullen, call 911." He took over the uterine massage. Ivy already had her baby at the breast, coaxing her to nurse. "That's good."

"So are you. I see why Tara loves you."

The IV was running, and Tara called out the meds she added to it.

The bleeding had stopped when the paramedics arrived.

The sheriff was with them—and a woman Tara didn't recognize. "Tara Marcus?"

Tara shut her eyes, then opened them.

Isaac and the sheriff saw each other at the same moment.

"Dr. McCrea, I didn't realize you were here. Could I have a word with you?"

Heart racing, adrenaline still surging, Isaac stepped out of the room with the sheriff, who introduced the woman. "This is Maxine Justice, from the Department of Health..."

Ivy said, "Tara, he's an angel."

"Yeah. He's the best." Ivy mustn't bleed again.

Isaac moved back into the doorway of the downstairs bedroom, the birth room. The sheriff asked if Tara carried any pharmaceuticals.

"No. No," Isaac lied almost reflexively and thought he heard Heloise laughing delightedly. Talk about sticking his neck out. He felt the blade already. "She's been helping me with this emergency. She's an EMT."

Maxine spoke to the sheriff, who shifted his bulk. The woman pointed at a Guatemalan bag on the floor. Tara's birth kit.

Isaac rubbed his neck. Thinking of Ivy, he guided both the sheriff and Maxine away from the room. "You can't upset that patient. She almost bled to death. You want her to go into shock? The EMT you want to arrest is her sister.''

The sharp voice of Maxine Justice rang through the hall. ''Tara Marcus is practicing midwifery without a license. This has been known for some time. A judge is presently issuing a search warrant for her apartment.''

Isaac eased back against the wall as the paramedics carried Ivy past. Tara, Cullen and Gabriela walked beside the stretcher, Gabriela carrying her baby brother.

The sheriff made eye contact with a deputy, who followed the group.

''Dr. McCrea, I'm sorry about this. I'm going to have to take her in.''

What to say without sinking Tara deeper?

Nothing.

But he kept opening his mouth, and the sheriff was waiting. Maxine Justice stood in the open doorway of the Victorian, keeping her quarry in sight.

Isaac said quietly, ''Can you…give her into my custody?'' He would gladly stuff the sheriff's campaign coffers if that's what it took.

The sheriff took his measure.

Isaac turned his back on the door. ''She was tortured as a prisoner in Chile.''

The other man made a deep, compassionate sound and slowly nodded. He patted Isaac's shoulder before he called, ''Deputy! Please read Miss Marcus her rights.''

Isaac's pager buzzed. The clinic. What time was it? Past two, no doubt. He headed back into the birth room, shut the door, and grabbed the phone.

His first call was to Beulah Ann.

TARA WAS PRETTY sure Butch Cassidy and the Sundance Kid had spent time in this cell. Besides their memory, she had the place entirely to herself. There were prisoners elsewhere, she could hear them, but Tara had been told she was a "security risk."

By the time Isaac showed up, she'd decided that was a joke. No strip search. None of the usual hell. They'd taken her barette and her charm from Beulah Ann—*So you don't hurt yourself, ma'am*—but that was it.

Seeing Isaac, she reached her arms through the bar. "Is Ivy all right?"

"Yes. And Cullen Michael. Gabriela picked it." Iron divided their hug. But his hands still found the place between her shoulder blades, found the back of her neck. "They're processing papers in the front room. I'm going to take you home."

She eased back from the cold bars and rubbed herself warm. "What about Beulah Ann and Chantel?"

Isaac glanced toward the door, then put a finger to his lips.

Tara drew a breath. Any thoughts she hadn't spent on her sister were for Beulah Ann.

"Did they search the apartment?"

"Yes. Your roommate borrowed a friend's Hummer and has taken her daughter and gone to Gunnison for a visit, taking her favorite possessions with her. She's not implicated in this."

Tara wiped her eyes. *He must have warned her.* "You know, you really come through, doc? At the birth, too." Composing herself, she asked, "Who called the sheriff? Dr. Scarborough?"

"I doubt it." If Isaac had to guess... Pat, the nurse

fired by the hospital, might have dropped Tara's name to Maxine Justice.

Tara glanced about. "How do I rate this nice, historical hoosegow?" Her hand caressed one stone wall. "No comfortable togs? No cellmate but a chipmunk? No glass on the window!"

"Cold?"

"Yes, I'm cold!"

He covered her hands on the bars, rubbed her skin warm. "Scared?"

"Never." She didn't move her hands. *Isaac.* "You don't have to...stand by me. I got myself into this."

"Having second thoughts?"

She shook her head, an emphatic no, then met his eyes. "I've done a lot of things for a lot of reasons, but telling you I'd get licensed was the sorriest decision I ever made—and for the worst reason. Not because I thought it was best, but just because I loved you and wanted you and thought I was letting the opportunity of a lifetime slip away."

"I'm not going anywhere."

"Do you know, in my whole life I've never known *passion,* except with you? I love you, I love your children, but I need to think for myself! I need to breathe. To live. Don't you see? I have to be free."

He scanned the walls of her cell, examined the bars. Looked at her.

"Oh, shut up," she muttered before he said a word. "Come here, so I can kiss you."

Between the bars, tongues caressing.

Some keys jangled, and a deputy cleared his throat. "Miss Marcus?"

CHAPTER SIXTEEN

But what is chance? How does it differ from odds? If you were in Rwanda in April of 1994 and you were Tutsi or believed to be Tutsi or believed to be part Tutsi, your odds differed from your chances.

—David McCrea

THE APARTMENT WAS a shambles, her records and anything else related to midwifery gone. Beulah Ann must have taken her birth bag and books to Gunnison. Tara would call her soon.

Isaac was already packing her remaining belongings when Leila came down. The pregnant woman hugged Tara. "Don't you two clean. I will."

"Oh, Leila." Tara sighed, shaking her head. Apologizing.

Leila said, "You stop that. I'm still going to become a midwife. Just not a stubborn one."

"Let me come up and write you a rent check. I haven't spoken to Beulah Ann yet, but I'm..." *You're coming to my house.*

There would be community reaction to her just moving in.

"I'm getting married."

Behind her, Isaac continued packing.

"Dr. McCrea! Congratulations. Isn't that what you say here?"

"Yes, Leila. Thank you."

OUTSIDE, BY THEIR CARS, with snow falling in her hair, she said, "I've made it awkward, haven't I?"

"Only if you don't marry me."

She noticed he couldn't quite smile. That old wound she'd inflicted at the Sajuarro Motel. She whispered, "I'll pay you. I'll pay you to marry me. Everything I own."

He did smile then, with snow on his eyelashes. "Is there a child involved?"

"Just yours. All of yours."

He hugged her tight and through the powerful waves of happiness felt Heloise gently leaving him— to her.

THEY TOLD THE CHILDREN when they went home, and David said, "D&D every night!"

Danielle climbed up on Tara's knee on the couch and settled against her as though to stay forever.

And Oliver asked, "Tara, do you like snowboarding?"

"I've never tried, but I'm willing to try!"

When the children had dispersed to their own activities, Tara remained on the couch with Isaac. "I need to call my parents. Gosh, how do I reach my mom? Every time she calls it's from Dad's house."

Her eyes suddenly shot to Isaac's.

He laughed.

Oh.

I won't think about this.

However— "I haven't warned you about my dad."

Oh, yes, she had. Daddy's girl. Isaac doubted that Charlie Marcus, for all his shortcomings, came up with twenty thousand dollars overnight for just anyone.

He touched her hair. "Give me your dad's number. There's a right way to do this." His eyes caressed her, and he said, "I'm a dad, too."

"MARCUS AVIATION. Charlie here."

Isaac thought of tigers and pictured Paul Newman. But Tara had gotten her brown eyes somewhere. "This is Isaac McCrea calling from Colorado."

A beat. "Dr. McCrea. Hello."

Keep going, Isaac.

Oliver started down the stairs, reading a snowboarding magazine as he walked, and Tara stood to head him off. "Hey, Oliver, show me your board."

"I'm sorry we haven't had a chance to meet yet," Isaac said. "But your daughter is the most beautiful—" He had to steady his voice. "The most wonderful, incredible woman...on earth. I love her and would like your permission to marry her."

Tara was on the stairs with Oliver. Her heart trembled at the emotion in Isaac's voice, and Oliver peered down into the living room with interest. Tara said, "Remember well, Oliver. That's how it's done. Now, let's go see your snowboard."

Charlie Marcus cleared his throat. "Yes. If Tara wants you...that's fine."

And Isaac heard a man who felt much more than he said.

MINUTES LATER, Tara was on the phone with her mother, whom she'd had to call at her dad's house.

After Francesca said how pleased she was, Tara said, "It's going to be soon. Can you come?"

"Oh. Oh, yes! I'll—We'll be there."

Tara touched her top teeth with her tongue. Glancing at Isaac, she managed to get out, "Should we arrange...separate rooms?"

"Ahhh." Her mother couldn't speak either!

You know—we'll make our own arrangements, Tara. Don't worry about anything, and ask Dad for whatever you need."

Soon after, Tara replaced the receiver and turned to Isaac. "They're making their *own* arrangements. Can you believe it?"

Isaac considered the voice he'd heard on the phone and Tara's mother and then imagined Tara in twenty years. "Actually. Yes."

ISAAC ARRANGED FOR the same judge who had issued the search warrant to marry them two weeks later, as soon as Ivy felt up to it. She'd be standing up with Tara. Dan—who had taken Tara's client load—was the best man.

Charlie and Francesca arrived from Alaska four days before the wedding, and Tara and Isaac met them at the airport. Listening to the plane making its final descent to Precipice's notoriously steep runway, Tara bit her lip and cast a glance at Isaac. She paced the small terminal, eyeing the glass cases from Precipice stores and shaking her head whenever she thought of her parents.

Isaac skimmed a copy of *The Denver Post*, then set it down and went to the window.

The minutes ticked by, and then the plane was on the ground, the passengers coming through the glass door. Francesca's hair was blowing slightly as she glanced over her shoulder at a gray-haired man in a flight jacket and jeans. Then she turned and saw Tara. She held out her arms, and her father embraced her next—"Hey, beautiful"—and shook hands with Isaac.

They collected luggage, and it wasn't until they were settled in Isaac's car, Francesca riding up front, that Tara turned to her father. "So…where are you staying?"

"The Springs." Precipice's finest resort and spa. "Thought we'd rent some skis and do it like rich folks."

Tara averted her face, trying to suppress a goofy smile. They'd made arrangements, all right.

On THE DAY OF THE WEDDING, everyone met outside the courthouse, children and families—her parents, Isaac's mother…friends. Leila and Asad. Beulah Ann and her boyish husband, Lane, cleaned up good in a black Stetson and Wranglers and a bolo tie, holding little Chantel. Beulah Ann was back from Gunnison. Back to stay. Tara had been on the phone to her parents several times in the past week, and she and Isaac had wedding gifts waiting at home from Charlie and Francesca.

The wedding party had brought champagne, plastic flutes and Oliver's boom box, and Raincheck and Dan's dog on leashes. The fiftyish judge had agreed to take a short hike with them up to a frozen waterfall, to marry them there.

It was snowing as they walked, and beside the waterfall, Tara found herself saying, "I, Tara, take you, Isaac, to be my lawfully wedded husband…" Her voice trembled, and a tear froze on her cheek. "…To have and to hold…"

The judge led her through the words, led them both through the vows. His eyes creased at the corners as they kissed.

Oliver yelled, "Now!" and the children pelted them with snowballs.

The dogs raced through the drifts.

A champagne cork popped.

Ivy switched on the boom box. She, Tara, Gabriela and Danielle had spent hours cooing over little Cully while they picked out and recorded songs for the tape. Now, the speakers sang one of Danielle's favorites from Walt Disney's *Sleeping Beauty,* "Once Upon a Dream," and Tara and Isaac danced with snow in their hair.

The music changed to Ella Fitzgerald's "Love Is Here to Stay," and Charlie took his tall daughter's hand to dance. He said, "I like him, honey. You be happy."

"You, too," she murmured, casting her eyes down.

Her father laughed a little.

After their dance, the Temptations began singing "My Girl," and he said, "Well, well, well," and crossed the snow to take Francesca's hands, to hold her hands and dance with her and croon to her with poetry and vulnerability and a bush pilot's certainty and snow falling all around. Cullen kissed Ivy as he danced with her, and Isaac, arms about Tara, murmured in her hair, "This is some party. And you're some woman."

Dan McCrea spoke to Gabriela, who stood holding her baby brother. "A little bird told me you want to be a midwife like your mother."

She seemed taken aback. "I'm a dancer."

"Oh." He nodded, assessing her. "Just thought I might try to point you toward medicine instead."

Gabriela looked thoughtful. Then said blandly, "No. Dance. If I don't break an ankle out here. Oh, little Cully. Look, he opened his eyes."

AFTER THE WEDDING, Isaac and Tara skied up to the miner's shack, leaving even Raincheck behind. At the cabin, he lit the stove while Tara put bedding on the new mattress they'd bought.

"Comfortable," Isaac said a while later.

"I like it."

He rolled on his side. "You know, our friends Leila and Asad have told me that in Sudan the man pays a bride price."

"*Before* the wedding. And the woman undergoes a terrible ceremony when she's a little girl."

"Well, you've had your own terrible ceremonies. But the bride price is a nice custom. All that gold. Leila loves hers very much."

Tara never wore gold.

From the floor, he brought up a box he'd concealed until that moment. He opened it.

White gold. Platinum. And the gems of the mountains. He draped necklaces on her, earrings and rings and bracelets. He brushed her hair with a jeweled brush, green stones set in silver.

"Isaac. You're crazy."

"You're sounding a little like Leila already."

She sounded happy.

"And since I have no cattle, I'm also giving you some property."

"What?"

"Now, be sure to act grateful and remember that it's possible to take something ugly and make it beautiful."

"What?" Tara repeated, not bothering to rise from the pillow, feeling like a queen. She wasn't taking these things off till she had to catch a baby.

"The Columbine."

She saw it at once in her mind.

The women's center.

But it could only become a reality if...

If I can stay out of jail.

And do it without compromising her principles. If she had to cave in, she wasn't sure she'd feel like practicing midwifery at all.

THE D.A.'S OFFICE was willing to cut a deal. If Tara could pass tests for a midwifery license as of January second and no later, they would drop charges. She knew the abruptio placentae, that long-ago emergency, was at issue. The hospital didn't want it to come out.

By Christmas, Tara was tired of holding up, tired of carrying the banner while the people who loved her begged her to drop it.

Everyone but Isaac.

Her family had all left the week before, but still she'd heard from them on the subject, as she had from Leila and Beulah Ann.

On Christmas Eve, after dinner with Ivy's family and putting out gifts for the children, up high where Raincheck couldn't reach them, Tara cuddled on the couch with Isaac. "It would probably be a great Christmas present for you if I dropped all of this."

"Actually, I have a better idea. Come on."

The bedroom.

As they made love, she felt some familiar cramping, which excitement eased and finally overcame.

But afterward, she remembered.

Menses. As usual.

She headed for the bathroom to deal with it. Remembering what she and Isaac had just experienced, the love they shared night after night, she stared down at her own blood, wishing there were fairy godmothers.

HER MOTHER CALLED in the morning from Talkeetna.

"Merry Christmas, Tara! How are you, sweetie?"

"Good. Really good." As she had many times in talking to her mother since the wedding, she contemplated those first nights after Laura was gone. How she'd told Isaac about Chile. She wanted her mother to know. To know, somehow, that she really was all right. It was Mia who had changed her, Mia's being missing, then dead, and her mother's response.

And everything Tara had never let Francesca do for *her*. The times she'd gone missing.

There were things she wanted to say, things she'd wanted to say when her mother came for the wedding. But Dad was always around, and this...this was for Francesca.

"Mom, I want to talk to you. Really talk. Is now okay, or shall I call you back?"

"Now is fine. What is it?"

Tara shut herself in the bedroom, away from her family. "I just...want to tell you—the truth about some things." She hesitated, unwilling to distress her mother. "I just want you to know...I've talked to Isaac about Chile. And Mexico. I kind of—spit it all up. Before you came. It was actually quite physical."

"Oh, darling."

"But I'm okay. I just— I'm sorry for worrying you. For being a jerk."

"Tara, you're not a jerk. You're a brave, strong woman. Thank you for telling me what you just did. He takes good care of you."

In the background, someone growled, "He'd better."

Tara giggled. "I'll talk to Dad in a minute." She sobered. "Oh, Mom. This is hard. This legal thing. I've always *sworn* that if it came to this I'd fight it out. But I never imagined someone would be offering me a halfway-pleasant alternative. And that's what makes me sick. At this point, it *looks* pleasant. They have me. Practicing midwifery without a license." She stopped talking.

Waited.

Finally, Francesca spoke. "Tara, many many midwives have stood in your shoes. The victory never tastes like victory, darling, believe me. Only attending births feels that way. You will come to resent every hour you're away from your work. And you'll wonder if you've done the right thing, after all." Her mother paused. "And, Tara—about Chile. And Mexico. You must know, I would kill those men, if I could. Every last one."

Boadicea.

A lump in Tara's throat gave way. Crying, she said, "Maybe I've always been afraid you'd try."

On New Year's Day, while Isaac's mother stayed in Precipice with the children, Tara and Isaac set out for Denver, for Tara's tests. Dan McCrea had passed her on practical skills, having seen her at the birth of Lorena Marie Preston. The hospital was talking "limited privileges." Now, she needed to sit for the written test.

Tara knew the questions backward and forward, and when she came out, Isaac said, "Well?"

"It could be tougher. Let's go honeymoon."

They stayed at his family's cabin, skiing and snowshoeing and making love in his parents' bed. Laura had been there with them the time before.

They were making love when Tara said, "I wish I could make a baby with you."

"So do I. Am I crushing you?"

"Yes. Don't stop."

"I wish I could make a baby with you," she whispered again.

"You want to see a fertility expert?"

"No. But I wish—"

He held his finger to her lips. "Be here, Tara. Just be here."

WHEN SHE CAME BACK to Precipice a certified and registered midwife, Tara turned, with Beulah Ann and Leila, to producing a book of local birth—and adoption—stories. They met with Rich Scarborough and Dan to explain their plans for the Columbine—a women's center—and both men were enthusiastic and agreed to spread the word to their clients. An olive branch had been extended and accepted.

Leaving Dr. Scarborough's office, Tara turned and grinned. She flashed the two men a peace sign.

Her brother-in-law laughed. "Get out of here."

But out in the parking lot, Beulah Ann, Leila and Tara banded together and let out victory whoops that echoed all the way to the ski slopes.

Between midwifery appointments and driving the

children to and from school, Tara edited the birth stories and formatted them on Isaac's computer. David presented artwork—snow scenes, ski scenes, a picture of the Columbine. A local historian wrote the history of the Columbine and the ghost town of Tomboy.

By Valentine's Day, the book was ready to go to the printer in Montrose, and by March, the books the printer had assembled were in the local bookstore. Two rooms in the Columbine were completed and already furnished—one as an examining room, the other as a playroom, library, and waiting room.

Tara, Beulah Ann and Leila had sent invitations throughout the community to a celebratory opening on the spring equinox, March twenty-first. Tara had even sent one to her mother in Alaska.

On the twentieth, she received a phone call in return.

"Mom, how are you?"

"Fine. Dad wanted to come down for your celebration. But he's busy now, flying."

"Oh, that's okay." Tara didn't ask how things were going. If she got into a real conversation with her mother, she'd end up talking about something else— something she didn't want to discuss until she was sure. Or at least until she'd had a chance to tell Isaac. "I wish you could be here. If we have enough people we're going to join hands and do a circle dance around the building. We're going to read selections from the birth book."

"It sounds beautiful, honey. And you and Isaac are happy?"

"*Blissful.*"

When she'd hung up the phone, Tara grabbed her coat to head for town and pick up the mail. Isaac had taken the children cross-country skiing, but she'd had an appointment with a client and couldn't go.

Inside the post office, she met Jack, her friend who tended bar at the Riviera. "Tara!"

"Hi." It seemed natural not to hug him, and he didn't hug her.

Instead, he said, "Heard you married the doctor man."

"That's old news. We just had our third anniversary. Three months, that is. Have you bought a copy of the birth book to support the clinic?"

"Tara, I do not want to read birth stories."

"It's for a good cause," she pressed.

He laughed and shook his head. "You look happy, Tara. Really happy."

"I am."

She opened the mailbox for Mountain Midwifery first. On top of issues of the *Birth Gazette* and *Midwifery Today* was a letter from Star. PHOTO ENCLOSED.

Tara tucked the other mail under her arm and tore it open. A picture of Laura fell out, a studio shot of her and Julia and Rob, her new husband. The family had sent the photo to Maternity House, and Star had sent it to Tara.

For a moment, it rushed back, the baby at her breast. Hugging all her mail to her, she rushed from the clinic and out to the Subaru. Behind the steering wheel, she drew deep breaths, thinking of her missed period. *It's okay. It's good that Laura is with her family.*

But her rapes came at her relentlessly and then the healing, the healing from the child she'd nursed. And from Isaac. *Isaac.* She pulled herself together enough to drive away from the post office, to drive up to the

Victorian. The tears fell again as she made her way up the Tomboy road.

I can't be pregnant.

She was alone in the house, and she threw herself on the bed she shared with Isaac, breathing the pillow that held his scent. *I want his baby. I want his baby.*

Door shutting behind her, his body covering hers. The picture being taken from her hand.

His lips drank her skin.

"I want your baby." *Could I be pregnant with your baby?*

"You are my baby, Tara. You're my lady, my lover, my wife. Shhh. I know it won't stop." Him peeling off her clothes, penetrating her. Slow. Good.

She clung to his hands on each side of her.

Skin and motion behind the locked door of their sanctuary, their place of love. Holding her, bodies together, moving.

His murmurings. Kisses between her shoulder blades and under her hair, caressing her jaw. Hands cradling her breasts.

Intimacy.

They separated, faced each other, came back together, were in each other's eyes.

They embraced, so tight.

He asked if she would like to adopt his children.

CHAPTER SEVENTEEN

The birth was very painful, but Dr. Dan McCrea
was patient, and it wouldn't have gone right but
not for trust—trust between all kinds of people
who wouldn't have trusted before. But my baby
was born, and she is safe. I have called her Tara.

—Leila

The equinox

EVERYONE WOULD ARRIVE at four-thirty, with food for
the celebration. But the day, until then, was a time for
their family. They went downhill skiing, the children
snowboarding, until two. Afterward, Tara and Isaac
collapsed on their bed for a half-hour's rest.

Isaac asked, "What do you say, tomorrow we go
down to the courthouse and start the paperwork?" For
her to adopt his children.

She kissed him.

He caught her eye. "What's going on with you?"

"Nothing."

"Tara, how bad is the scarring on that tube? This
one." He touched.

"Bad." *I can't be pregnant. I can't.*

"Do you know what it looks like?"

"Not recently. Can we drop this?"

"I was thinking we could *do* something about it."

She shook her head. "Uh-uh."

The side he'd touched hurt. A sharp, stabbing pain. It went away, but suddenly she was frightened.

THERE WERE MANY HUGS outside the Columbine in the spring snow. Many children throwing snowballs as parents tried to corral them and interest them in holding tapers that would soon be lighted.

Tara's friend Scooter had set up a public address system, and Tara and Beulah Ann and Leila had decided, as a gesture of community, to give the microphone first to Richard Scarborough, head of obstetrics at Precipice Peak Hospital.

"I'm proud to be here at the christening of this structure, to help take it from its painful past to a new future honoring women and families in the community of Precipice."

Everyone cheered.

"We are going to start by remembering this building's past history, with a reading by local historian Cassandra Grey."

The head of the local history museum stepped forward to read from one of Colorado's many books about its prostitutes. This reading was about the madam of Tomboy, Lucia Mae.

"Lucia Mae lost her family on the Kansas prairie, all of them one same cold winter…"

Tara, holding Isaac's left hand and Leila's right, listened to the history of the woman who founded the Columbine and the history of the region's prostitutes.

"…The year the mine caved in, it was Lucia Mae and her girls who nursed the miners…"

Steam blew through clear air turning to twilight.

Stars came out. The moon rose like a wish, and it was growing full, pregnant like Leila.

"And now, I'd like to introduce our local midwife, Isaac McCrea's wife, Tara."

Tara hurried to the microphone. "It's getting cold, so let's warm up by lighting those tapers." Her voice reached back to her in the night, and the sheer number of faces lifted her heart, filled her heart and her dreams.

She saw that compromise could be peace.

"We've selected some songs to remind us of birth and of love in this beautiful community where we all have so much. Some people say, 'He who sings prays twice.' And so we will honor those who have used this building in the past, in their caring and their suffering, and ask to bring the Columbine to new blossom, honoring women and families of Precipice, their life cycles, their health, our peace and unity as a community. I'd like to ask everyone now to circle the building with your lighted tapers. And we're going to start off with the first song on your sheet, an old one many of you will know and the rest can pick up. 'When You Walk Through a Storm.' But before we start, introduce yourself to the neighbor next to you— kids, too. And let's remember that we're a community here and make this an occasion of peace and love."

She went to join her own family and found herself between Danielle and David. She raised her voice with the others, and as the circle moved to the next song, they separated and filed through the building, in one door and out through another, their tapers filling the building with light.

She was in the new examining room when the stabbing pain returned. "Isaac!" He had started to duck out of the room, and she grabbed his arm. "I have to go to the hospital. Now."

DR. SCARBOROUGH AND Isaac's brother stood near the table, watching an ultrasound monitor. Isaac held her hand.

"There it is," said the senior physician. "Tara, your guess was right. You have an ectopic pregnancy two and a half centimeters in diameter. We can remove it with a laparoscope, but I'm going to suggest instead that we get you on a plane to Denver immediately. They have a microsurgeon there. He'll do a much better job on that tube."

"What does that mean?"

Dan spoke. "An abdominal scar. Fewer adhesions. Better chance for conceiving and carrying a baby to term."

"What's the alternative?"

The gynecologists exchanged looks and launched into the options.

Isaac saw Tara's brow furrow. He could imagine the ethical fields in which she was wading and shook his head at her. "Tara. Denver. Let's go. My turn to choose."

Her eyes flickered at his, and his were kind.

Slowly, she nodded.

He said no more. There was time later to point it out—*The number one cause of maternal death in the country, Tara. Number one.* But he'd never say it. He had always known—and assumed she had, too—that this was a possibility.

He just hoped that after surgery it wouldn't happen again.

That something much sweeter would happen instead.

THEY WERE THERE FOR more than two weeks, and Isaac's mother came from Silverton to stay with the children. On the day Tara returned home, Leila went into labor. Beulah Ann called with the news. "I'm riding with them," said Beulah Ann. "Chantel's sitter's already here."

"I'll have Isaac bring me over."

Isaac stood listening to the call. "You're not going to a birth."

"I'm not assisting."

"I said no."

"You two work it out," Beulah Ann said. "And Tara, you keep wearing that charm. It's working just fine." She hung up.

Tara faced Isaac. "It's *Leila. Please.*"

"I'm staying with you."

On the ride to the hospital, Tara fingered her charm. Beulah Ann had said it was working.

A love charm?

Or...

A fertility charm.

She had never conceived a child before her tubal pregnancy.

She touched her tender abdomen, glad Isaac was taking the road slowly. Granted, she could have another ectopic pregnancy. But the surgeon in Denver had said her chances of conceiving and bearing Isaac's child without further intervention were around thirty percent.

That seemed very good.

"LEILA, I CAN GIVE YOU something for this pain."

Some things never change, Tara reflected. But she understood Dan much better than she once had—and felt gratitude to him and Rich Scarborough for suggesting she go to Denver. Now she and Isaac had a small chance—which he said they would increase by making love more often.

Leila had not yet moaned or cried out. She had displayed amazing calm through the episiotomy that had allowed the dilation of her cervix. Now, she was in transition, but the baby was descending slowly.

When Dan allowed it, Asad applied sterile compresses, stretching the tissue. He spoke to Leila in their native language, excluding the others and bringing a deeper flush to her cheeks.

Leila said, "I must stand."

They all checked the monitor. The baby was doing well. Beulah Ann crouched on the floor to look up at Leila. "Dr. McCrea, he's crowning."

Asad and Isaac helped the laboring woman back onto the bed.

Dan took over. "Okay, a slow push."

Tara grabbed Isaac's waist, holding him, and his eyes ran tears as the baby was born, perhaps because of the color of this child. Perhaps because of the child he and Tara had conceived and lost, the tubal pregnancy that could have killed her.

In part, because of their dreams of what could be.

*Turn the page
for an excerpt from
Margot Early's third book in*

the MIDWIVES miniseries—

THERE IS A SEASON

—available December 1999

PROLOGUE

Talkeetna, Alaska
October

CHARLIE MARCUS was using a pay phone in sight of Deadman's Wall in Talkeetna's historic Fairview Inn. Whatever wasn't new in Talkeetna was historic. In fact, he was history in the making. But, being too smart to climb Denali, he'd never be found on Deadman's Wall.

No Walls for Charlie Marcus.

That still left some ways to die. Like whatever way Mia had.

Francesca's shout rang through the receiver, all the way from Colorado, so loud Charlie had to hold the phone away from his head. "*I am not scared!* Stop saying I'm scared."

"Of course you are." Glasses banged behind him at the U-shaped bar, where off-season mountaineers from Italy were celebrating the gift of life, recently returned to them by Marcus Aviation. "Cesca, it's been thirty-two years since you've seen Talkeetna, and the only excuse for that is fear. You're chicken. Scared, scared, fraidy-cat."

"I cannot believe a fifty-four-year-old man is talking to me this way."

She was thousands of miles away in Precipice, Colorado, where she practiced midwifery, but Charlie could imagine his ex-wife's pale cheeks flushed beneath her auburn hair, maybe going gray. He'd turned gray a few years ago, second time he'd lost a plane, making his own way down the glaciers, off Denali, after two weeks without being found.

She said, "I have no reason to be afraid. *You* may have forgotten why I left Talkeet—"

"No, Cesca, I haven't forgotten. I should add seeing your own flesh and blood to the list of things that frighten—"

"That old man does not frighten me! And neither do—"

"Probably not like the thought of his dying without your seeing him again, but—"

"He's not dying."

Yes, she sounded worried. Eighty was getting on in years. "Cesca, you know you should come up here and see about Mia but the fact is, you're scared, scared, scared." One of the Italians tried to hand him a beer, and Charlie shook his head, indicating his unopened Surge. "And I know why you're scared. Growing up with—"

"Oh, I get to be psychoanalyzed by the man who spent the first sixteen years of his life running cons with his father and the next twelve running away from his own wife and daughter."

"Don't forget the VC."

She ignored that. "One thing's for certain. *If* I come to Alaska, it will be for Mia—to learn what happened to Mia—not to see you. I'd prefer not to come within seeing distance of you."

And blood relatives who weren't dying didn't bear mention.

"Alas." Charlie pulled up a steel-leg cushioned stool, but someone had spilt a beer on it. He passed. "A woman like you is rare anywhere, but especially here. Men will queue up to hunt meat for you and sew your mukluks. You know what women say about finding partners in Alaska. 'The odds are good, but the goods are odd.'"

"I *did* find a partner in Alaska."

"Ah, Cesca. For those days we gathered berries in Denali, seeing our daughter, Tara, in each other's eyes. You can stay with me." He'd told her Talkeetna had changed, that now it was just like the place on "Northern Exposure." It *had* changed since 1967— changed plenty. But it was still Talkeetna—launching point for Denali and famous for its annual Moose Dropping Festival. "You're talking to one of the few people in town who doesn't shower at the Laundromat. And my house is *warm*."

That should cinch it. In January of '68, when he'd rescued Francesca from a life of waiting tables in Anchorage and taken her to Hawaii, she'd shown her gratitude by marrying him, in the most dire circumstances.

"You'll have to do better, Charlie. I grew up there. Remember?"

"Think running water. Think *bathtub*. Indoor plumbing. But maybe you could stay at Mia's. To look after the dogs. She's got a big dog-food cooker. You can melt snow for water." Before she could react— and before he himself could think too hard about Mia—he added, "Probably room for another midwife, too. I could fly you to nearby villages for births—"

"Like you did for Mia?"

A little jealous, Cesca? "Now and again."

Roy Walcott Jr., Francesca's brother and the son of Talkeetna's oldest surviving bush pilot, entered the bar. Charlie turned his back. The day Roy Walcott Air Service closed its doors Charlie Marcus would begin observing an annual holiday in honor of the event.

Yeah, and that's the day the state bird stops drinking blood.

Roy Jr. told the bartender, "Haven't you got some air freshener, Spike? I smell *Charlie*."

"'Scuse me, Cesca." Charlie dropped the receiver and strode six yards, making sure the Surge had a rough ride along. "Well, if it isn't Roy Pilot-Error Walcott Jr. How's Trix, Roy?" He opened the can.

From her phone in Colorado, Francesca Walcott heard the sound of a table crashing, wood splintering, glass breaking. Someone yelled, "Take it outside!"

She heard another explosion.

"You're paying for that table, boys!"

"You've lived too long, Marcus, after you killed my—"

"Marcus, finish your call and hang up my phone! Get out of here! You can kill each other in the street!"

A crack that was fist on flesh.

This does not attract me, Francesca told herself calmly. *Charlie Marcus is a barbarian, and he lives in a place filled with other barbarians. I know this better than anyone. I will eat this house before I return to Talkeetna, Alaska.*